I0619209

Stonyford Submission II

Stonyford Submission II

Bennie Ray Murdock

Wagoner Oklahoma

Copyright © 2025 Bennie Ray Murdock

All rights reserved. No part of this book may be reproduced or transmitted in any form or by any means, electronic or mechanical, including photocopying, recording, or stored in any information or retrieval system, without the prior written permission of the publisher, except as authorized by law.

All rights reserved.

Published by Word Out Books
An imprint of AZ Entertainment Group LLC

cover design by AZ Designs

ISBN: 978-1-947035-60-7

For inquiries, including bulk orders of 100 or more, please contact:

AZ Entertainment Group LLC
PO BOX 854
Wagoner, OK 74477-0854

Email: info@az-entertainmentllc.com
Website: www.az-entertainmentllc.com

Printed in the United States of America

In Memory of

Roxanne Manuel Murdock
Radelle Renee Murdock
Vanessa Elaine Murdock

CHAPTER ONE

ENTERING THE CAMPGROUND, Randy, and his passengers wandered aimlessly, shrugging their shoulders in doubt, while some kind of transmission—radio, television, or another device—blared loudly through the air, apparently coming from one of the few mobile home trailers abandoned by its owner.

The entire campground appeared deserted, except for a well-fed, unusually large pit bull clawing and wriggling under a small fifth wheel that had somehow dropped, flattening its tires and trapping him. The dog's howls echoed loudly beneath it.

"Somebody give me a hand over here," Randy yelled, heading toward the howling. "He's trapped under there. But I think we can just, you know, lift this thing a little on one side."

"Come on, Brian," Terry said, jumping out of the Jeep. "Melody isn't strong enough to help him pick that thing up."

"Hold on, Randy," Brian called. "Let us help you with that."

"Christine!" Terry shouted. "See if you can pull him out."

"But what if he tries to bite me or something?" she asked.

"See if you can find a chain on him or anything," Terry said, reaching down and grabbing the bottom of the fifth wheel along-side Randy and Brian.

"No, I don't think one is on him," Lori said.

"Well, you better back away a little if you think he's going to bite you," Brian told Christine, lifting the fifth wheel.

Backing away from the fifth wheel as quickly as she could, the pit bull ran out from underneath it, charging toward Christine but running past her, climbing a nearby hill, and disappearing into the thick brush.

"Oh, God," Christine screamed. "I just knew that dog was going to attack me and bite me."

"Here, boy! Here, boy," Brian called. "Come on, boy! Come on, boy! We're not going to hurt you. Come on, boy!"

"Man, you guys," Randy said, trying to spot the dog. "I think that dog is scared shitless about something. Didn't you see that? He came charging out from underneath the trailer and just kept running."

"Damn!" Terry said, laughing at the thought of what had happened. "And he didn't even stop to say thank you, or even to lick Christine on the face."

"Yuck!" Christine said in disgust. "That is so gross."

"Everything's gross to you, Christine," Brian said. "I bet Terry is gross to you, isn't he?"

"Hey, you guys?" Lori called, trying to get their attention. "Listen to that."

"Listen to what?" Terry asked.

"What they're saying on the radio," she said.

"What radio?" Christine asked.

"Wherever that's coming from," Lori said again.

"What'd you hear, Lori?" Melody asked.

"Listen to it," she said. "They're talking about it right now."

"I think it's coming from over there," Randy said. "See? The trailer with the door left open."

"Let's go over there and find out what's happening," Brian said.

"And just what are we going to tell the owners when they return and find you snooping around in their trailer, Brian?" Christine asked. "You were just stopping by to listen to whatever it is Lori said she heard?"

"That's exactly what I'm going to tell them, Christine," Brian said.

"Yeah, I'm sure they'll understand without getting upset at you."

"Man, you guys," Randy exclaimed. "Just look at this thing. It's one of those gigantic motherfuckers. I mean, just look at it."

"You know what I'm thinking?" Brian said, looking around suspiciously toward the road they had traveled to get to the campground.

"Who cares what you're thinking, Brian," Lori said, expressing her distrust in his judgment.

"Well, I'm going to tell you anyway if you want to feel that way about it, Lori," Brian said, smiling seriously. "I think this campground is probably where that thing that got Travis came from."

"Brian, how could you say such a thing?" Melody yelled. "He's still out there somewhere, and here you are being inconsiderate about it. You thoughtless bastard!"

"Now why would you want to go and say something like that about me?" he asked, still slyly smiling. "That's not a nice thing for you to say about your good old pal, is it? Hey, I'm the one who just might end up taking Travis's place."

"Like hell you will!" Melody yelled again.

"Okay, you guys," Terry said to both of them. "That's enough. We still have to, most likely, go back and try to find Travis."

"That's what Randy should be doing anyway," Melody cried. "He's the one who drove off and left him."

"I was only doing what everybody was telling me to do, Melody," Randy said, shrugging. "And you know it! I didn't know he wasn't in the Jeep."

"Well, we still have to go back and see if we can find him," Terry said again, staring in the direction where they'd left Travis. "And I think she's right, Randy. The two of you should go back and see if you can find him."

"He just might be trying to find us," Christine said, looking down. "He might be out there somewhere, walking down that dirt road looking for us."

"Well, if he is," Randy said, "he would have yelled out for us by now."

"But what if he can't yell?" Lori said, shrugging. "What if something happened, and he can't yell?"

"Something like what?" Brian asked curiously. "Like what? That monster got him or something?"

"Man, do you really see what I mean about this conversation?" Terry said, shaking his head in disbelief. "That was no monster. And really, none of us can say what it was. You guys need to just cut the crap. Travis is still out there, and we're all going to go back and find him."

"Well, until you guys figure out just what we're going to do," Melody said, "I think I'm going to, for once, agree with Brian. I think we need to find out what's happening. Why aren't the owners of these things here watching them?"

"Because they're probably doing like everybody else—fishing," Randy said, walking toward the door of the mobile home trailer.

"Are you guys listening to what they're saying?" Christine asked, as if what she was hearing was important enough to make her follow Randy, who was now stepping up onto the few steps leading inside the trailer.

"I could only make out bits and pieces," Lori said. "But what did you hear?"

"I heard them say something about body parts," Terry added.

"And then something about them being found miles away, or something like that."

"Hey, you guys," Randy said. "You need to check this out. Man, this is no ordinary mobile home trailer. I think this is a lab or something. I mean, just look at all of this stuff."

"Sure isn't any meth lab either," Brian said, staring inside the trailer, curious about what Randy was talking about. "I don't know about this."

"Here, let me see," Melody said, squeezing between Randy and a long, narrow-backed sofa with stretched arms. "Oh, yeah," she said, looking around and showing her knowledge of mobile homes. "I could definitely live in this one."

"Okay, you two," Christine said, climbing inside the trailer. "Sounds like you're having a little too much fun up here. Move over and let the lady check things out."

"You coming in, Brian?" Randy asked. "Or are you just going to stand there staring at all this expensive luxury and comfort that only the rich get to enjoy?"

"Go ahead, Brian," Lori said, snickering. "You know it's hard for a guy like you to resist."

"What's your problem?" Brian asked. "I don't see you trying to make an effort to get inside this thing. What's wrong? Are you afraid the owners might return and catch you or something?"

"Well, in case you didn't know it, Brian," she said, smiling slyly and squinting her eyes, "I'm not Christine. I'm not worried about the owners returning and finding me. Plus, I know how to charm my way out of anything I get into. So, what about you, Brian?"

"Hey, Randy?" Terry called out. "Man, why don't you guys do something to turn that thing down a little?"

"Move out of the way, coward," Lori said to Brian. "Staring seems to be the only thing you know how to do."

"Oh, yeah," Brian said, moving to one side, so Lori could gain entrance to the trailer. "Is that right?"

"That's right," she said again in a seemingly flirtatious manner. "And by the way, Brian, what you see, you'll never be able to touch."

"I know I didn't just hear what I think I heard," Terry said, smiling broadly at Brian.

"You too, man, Terry," Brian said. "She knows I'm digging on her. Fuck!"

"You going in?"

"No, not yet, man," Brian said, turning toward the picnic tables arranged in a wide circle, surrounded by a group of motor homes—Winnebago Campers, Gulf Streams, Coachmen, Dynamaxs, and Georgetowns. "I think I'll just hang out here for a few minutes, you know, and maybe check for the owners of these things. I mean, I just can't see these things being left here with no one attending to them. You know what I mean?"

"Yeah, man," Terry said, staring around at the trailers. "I was thinking the same thing... but first, I gotta see what's happening in here."

"Yeah, man," Brian said, puzzled by the entire situation. "It's the way everything is arranged out here. I mean, it's like a group of people were camping and then just vanished or something. Kind of hard to explain."

"I know, man," Terry said, smiling and nodding his head. "But who knows—they'll probably be back before we know it."

"But what if they don't?" Brian asked. "Maybe something really did happen to them. You know, just like Travis?"

"Hey, Brian," Terry said, giving Brian a subtle signal not to scare anyone. "Let's not trip on that scary stuff, okay? I mean, you already know how the girls are feeling about everything as it is, and the one thing we don't want them thinking is that there's some crazy person out here running loose, slaughtering people. Can you just imagine how much panic that would cause, considering we don't have any possible way to make contact with anybody?"

"So what about that thing we saw coming down the hill?" Brian asked. "I mean, didn't we all see it?"

"Look," Terry said, shrugging his shoulders, "man, I really can't say what we saw, and neither can you, and you damn well know it. Whatever it was, it didn't do anything to us... well, except for Travis. But we're really in no position to say that the thing got him or did anything to him. He just might be somewhere trying to find us right now, as we speak."

"Well then, why don't we go and see if we can find him?" Brian suggested. "Just you and me can do that by ourselves. Randy can stay here and keep an eye on the girls."

"To be truthful, I think that's a swell idea," Terry said. "But there is one problem."

"And what's that?" Brian asked.

"Only an hour or two before it'll be completely dark out here," Terry said, looking at the sky. "And man, when it gets dark up here in these parts, you know it."

"Just hate that Travis is out there, somewhere, by himself," Brian said. "I mean, he might be hurt or something."

"I know just how you feel, but man, I promise you—we'll go search for him first thing in the morning."

"So tell me something," Brian asked, trying to ease the tension he felt. "Just what are we supposed to do until morning? Man, I've never been so confused."

"Well, for one," Terry began, "just be cool and don't worry yourself to death. Try not to cause a panic."

"Okay, man. I might as well check in with the others and see what they're listening to," Brian said and headed toward the tables.

"Go ahead. I'll catch up in a minute," Terry said. "I gotta check out what's happening inside this trailer first."

Just as Terry was about to enter the trailer, he glanced at

Brian. He thought maybe he should have gone with him instead of joining the others.

*

KRTV NEWS: Here we are once again bringing you the very latest. Is one serial killer responsible for the killings throughout the region? Could there be two? Or possibly even—at a guess—multiple killers at large?

The mystery continues. It's baffling to everyone involved in the investigation. Police are working tirelessly, searching for the killer—or killers.

Bodies and body parts have been found scattered along remote areas. Some speculate that multiple killers are at large. Theories suggest the perpetrator or perpetrators may be residing within the neighboring communities.

Our affiliates are reporting that men, women, and even little babies have been found along seemingly very remote parts of the area that surrounds a vast portion of the small towns nearest to the Stonyford region. But it's even more shocking to note that body parts were also found as far away as the humble communities of Williams, Colusa, and even there in Maxwell and just about every small town community leading up to Stonyford.

One of the County Police Commissioners, Garnet Tolen, previously spoke with us and speculated that as many as a dozen or more killers could be responsible and are on the loose, freely committing these horrible crimes. "Just looking at the common denominators... my theory about this situation is that it's probably an extremely sick group of people out there on a violent, destructive rampage needing to be restrained, dead or alive—immediately!"

POLICE REPORT: Body parts have been found scattered over at least fifty miles in nearly every direction. Some of the corpses are believed to be teenagers from Maxwell and Colusa, and as far north as Coveo. There is also speculation that possible bodies have been discovered in the mountain region of Garberville.

Our theory is that the perpetrator is probably an extremely mentally ill individual with a severe mental disorder. Worst-case scenario: the responsible person may be someone going through a divorce, someone who recently lost a job, or someone lacking the confidence or ability to find work—or even a girlfriend.

One thing is certain: this individual is extremely depressed about his misfortune and is taking his frustration out on innocent people who have nothing to do with his problems. Whoever he is, he should be brought down immediately—without further delay.

KRTV NEWS: We here at the station want to thank you for that update on the terrible situation currently unfolding throughout the northern region of California. We at KRTV will continue keeping you informed and up to date on any information received from our affiliate stations, even as we speak.

Again, let us update you, our listening audience, on this ongoing crisis, which appears to have begun in the small-town communities of Stonyford and Elk Creek, with the main focus on Stonyford.

Bodies are being found throughout the region. We at KRTV have been extremely busy gathering information so we can report it directly to you, our listening audience.

Before we switch you back to your regular programming, we are issuing an alert: be watchful and vigilant for anything out of the ordinary. We are also asking you to be on the lookout for several teenagers who went missing while attending the festival celebration in Stonyford. At present, the only information we can provide is that they were last seen speeding off toward the boys' ranch, which we understand is located at the lower basin of Snow Mountain.

The missing are Terry Gilbert and his younger brother, Randy

Gilbert, along with Christine, Lori, Melody, Brian, and Travis. All are white. They were last seen riding in two new orange Jeep Wranglers with removable black tops.

If anyone knows the whereabouts or approximate location of these teenagers, you are urged to contact the local police department immediately. These are the only pictures we have to show you.

Again, KRTV is making a plea to its listening audience to help find and locate these missing teenagers. Reports state they were last seen speeding on the road leading toward the boys' ranch, located at the lower basin of Snow Mountain.

*

Terry stepped into the trailer and froze, pointing at the fifty-inch plasma HDTV mounted on the wall. "Do you guys believe this? That's a picture of me they just showed."

"A picture of all of us," Lori said, looking around the trailer, curious as to what it was being used for. "I wonder if they left something in here I can use to try contacting somebody with?"

"I don't know," Randy said, still staring at the screen. "But, man, they think we're lost or something. You know, it's like nobody knows where we are, and that's scary."

"I could've sworn I saw people down here," Christine said, staring out the window. "When we were coming down that hill, some were standing, some were walking. They were watching us as we came around that curve."

"Yeah," said Melody. "I even thought I'd seen somebody, you know, wave or something."

"Well, just where are they now?" Terry asked, looking around nervously. "I think what we had better do is start checking all these trailers to see what we can find before dark."

"Yeah, cause," Christine began, "it's starting to get dark, and the one thing I don't want to be doing is thinking that thing is outside this trailer waiting on us. We gotta hurry up and find something so we can try contacting the sheriff or somebody to come up here and help us."

"Sounds good to me, Christine," Randy said. "I think you're right. Whatever that thing was, I'd hate to see it again. It's like I can feel it watching us."

"Yeah, I know what you mean," Terry said, looking out one of the side windows at the hill they'd come down to the campground. "I thought it was just me feeling somebody watching us."

"I've felt that way too," Lori said, pulling on the door to a small cabinet. "Ever since that thing started coming down the hill after us, it seems like something has been watching us. I can just feel its eyes on me, watching everything I'm doing."

"Whatever it is," Melody said, "it's really giving me the creeps."

"Hey, Terry?" Randy called from a room near the back of the trailer.

"Yeah, what's that?" Terry answered.

"Man, what's happening with Brian?"

"Oh, he decided to go searching on his own for now."

"I thought not too long ago I'd seen him going inside that trailer over there," Christine said, pointing toward the Winnebago with its door wide open.

"Randy, I thought you said that Margaret's sister was the only one attacked and murdered up here? You never mentioned all the others. Why didn't you tell me about the other bodies found?"

"That's because I didn't know anything about them, Melody," Randy said, coming out the back of the trailer carrying a small black laptop and a new netbook still wrapped in plastic. "If I had known anything about them, don't you think I'd have told you by now?"

"Man, what is this you're carrying?" Terry asked. "Where'd you find this stuff?"

"Yeah, Randy," Melody asked, reaching for the laptop. "Where was this at?"

"It was lying on a table in one of the rooms. There's some more things back there," he told them.

"Just follow me, Terry," Randy said, handing the netbook to Christine. "Come on, I'll show you."

"Hey, what about me?" Lori asked. "Can I help?"

"Sure, come on," Randy told her. "Just try to be careful not to trip over all these wires lying around on the floor back here."

"Damn, man," Terry said, looking around. "I wonder what these people were doing up here, using all this stuff?"

"I'd guess they're probably scientists or something, from the looks of things," Randy answered, opening another door that led to a much larger room. "But I'm sure there's an explanation for all this stuff."

"Yeah, maybe one about that thing we saw," Lori said as she tripped over a wire leading inside a closet. "Oops, I think I just kicked something loose. This plug came out," she said, showing a set of RCA plugs caught on her shoe.

"Hold up, Randy," Terry said. "Let's see what's in this room. She might have unplugged something important."

"What's happening?" Randy asked. "The door won't open?"

"It feels locked," Terry replied.

"Pull on it," Randy said.

"That's what I'm doing, but it won't budge," Terry said, twisting the doorknob.

"Here, wait a minute," Lori said. "Let me get down here and see if I can see anything from underneath this door."

"Go ahead," Terry told her. "But I doubt there's much room for you to see anything from that far down."

"Oh, shit! You guys!" Lori exclaimed, jumping up from the

floor. "Oh, fuck! Just what in the hell is that in there?"

"Jesus Christ, Lori," Randy said, laughing at how fast she suddenly shot upward from the floor. "What's your problem? You're acting like you've seen a ghost or something, the way you came leaping up off this floor."

"Lori, what's the matter?" Terry asked, backing away from the door and peering down at the bottom. "What's happening? What did you see? Could you even see anything?"

"Yeah, I did!" she screamed at Randy. "And I think you know exactly what's in there. Don't you, Randy?"

"Now wait a minute, Lori," Randy said, still laughing. "I had nothing to do with whatever you think you saw in there. I didn't! Honest."

"Like hell you didn't," Lori shot back, squinting her eyes.

By this time, both Christine and Melody had entered the hallway, trying to figure out why Lori was so upset at Randy.

"What's happening?" Christine asked Lori, who stood frozen in place.

"He knows what he did!" Lori yelled. "That stupid, rotten son of a bitch! You good-for-nothing bastard!"

"Look, I promise you," Randy said. "I had nothing to do with whatever it is you think you saw in that room. That's the honest-to-God truth. I swear on my dead grandma's grave—you know how much I loved my granny."

"Everybody just back away from the door," Terry said in a low whisper. "At least until we figure this out."

"Figure what out?" Randy asked, glancing down at the bottom of the door. "Why don't you just tell us what you saw, Lori?"

"Yeah, what was it?" Christine asked.

"All I know is, as soon as I got down there, I didn't know what I was looking at. I thought maybe Terry shook the door so hard that something on a hook fell to the floor. I didn't pay much attention at first—not until it started moving and its eyes blinked at me."

"Oh shit, Terry," Lori said, her voice shaking. "We gotta get out of here. I don't want to end up like those people on the news. They're already thinking we could be next, possible victims, probably murdered like the rest."

"Lori, get a hold of yourself," Christine said, pulling her toward the front entrance of the trailer. "Nobody is going to die. Whatever you saw in that room, Terry and Randy will get in there and find out. So don't worry—everything's going to be all right."

"But I did see something," Lori said, trembling. "It was just lying there, like I was, staring back at me—blinking those huge, ugly eyes. I even think it smiled at me."

"Melody, why don't you take the rest of these boxes and see what's in them?" Terry said quietly. "Whatever Lori saw, if there really is something—or somebody—in there, I don't want them knowing what we're doing."

"You know something?" Randy whispered. "You're right. Whoever it is might be listening to us."

"I know," Terry said. "That's why I want everyone to keep talking in a low voice so he can't hear us."

"Maybe one of you should try asking him something," Melody suggested. "Maybe he's hurt or something."

"You know, Randy, she's got a point."

"Okay, then," Randy said, smiling at Terry. "Why don't you just go ahead and knock?"

"Why don't you? You're closer."

"But you were already trying to get in there, Terry."

"No."

"So just knock on the door and see if he answers."

"Why don't you, Randy?"

"Man," Melody said, shaking her head. "I really don't believe what I'm hearing from you two."

"But what if it isn't a he?" Randy asked. "It could be a she."

"And that'll be even better for you, Randy," Terry whispered.

"If it's a nice-looking chick in there, that'll be right up your alley. Just think about it—you feel me?"

"Move out the way, Terry," Randy said, stepping up to the door. "I got this, my man."

Randy knocked lightly on the door. No answer. He tried a second time—still nothing. Then a third, fourth, fifth, and sixth attempt—all unanswered.

"Uh, check this out, Randy. Why don't you just get down on the floor like Lori did and see what you can see?"

"Uh, are you all right in there?" Randy asked, pressing an ear against the door, ignoring Terry's suggestion. "Hey in there, can you hear me? Are you all right?"

"I told you what you need to do," Terry replied.

"Well, why don't you do it, Terry? What's wrong? Are you afraid? Scared of the big bad wolf?"

"Are you guys still at it?" Melody asked. "Hey, if it were me in there, listening to the two of you, I'd be long gone by now."

"Yeah, right," said Randy. "And just how would you do that? I mean, get past us?"

"Simply," Melody said, pretentiously. "Windows and ventilation systems exist for a reason."

"Oh, fuck, Randy," Terry said, looking up at the ceiling, then slowly turning and heading toward the trailer entrance. "The window! I forgot all about the window."

"But only if there's even a window in this room," Melody whispered, heading back to the other room to check the boxes. "There's a lot of stuff in here."

"Like what?" Randy asked.

"Uh, you know," Melody said. "boxes with cameras, memory cards, camcorders, battery packs, iPhones, and all kinds of accessories. Plus a few mobile hotspots, and some other gadgets I'm not even sure what they do."

"That's it?" Randy asked.

"No way," she said. "There's a huge refrigerator, a microwave, a stove, even a dishwasher. And a countertop grill and griddle, a big food processor, and some strange-looking vacuums with long attachments."

"Sounds like they were eating pretty well," Randy remarked.

"Yeah, and there's more," Melody said. "Seriously, this place has it all."

"What are you guys talking about?" Terry whispered, trying not to talk too loud.

"Melody was just telling me about all the things she found in these boxes," Randy said to Terry. "Man, you really need to hear this."

"Oh, yeah," Terry said. "Like what?"

"Well, back there in one of those rooms, I saw two high-efficiency washer and steam dryers, Samsung Galaxy Tab 27.0 Media Hubs, multiple tablets over ten inches, Asus TF300 Transformers, Nook Simple Touch with bright GlowLights, hundreds of DECT 6.0 cordless phones with digital answering machines, all kinds of processors, TI-84 Silver Edition graphing calculators, disc spindles, wireless printers and routers, and loads of GPS maps."

"And you already took all of that stuff up front?" Terry asked.

"Now, really, Terry," Melody said. "You think I'm packing all of that by myself? You're crazy."

"What about the window?" Randy asked.

"Ain't no window," Terry said. "Whatever it is, it's still in there listening to us."

"Oh man, Terry," Randy said, closing his eyes. "Damn! You just had to say that, didn't you?"

"Nah, I could've said something else," Terry said, pointing at the ceiling. "But the truth is, I really couldn't find a window in this room. We could use some fresh air."

"Fresh air?" Randy whispered. "What?"

Terry stood a few feet from Randy and Melody, pointing at the ceiling, and suggesting that whoever it was in the room had somehow made its way into the ventilation system and could be heard crawling slowly, as if searching for a way out.

"Whoever it is, he's moving like a worm," Randy said, looking intently upward, trying to follow the slow, dragging sounds from the vents.

"I think he stopped right about here," Terry said, pointing to where the sound ended. "Don't say anything. Just be quiet."

"Wait a minute," Randy said, glancing at the ceiling. "You mean there's nothing, nothing at all up there?"

"Nothing," Terry confirmed. "Not even a vent you could open. Whoever it is, he's still in that room. That's what I'm worried about."

"Man," Randy muttered, shaking his head. "This is getting serious. We can't just sit here."

"Exactly," Terry whispered. "We need to be careful. Don't make any noise, don't do anything stupid. Just wait and see."

Randy nodded, his eyes following the direction of Terry's pointing. Melody stayed close, watching both of them, silent, her hands folded in front of her.

"That didn't sound like any human being up there," Melody whispered. "I think it's something else crawling around. Some weird little lost creature that got stuck in here and can't find its way out."

"What?" Terry asked. "A snake or something?"

"I don't know," she replied.

"Well, whatever it is, it was creeping and sliding really slow up there," Randy said. "Fuck! The thing isn't moving anymore. It's like it just came to a dead stop."

"No, it didn't stop," Terry said, straining to hear. "I think it's right above us, listening to see what we're doing."

"Hey, you guys?" Christine said out loud, forgetting she was supposed to whisper. "What?"

"Christine!" everybody said at once, shouting in unison but still in a whisper, signaling her to be quiet while pointing at the ceiling.

"What is it?" she whispered.

"It's right above you," Melody said, leaning in and whispering. Just as Lori turned to see what was happening, Melody and Christine put a finger to her lips and guided her slowly and quietly outside the trailer.

"What?" Lori asked. "What's happening? Did they find out who he is?"

"Let's go over there," Melody said, pointing toward the picnic tables.

"What's happening?" Lori asked again.

"Whatever you saw in that room—it's playing some kind of game with us," Melody told Lori and Christine.

"What do you mean?" Christine asked. "A game? What kind of game?"

"We really don't know," Melody said. "But it was following us all over the place. From this point on, everything we say to each other, say it in a very low whisper. Very low."

"But, Melody," Lori said, her voice worried, "it's really getting dark, and I don't want to be stuck out here all night. Especially after everything we've already been through."

"Yeah, I know exactly what you mean, Lori," Christine said, looking at the hills and large mountains around them, which were beginning to swallow what little light remained. "I think we should sit in one of the Jeeps."

Just as they started toward the Jeeps, Brian walked over, having noticed them talking and scanning the area near the picnic tables.

"Hey, you guys," he called out. "What's going on? What's all the whispering about?"

"Oh, man," Melody and Christine said at the same time.

"Brian, are we glad to see you."

"Hey, I'm glad to see you too," Brian replied. "But it hasn't been that long since I last saw you. So what's up? Where are Terry and Randy?"

"They're still over there in that trailer," Melody told him. "Something really weird is crawling around up in the ceiling. They're trying to figure out what it is."

"Didn't they ever think it might just be a raccoon or a possum?" Brian asked. "Or maybe a squirrel got trapped in there."

"No, Brian," Melody said, trying to clarify. "Whatever it is in the ceiling was following us around, trying to listen to everything we were saying."

"Yeah, it was first locked in that room," Lori said seriously. "And when I looked under the door, that ugly thing dropped down from somewhere and stared right at me."

"Are you sure it wasn't a raccoon or something, Lori?" Brian asked.

"No, Brian!" Lori shouted. "It wasn't any of those animals. It was something else, with big, ugly, round eyes. And it even smiled at me—like the thing that came down the hill."

"Up in the ceiling," Brian muttered, puzzled. "Something up there, and you say it was following you, trying to listen to everything you were talking about? Like following you around?"

"Yeah," Melody said, "it's up there just like I said. I heard it crawling slowly, and then it suddenly stopped, like it was trying to hear us."

"So, what are you guys going to do?" Brian asked.

"After Lori reminded us how dark it's getting, I suggested we sit in one of the Jeeps," Christine said. "Look at how fast the light's disappearing. Before long, it'll be completely dark, and Travis is still up there somewhere."

"Maybe we should be looking for him, Brian," Melody added, staring regretfully at the hills, thinking of leaving Travis behind.

"Okay, you guys, check this out," Brian began. "See that huge trailer? The one with the two slides open really wide?"

"That one, right there?" Melody asked, pointing at the forty-eight-foot Winnebago Camper Custom Coach.

"Uh-huh," Brian said. "That's it. So why don't you guys go sit in it for now? I mean, hey, it's really loaded with just about everything."

"And what about all the stuff we can use in that one?" Melody said, pointing at the trailer where Terry and Randy were still trying to find whatever it was in the ceiling.

"What stuff?" Brian asked.

"Lots of boxes in there," she said. "I checked them—they're full of things we can use."

"What kind of things?" Brian pressed. "What do you mean?"

"Come on," she said, motioning for him to follow her to the trailer. "I'll show you."

"No, wait a minute. Hold up," Brian said. "Let me show you what's inside this trailer first."

"Come on, you guys," Melody called to Lori and Christine. "I wanna see what Brian's talking about."

Just as they were about to head to the Winnebago, Terry came out of the trailer he and Randy had been searching, looking for whatever was crawling around in the ceiling. "Hey, what's happening?" Terry asked. "Where are you guys going? What's happening, Brian?"

"Hey, Terry," Brian said, waving and pointing toward the Winnebago. "I'm just taking them over here to this motor home for now until you can figure out what that thing is they told me about."

"Ah, man, dude," Terry said, laughing while looking around. "Whatever that thing was, I think it's gone. I mean, we ain't hearing it no more. You feel me?"

"Are you sure, Terry?" Christine asked, wanting to be certain.

"We've been out here and didn't see anything leave."

"Well, it all depends on which way the damn thing left," he said. "It could've run past you without you seeing it."

"Nothing ran past us, Terry," Melody said, looking toward the Jeeps parked near the entrance to the campground.

"Yeah, Terry," Brian said, looking behind the trailer. "We didn't see anything come past us. Not in this direction."

"Well, it sure isn't in here anymore," Terry told them. "I've been using a long broom handle and an old rusty steel bar, poking holes just about everywhere in the ceiling. But I didn't hit anything. It's been really quiet up there for a while. I've been jamming those things up there hard, trying my best to kill whatever it was. But nothing happened. Not a single drop of blood. So I figured it must have found a way out."

"Are you sure, Terry?" Christine asked again.

"Yeah, 'cause we can really use everything in those boxes," Melody said, slowly walking toward him.

"And I don't want to see that thing again," Lori added, grabbing one of Brian's hands.

"Look, you guys," Terry said, turning toward the entrance to the trailer. "Randy's still in there, searching this motherfucker up and down everywhere. If anything is still in there, you can bet he'll find it." "Okay, you guys," Brian said. "Go ahead, get everything you need, and bring it back over here. We can just put it all in here." "What about the Jeeps?" Christine asked. "Are we going to move them over here?" "Nah, don't worry about them," Terry told her. "We'll leave them where they are for now, in case somebody comes up from the festival. They'll see the Jeeps and know we're here."

"But that's if they'll even stop," Brian said, shrugging and pointing upward, reminding everyone how dark it was getting. "You guys already know how dark it gets out here. People just don't stop in these mountains at night—well, not unless they really have to."

"Well, let's hurry up and get this stuff," Melody said, hastening toward the trailer. "Aren't you coming, Brian?"

"On my way, Melody," he said. "Right behind you."

"Isn't it too heavy, though?" Lori asked Melody. "I mean..."

CHAPTER TWO

SUDDENLY, THERE WAS A LOUD NOISE. An extremely violent eruption that sounded like a rapid, moving explosion. A sudden release of energy—loud and sharp. A burst with such force and intensity that the entire campground shook, as if two fast-moving freight trains had collided.

"Jesus Christ, Terry," Brian screamed. "Man, what the fuck was that?"

Terry and Melody rushed out of the trailer, where they had been gathering the few remaining boxes.

"Man, Brian," Terry shouted. "What did you do?"

"Yeah, Brian," Melody cried angrily. "Just what was that all about—dumbass?"

By this time, both Lori and Christine had rushed out from inside the Winnebago, terribly frightened by the explosion, puzzled, and confused just as everybody had become after the violent outburst.

"Look, man," Brian pleaded. "I had nothing to do with that, I swear."

"Well, what just happened?" Terry asked him, staring at the remnants of the explosion. "Like, just where is all this dust coming from, Brian?"

"Man, I really had nothing to do with what just happened," Brian exclaimed again. "I was just standing here, about to come down these steps, when I heard the explosion and saw it happen."

"Seen what happened, Brian?" Melody asked him angrily, thinking that he had caused the explosion. "What happened, dumbass?"

"It's all right, Melody," Terry said. "I really don't think he had anything to do with it. I mean, if he did, he'd have told us by now."

"But just what did you see, Brian?" Melody asked again, walking slowly toward him. "You were out here—so what happened?"

"Was that you who did that, Brian?" Christine asked. "Where did you get the explosives?"

"Look, Christine, you guys, I had nothing to do with that," Brian told her. "I swear, man. I had nothing to do with it."

"Well, what happened then?" Lori asked. "You were out here."

"I know, but it wasn't me," he said again. "It wasn't me."

"And where in the heck is Randy?" Christine asked.

"He's probably still in there in the back, packing those boxes," Terry said, turning and heading back inside the trailer while calling out Randy's name.

"Oh, no. This can't be happening," Brian said, looking around.

"What can't be happening?" Christine asked him.

"Hey, you guys," Brian said to get their attention, shrugging. "Man, I really don't think that was an explosion that we heard."

"No?" Terry questioned. "Then what was it?"

"I think it was that thing you guys were searching for in the ceiling that made the noise," Brian said.

"The thing in the ceiling?" Terry again questioned. "And what makes you so sure of that?"

"Just look at the top of the trailer," Brian said, pointing at all the damage done to the top side paneling above the entrance. "Just look at all of that. And you guys were inside? Well, whatever it was that did that, it was done from inside the trailer and not from the outside. It's pushed outward, not inward."

"Then where is Randy?" Melody asked, confused. "Where is he?"

"Hey, Randy?" Terry yelled. "Randy?"

"Where is he?" asked Christine. "Didn't he come out with you guys?"

"No," Terry told her. "I don't think so. Last time I saw him, he was doing something to those boxes. And then he headed to the front entrance of the trailer, you know, to poke holes in the ceiling."

"But that's what you were doing, wasn't it?" Christine asked Terry.

"No, but by then, that's when I started helping Melody," he told her. "She couldn't carry all those boxes by herself. But Randy was—"

"What did you see, Brian?" Melody pressed. "You were already out here. Why don't you tell us what you saw?"

"Yeah, Brian," Terry added. "Man, dude. Just tell us what it was you saw. You know, when that loud noise happened."

"Look, you guys," Brian began. "Man, all I saw—you know, hey—it was like something just exploded up there. You know, on top of the trailer. It just didn't make sense to me."

"What, Brian?" Christine asked. "What didn't make sense to you? What was it?"

"Randy!" Terry shouted again. "Hey, man! Answer me!"

"Hey, you guys," Brian said, puzzled. "I'm telling you, it was whatever that thing was in the ceiling that did this."

"But did you see it, Brian?" Christine quickly asked him angrily. "I know you saw it. Just tell us what it was that you saw."

"Hey," Brian began, shrugging his shoulders and pointing one of his hands aimlessly in the air. "All I can say is that I think it was a, ah, man, you guys. It was a for real 'chimera,' except it didn't have, you know, a head like a lion."

"A 'Chimera?'" Terry asked, confusedly. "Man, just what the fuck are you talking about? A chimera?"

"That's exactly what I said, Terry," Brian told him seriously. "It was a for real chimera that I saw, seemingly like it exploded out from up there on the top of the trailer—carrying Randy underneath it."

"Come on, Brian," Terry pleaded out loud. "Man, you ain't making no sense at all."

"You really think you've seen a 'chimera?'" Christine asked him while holding both of her hands over her chest area. "Are you sure, Brian? Are you really sure?"

"Hold up, dude," Terry said, staring upward. "Just what the fuck is it that you're saying you saw—carrying my kid brother underneath it up there?"

"Look, Terry," Brian said. "I didn't see him underneath it up there. I saw him just after it started to fly away. Like, Randy was struggling, trying to get free or something. You know? He was really trying to get free, but the chimera's huge, monster-like claws were gripping him tight. He just couldn't break free."

"Just what the heck is a chimera?" Melody asked. "You guys are really freaking me out. First Travis, and now Randy. I'm really scared out here."

"Just what the heck is a chimera?" Lori exclaimed. "I'll be glad to tell you, Melody. It's an imaginary monster. It's not real. It's like this huge, ugly-looking creature with a body like a goat, a head like a wild, angry, ferocious lion, and a huge, long, violent serpent tail that swings widely, striking its victims dead."

"Yeah, but Lori," said Brian, nodding, "it didn't have a lion's head. I saw it with my own two eyes, and this thing had something like a human head on it. And believe me, it was definitely huge!"

"But how tall would you say it was, Brian?" Terry asked, pointing toward the Jeeps after noticing that one of them had been smashed completely to the ground. "Man, you guys. What the fuck!"

"Holy shit, you guys. Look at that!" Brian cried out. "I told you that thing was huge. Look at that."

"Hey, Randy," Terry yelled again, hoping Randy would answer. "Come on, man, answer me. Are you still in there?"

"What are we gonna do?" Christine asked, staring at the crushed Jeep.

"I don't know, but I think we better get back inside that motor home," Brian told everybody. "At least it's got a transmitter and a few other things we can use to try contacting somebody for help."

"Randy!" Terry continued to call, but there was no response. "Hey man, you gotta answer me. You know?"

"Terry, man. Come on, dude," Brian said, trying to comfort him. "Hey, bro, there isn't anything we can do. I mean, look at it—it's really starting to get dark out here, and we need to try to get some help."

"I don't believe this is really happening," Melody said. "It's like a bad freakin' nightmare."

"Okay, you guys," Christine said, trying to get everybody's attention.

"What's happening, Christine?" Brian asked, wondering what was on her mind.

"We gotta get a grip on ourselves. It's like everything has been going really crazy ever since we came up here. We should have stayed in town, because everybody's thinking we're lost—or even dead or something. I mean, you guys heard what they were saying on the news about us. They even showed our pictures. That's just how serious it is. Something isn't right."

"Why don't we just hurry up and get inside this thing?" Lori said. "I don't want that thing coming back again. I don't wanna be out here—not in the dark."

"I gotta take a look inside that trailer," Brian said, staring at the damage the thing had caused. "You coming, Terry?"

"No," Melody said in a whisper. "I mean, why don't we all, you know, stick together? Let's take a look together."

"Yeah, I would agree," Lori said. "Let's stick together. I don't want to be by myself."

"Well, let's do this," Brian said, heading toward the trailer. "Whatever that thing was, it's long gone by now."

"That's easy for you to say, Brian," Melody told him. "What about what it did with Randy?"

"Randy, are you in here?" Terry called again, stopping at the entrance of the trailer, hoping to get a response. "Are you in here, dude?"

"Oh, shit, you guys," Brian exclaimed in a low voice. "You gotta see this. I mean, fuck! Just look at this."

"What is it, Brian?" Christine asked nervously, moving aside from Terry, who was still standing within inches of entering the trailer. "What do you see?"

"Hey, somebody help me!" A troubling voice called out from the back of the trailer, shivering with fear. "Somebody, help me!"

"Randy, is that you?" Christine yelled. "Is that really you?"

"Where?" Melody demanded. "Where is he?"

"Randy!" Terry cried out. "Man, dude. Is that really you?"

"It's him," Brian said. "Come on, you guys, we gotta get him out of there."

Everybody entered the trailer.

"Where is he?" Lori asked excitedly. "Where is he?"

"Man, fuck!" Brian said, searching for Randy. "Hold on, man. Here we come. We're right here. Just hold on."

"Randy, where are you?" Terry frantically called out. "Where are you?"

"Randy!" Melody shouted, distraught with worry and fear.

"Please let us know where you are."

"Everybody stop for a minute," Brian told them, looking around. "Hold up right here. Something isn't right about this."

"What are you talking about, Brian?" Melody asked. "What's wrong?"

"Where are you, Randy?" Terry called out. "Where are you?"

"Yeah, Brian," Christine said, looking around. "Isn't he in here?"

"I don't know," Brian admitted.

"But we all heard him calling for help," Lori said, worried. "We did, didn't we?"

"Yeah," Brian said. "Though..."

"Hey, man," Terry said, moving slowly past Brian. "That's my brother in that room, and I'm going in there to help him. Didn't you guys hear him? He needs our help."

"But why would he call us to help him?" Christine said. "And then—"

"I mean, just look, you guys," Brian said, nodding toward the back of the trailer at the open door of a dark room. "We don't know what's in there. I mean, why isn't he still calling us for help?"

"Wait a minute, Terry," Melody cried out. "You know, I think he's right. Why isn't he calling us for help right now? I don't think it was really him."

"Well, then who was it, Melody?" Terry asked angrily. "Just who was it if it wasn't Randy?"

"I don't know, Terry," Melody said, shaking her head. "But really, I don't think what we heard was him."

Suddenly, Terry slowly began to back away from the entrance to the dark room. While he did, everybody could sense that something wasn't quite right about the voice they'd heard—supposedly Randy crying out for their help.

Fragments and pieces of debris from the ceiling were scattered about the entrance to the trailer as Melody and Christine began tapping on boxes and collecting scattered documents and important manuals from the boxes.

"Let's hurry up and get everything we can," Brian said. "Don't need to be coming back in this thing for nothing."

"Why don't we go ahead and take this stuff over to the Winnebago?" Christine suggested while loading some of the boxes onto a hand dolly.

"You, Melody, and Lori go on," Brian told her. "Me and Terry will be over there in a minute."

"I thought we were going to stick together?" Lori asked, questioning what they'd agreed to earlier.

"She's right, Brian," Christine said. "We should continue just as we planned."

"Let's hurry up and get out of here," Terry told everybody. "Before I'm tempted to go ahead and see what's in that room."

"I know just what you mean," Brian said, looking down the hallway toward the dark room. "I wanna see what's in there too."

"You guys hurry up and get this stuff out of here," Terry told Melody. "Brian, you keep an eye on the hallway. I'mma see if I can move this thing from where it is."

"What?" Brian asked, curious about what Terry meant. "Man, I know you're not thinking about trying to move that big-ass monitor all by yourself. Are you?"

"Just wanna see if it'll come loose from the wall," Terry said. "I think we can use it."

"That size?" Brian questioned.

"Uh-huh," Terry mumbled. "It'll be just right for us to use."

"But it's already three—or maybe even four—of them over there, if I'm not mistaken," Brian said.

"Man, are you sure about that?"

"Yeah! I know I'm sure."

"And you're just now saying something about it?"

"I don't know. I thought I said something about it a long time ago."

"Man, I don't remember—"

"Wow!" Brian whispered intently, staring down the hallway. "Hey!"

"What's happening?" Terry asked, backing away from the monitor. "What's happening, Brian?"

Whatever it was that caused Brian to suddenly say "Wow!" as if he'd been startled, it made everybody stop what they were doing.

"Hurry up and get that stuff out of here," Brian told Melody. "I know I just saw something walk past that door back there."

"Back there where?" Terry asked, staring down the hallway.

"In the dark room," Brian said. "Or rather, the black room."

"You mean the death room," Christine said, pushing the dolly outside the trailer and onto the steps. "Let's go, you guys," she added, referring to Lori and Melody. "See the hole up there in the ceiling? I ain't gonna let that thing do me like that."

"What was it, Brian?" Melody asked.

"And here we go again with all the questioning," Brian said. "Didn't we already go through this once? I know I saw something moving around back there. Isn't that enough for you to believe? Something is moving around back there, and it sure as hell isn't Randy. Whatever it is, it's our size!"

"Brian," Terry said in a low whisper. "Hey, you can't blame her for asking so many questions. She feels the same way I do about Randy."

"Yeah, man, I know. I guess we're all on edge about this. I know I am—except one thing: I just don't want whatever that thing is coming after me."

"None of us do. That's why it's important to try to understand what Melody is going through. We're all going through it—whatever it is."

Before Brian could respond, Melody, Christine, and Lori were already headed to the Winnebago with everything they could carry. Thankfully, everybody remained near the front entrance of the trailer instead of venturing into the back.

*

It was definitely a chimera that Brian saw bursting through the top of the trailer. From humanity's perspective, it was an imaginary monster, a creation of the mind in relation to ideas of what it means to be human. But one might wonder if the chimera could ever truly be a living being instead of just a fanciful fantasy. I would guess it depends on whom you are sharing this fantasy with. We all seem to have such vivid imaginations when it comes to monsters, and a strange taste for letting fiction feel real—marked by highly fanciful and supernatural elements conjured from our minds.

A creation from our very own imaginary world, which we hold deep inside these bodies of ours.

The almighty chimera is described by Webster's as a monster with a lion's head, a goat's body, and a serpent's tail.

What Brian saw forcefully blasting its way through the top of the trailer could have been just about anything when one is afraid. I would like to emphasize—and I do stress—that whatever it was that our man Brian saw coming from the top of that trailer, it was indeed in the likeness of a chimera, but it wasn't a "chimera," nor was it a "wart hog."

From a genealogy account of the descent of a family, group, or person, what Brian saw were the descendants of Lucifer himself —the Devil, Almighty Satan, and his children from the pit of Hell. *The Dragon* by Bennie R. Murdock describes the spiritual ramifications of the philosophical system more commonly referred to as the "Dialectic."

The facts here are that Brian had just come out of the Winnebago and, upon staring into the darkening sky, became startled by the loud sound of a violent explosion. At that moment, while he stared intently into the darkening sky, a figure—which he immediately described as a chimera—came blasting forcefully from the top of the trailer. Both Terry and his kid brother, Randy, were inside, as the figure poked holes in the ceiling, searching for what they had thought might possibly be a human—or perhaps a raccoon—following them, and at times listening to their conversations.

*

"It was something with big, ugly, round eyes," Lori told everybody, describing what she'd seen staring at her from underneath the door while she lay flat on the floor, trying to see from that angle. "It was just staring directly at me. It even smiled at me."

Having already said that whatever it was had smiled at her, Lori realized that something was indeed inside the room—something that frightened her terribly. Her only explanation was to blame Randy for what she'd seen.

"Jesus Christ, Lori," Randy said, laughing at the thought of how fast she had suddenly leaped up from the floor. Still laughing, he said, "What's your problem? You're acting like you've seen a ghost or something."

"Yeah, I did!" she said, screaming at Randy. "And I think he knows just what it is that's in there. Don't you, Randy?"

*

The truth is, whatever was crawling in the ceiling can best be described in the book of Revelation. The Beast—Lucifer himself cast out of Heaven—wasn't alone. His entire flock received the same penalty for their crime and offense. This phenomenon represents a conflict generated between the residents of the town of Stonyford and Lucifer for their failure to comply with his demands.

He's now seeking compensation.

The huge beasts described—without any recognizable identities—under the conditions of Stonyford and the surrounding communities are, in fact, the spirits presently inhabiting this entire region.

"Lucifer's army of fallen angels." The same group of immortal beings that once attended upon God—both kind and lovable—played an extremely dramatic role during the creation of all existing space and matter, once regarded as a whole. This teaching is difficult to assimilate if you've never heard about it. But the question remains: Is it really the truth?

As in the small community of Stonyford, California, Margaret Johnson was indeed the victim of something deadly. The threat could be felt as far away as Medford, Oregon, where residents of the northern California region fled, trying to avoid becoming victims. However, false prophets ventured to Stonyford to engage in deceptive teachings designed to ensnare residents into believing in the Antichrist. This entire practice was specifically linked to the old snake hunter and his snake. In the beginning, there was the savage slaying of Wanda, prompting Christians everywhere to believe the fulfillment of all prophecies was imminent. This theory was being systematically demonstrated and integrated throughout the region.

The spirit of Lucifer, which many had thought bound deep in the bottomless pit, could be seen in a glossary-like form—a "list of describable messages expressing precise definitions" about Stonyford's failure to submit to "HIS" theology and its demands for submission.

*

"Okay, Terry. Check this out. Uh, I'mma go out back to see if I can, you know, see anything. I mean, that's if there's a window back there. While I'm doing that, you can keep an eye on this room. OK?"

"Whatever, man. Just don't be gone too long. You know what I mean?"

"Hey, I feel you, Terry. I just wanna see if there's a window so I can see inside this thing."

"Wait a minute. Hold up, Brian."

"What's the problem?"

"I think something just moved. You know, like, it walked past that door and went to the other side."

"Are you sure?" Brian asked, slyly looking down the hallway. "Damn."

"Wait a minute," Terry said, about to suggest something. "Let me see. I thought I'd seen a flashlight in here somewhere."

"It's a box of them over there, behind you."

"Where?"

"Right there. Well, that's if the girls didn't take them."

"Oh. Damn. Here's a few right here."

"And okay, Terry. Just what the fuck are you thinking about doing?"

"Well, for one thing. And that's if I can find one that'll really do the job by lighting everything up. I'm going to throw this baby down there and into that room, and light that motherfucker up big time."

Brian smiled.

"What, Brian? You don't think it'll work?"

"No, dude. I think it's a great idea. But only one thing."

"Yeah. What's that?"

"I'mma throw one too."

Both nodded in agreement.

"What, you say we throw all of them?"

"Let's do it. I'm following you."

"But what if it comes after us?"

"Terry, I know you'll deal with it. I got faith in you."

"Oh, that's right. Put me out there to fight this thing by my-self."

"But if it turns out to be Randy?"

"Man, Brian," Terry suddenly stared at the room. "I gotta try calling him again, man. I mean, that's my kid brother. Let me see first, you know. I gotta see if it's him or not."

"Go ahead, Terry. See if he'll answer you."

Terry hesitated for a few seconds, peering intently down the hallway as if trying to make a connection with whatever was in the room. "Randy, is that you?" he called in a soft voice. "Randy, is that you in there? Answer me, man. Is that you?"

"Hey, Terry," Brian said, checking the flashlight. "Man, this is kind of, you know, ridiculous in a way. I mean, here you are calling him, but he ain't answering. Maybe we should just go on down there and see for ourselves?"

"Brian, do you see that hole up there?"

"And? What's your point?"

"Just look at it. Whatever did that, I really don't think either of us needs to be trying to fight it."

"Mmm, I know what you mean."

"And think about the Jeep. Who crushed it like that? Or rather, what was it that crushed it, Brian? Didn't you say you saw it? Was it carrying something? I just hope it wasn't my brother."

"I'm really sorry, man. But I know what I saw. It was really moving fast, and then, all of a sudden, it just, like, landed on top of the Jeep."

"Now that's what I'm talking about, Brian," Terry said, refer-ring to how Brian described whatever it was landing on top of one of the Jeeps. "It didn't crash into the Jeep, but you said it landed—

meaning, damn! Just the weight of that thing flattened our Jeep."

"Hold up, Terry," Brian said, motioning toward the back of the trailer when he felt movement again. "You feel that?"

"On the count of three," Terry suggested. "Let me throw mine first."

"Better make sure it's fully on, all the way. High beam."

"Switch all of them to high beam."

"Thought you knew."

"All right then," Terry said, smiling. "Ready?"

"Let's do this," Brian said in a deep, low tone. Counting to three, he first tossed a medium-size, five-hundred-watt portable halogen work light down the hallway, partially lighting the room as a small fluorescent light would. Both Terry and Brian then stood quietly, trying to get a quick glimpse of the figure in the room.

"You see anything?" Brian asked.

"Hell no, man. I think that motherfucker's hiding behind something," Terry whispered.

"Damn! And just think, Melody was back there moving those boxes around and didn't even see that thing," Brian said.

"And it was probably watching her the whole time," Terry added, nodding his head.

"Hey, Terry. Man, check this out," Brian said, pointing to an area in the room where a long, narrow, rusted metal crowbar rested against a wall. "See how it's got that chisel-shaped part on one end?"

"Yeah, dude. I see it," Terry said. "What about it?"

"Well, I was just thinking about how sharp the edge is on that thing," Brian told him. "I bet it'll cut through just about anything."

"So whatcha thinking, Brian? Running back there and cutting that thing into pieces?"

"Naw, Terry," Brian said seriously. "I was thinking that if we can get it to move past the door again, I'mma throw that mother-fucker as hard as I can."

"And what if you miss?"

"Hey," Brian said with confidence. "Throwing shit is my specialty."

"So, what do you wanna do? Think we should go ahead and throw a few more of these flashlights down there, or what?"

"Gotta get that thing to move again," Brian said. "You start throwing them, and I'll get this crowbar and aim it at my target."

"Okay, here I go," Terry said. "Count to three, Brian."

"One. Two. Three!" Brian said, counting in a whisper to the number three, giving Terry the go-ahead to start throwing the flashlights. "That's right, you freakin' motherfucker!" Brian shouted out loud. "Come on out so we can see your fuckin' ass, you motherfucker. Come on! You bastard!"

"There he is," Terry shouted, pointing at the figure. "Get 'em, Brian! Get 'em!"

Upon seeing a slight resemblance and possible appearance of the figure moving slowly past the entrance to the room, Brian was already highly tense. He then very nervously, and suddenly, drew back his right arm, firmly gripping the rusted crowbar. Then he threw it as hard as he could in the direction of the door, observing it as it sped through the air, puncturing its way through the door and leaving a shattering gaping hole in its wake.

"Yeah, man!" Terry yelled after seeing what happened. "I think you got that motherfucker, Brian.

"Fuckin' yeah," Brian yelled, looking intently down the hallway. "What you think about that, you freakin' son-of-a-bitch? Whatcha think about that?"

"Come on out and show yourself now, motherfucker," Terry called out to the figure, daring it to come out. "What's wrong? Afraid to show just who the fuck you are? Come on out and show yourself now! You ugly-ass looking motherfucker. Yeah, that's right! Brian nailed you, didn't he?"

"Hold on, Terry," Brian said, slightly pulling back on one of

Terry's arms in an attempt to stop him from going down the hall-way. "Wait a minute."

"Wait for what?" Terry asked. "You nailed that mother-fucker."

"Hold on, man," Brian told him. "Just hold on for a minute and let me find something else to throw before you go down there. That thing just might be waiting for us. Who knows?"

"Man, Brian," Terry said, laughing loudly. "Man, I heard it hit. That motherfucker is dead, and I bet you anything he's hanging stuck on the other side of that door somewhere."

"Easy for you to say," Brian said, shrugging his shoulders. "But, man, I swear. If that thing comes my way, I tell you, Terry, I ain't taking no freakin' chances."

"Well, hurry up and get whatever you think you can find and throw it. You'll be wasting time otherwise. That thing is DEAD!"

This time, it was an old hand-size ball bearing that Brian found on the floor underneath a desk.

"Got something," Brian said, coming up from underneath the desk.

"Man, Brian. What's that? A goddamn miniature bowling ball you got in your hand? What? Next you'll be under there looking for the pins. This ain't no time to be playing around, dude."

"It ain't no freakin' bowling ball, Terry. It's a small ball bear-ing."

"Oh, yeah. That's right. I guess you're gonna try throwing that thing all the way down there to that door?"

"Yeah! Why not?"

"And just how heavy is it? Let me see."

Terry took the ball bearing in one of his hands to see how much it weighed.

"Not bad," Terry said, lifting the ball bearing up and down. "Really not bad at all. I thought this sucker would be heavier. But it's like one of those small anchors you put on your line when fishing. Just a little bit heavier. So what's up?"

"You ready?" Brian said, grinning foolishly.

"Hell yeah," Terry said, grinning back. "Just let me move back a little before you do it."

Brian stepped back with Terry. Clutching the ball bearing in his right hand, he swung it in a slow backward arc, preparing an underhand throw, his hand kept below shoulder level like a softball pitch.

He took a few steps forward, swung the ball bearing in a wide circle as fast as he could, and then released it.

CHAPTER THREE

SUDDENLY, THERE WAS A LOUD ANGUISHING SCREAM, so agonizing it could be heard for miles in every direction. Windows began to shatter, and every form of wildlife fled swiftly from its natural environment.

Residents and out-of-towners as far away as the town of Stonyford, who were busy enjoying the celebration, found themselves deeply startled by the violent jolt of such a scream.

"Oh man, Terry," Brian yelled. "My ears! Man, I can't hear anything."

"What the fuck!" Terry yelled out loud. "Motherfuck! Man, Brian, what the fuck did you do?"

Just as Brian turned toward the trailer entrance, thinking Terry was close behind. He caught a fleeting glimpse of the crowbar streaking through the air, aimed straight at Terry's head like a bullet.

The impact shattered Terry's skull instantly, sending fragments flying in every direction throughout the trailer.

The impact was so powerful, and the continued scream so enormous and excruciating, that Brian found himself blown a considerable distance from the trailer, tumbling over and over like a rolling somersault, finally coming to rest near the flattened Jeep.

After realizing he wasn't badly hurt and could still feel all his limbs, he regained control of himself and staggered unsteadily toward the Winnebago, overwhelmed by a loss of coordination.

Reaching the Winnebago, he was met with a barrage of questions from Lori, Christine, and Melody, who were screaming, frantically and emotionally distraught with worry and fear.

"What happened, Brian?" Melody screamed. "What happened? Where is Terry?"

Not realizing he was temporarily impaired in hearing, he had to point to his ears before they understood he was having trouble comprehending what they were saying.

Though confusion still reigned, pieces of fire, debris, and scattered remains of Terry continued to fall from the dark sky after the trailer exploded. Discarded waste littered the entire campground. Yet the scream persisted, as the figure they were after—during the explosion—ejected itself just as it had intended, mirroring the action of the first figure they had pursued from the ceiling.

*

However intentional the explosion, the two "Beasts" from Hell are among those described, along with the pale horse in doctrine, as "Death and Hell" in close proximity. This, of course, is the beginning of the end for the Stonyford region. Submission is at hand, but for the refusal of others, Lucifer's covenant with the elder residents of Stonyford has internalized their benefits. As for the others, Satan has already planned a place for them in the pit of Hell.

The deaths of Travis, Randy, and Terry are invariably and undeniably a departure anticipated by Lucifer himself. In other words, they have become primary examples, as so many others have throughout the northern region of California.

Garberville is doomed, just as the town of Covelo is about to be. A highly contagious disease, prone to rapid spread, is about to be unleashed—carried by the manipulations and false deceptions of old Lucifer himself. Sounds familiar, doesn't it?

*

"Melody, can't you see he's hurt?" Christine screamed, grabbing Brian and helping him into the Winnebago. "Somebody help us!"

"Where's Terry?" Lori asked, frantic and confused, scanning the falling debris from the darkened sky. "What happened? Where's the trailer? Where is everything? Are we on fire too?"

"Watch him while I go check," Christine told Melody, looking outside the door to see if the Winnebago was on fire. "This stuff is everywhere. It's all over the place. But I don't see anything burning on top of us."

Realizing Christine needed help, he began straightening up to assist her.

"Brian! Brian! Are you OK?" Melody and Lori both asked. "Are you all right, Brian?"

"Ah, man," Brian moaned. "Damn! I thought I'd lost my hearing. I couldn't hear anything except that loud ringing and somebody screaming."

"What happened over there, Brian?" Lori asked again. "Where's Terry?"

"Lori," Melody cried. "Can't you see he's trying to get it together?"

"Where's Christine?" he asked, looking around at everything. "Where is she?"

"Outside, checking to make sure we're not on fire," Melody told him.

"Outside!" Brian yelled. "What? Move out of the way. I gotta go get her."

"Brian!" Melody shouted at him. "Just let me try stopping this bleeding from your head."

"What? My head?"

"Yeah," she said, trying to place a towel on the front of his head. "You have a small cut that's not really that bad. I'm just trying to stop a little bleeding. It's just a little cut."

"Here's a bandage I found in the desk next to the door," Lori said. "If you need more, there are plenty."

"Ah, man, Melody. My head is killing me," Brian said, glaring down at his torn, bloody jeans below the knees. "My leg might even be broken. Just look at me."

"What happened to Terry, Brian?" Lori asked again. "Where is he?"

"Tell you in a minute, Lori," he said. "I promise. You just don't know what we're up against. None of us do, but we gotta get outta here. Why don't you check if the keys are in the ignition while I go get Christine? She doesn't need to be out there by herself. What is she doing out there anyway?"

"Uh, she's checking to make sure we're not on fire," Melody told him.

"Yeah, after that explosion, everything really lit up," Lori said. "It was like the whole campground was on fire. It's still slowly coming down, landing on everything."

"That's why I have to get out there," Brian said, reaching for the door.

"I'll go with you," Melody said, following behind him.

"No, Melody," he said firmly. "Stay in here with Lori and help her find the keys and anything else you can. We need a way to make contact with somebody. We need help."

"What about that thing in that room, Melody?" Lori asked. "I think it's something you use when trying to talk to people. I saw my uncle Tony using one of them in his pickup."

"What did you say, Lori?" Brian asked, interested in what she was referring to. "What? I mean, where is it? You know, the thing you're talking about?"

"They're back there," she said, pointing to the back of the Winnebago. "Where I put some of these boxes."

"You mean there's more than one?"

"Uh-huh," she answered. "There's even one right up over the driver's seat. But that's a CB radio, I think."

"Christine!" Brian called as he stepped out the door. "Christine, where are you? Are you out here? Can you hear me? Where are you, Christine?"

Silence.

The only sounds were tree branches, dry twigs, leaves, and burning stems, crackling sharply as they fell to the ground.

In the far distance, the piercing scream could still be heard, like a child crying out for its mother.

*

Still, the story begins with a timeline. The events have largely unfolded in Stonyford and the surrounding region. The persecution and impregnation of many people here—through incestuous relationships, often disgusting and brutal—is not entirely unthinkable.

Not in the small, diminutive town of Stonyford, where such relationships are, in fact, permissible.

Lucifer is by all means the caretaker, satisfied with the elders who have fully stretched themselves outward toward this specific, established, ongoing tangle of obligations set forth through false fundamental prophecies and miscalculations. Although stunning to realize, this miscalculation about the Stonyford region has caused intensifying waves of undeniable events and sequents in unnatural forms. The clock is steadily ticking and indeed intensifying. The rapid escalation progresses well aligned with the facts, sequentially occurring throughout the northern region of California.

The media have been extremely skeptical of false doctrines. The most important aspect brought forth is Margaret Johnson, directly related at the very beginning of this phase, providing basic versions of the horrific, horrible fall of the entire region.

"Oh, my gosh. Gee," Margaret whispered to herself while thinking back on the events that brought so much anguishing pain into her childhood life—tormenting hundreds of people with its mad, seething wrathfulness. "It was irate and full of anger. It was enraged, with inflaming fire emitting from its wide, ugly-looking nostrils. I saw that face staring directly at me. Smiling as if it were telling me something wonderful about myself.

But it was surely Death! Death was standing right there in front of me, about to take me as it pleased. Everything was disgusting about that place of horror—pure horror, seemingly intensifying rapidly every day."

Progressively escalating amongst everybody living in that town. And there I was, satisfying the elders of Stonyford sexually. On most occasions, I also witnessed others being brutally assaulted by the so-called elder citizens of Stonyford. And do I really give a rat's ass about their fate? Surely not!

Even when Margaret attempted to get her parents' attention, it was as though they cared more about Wanda than Margaret. She was intentionally confined to one room of the Johnson family estate, allowed only one meal per day, with no means of education or association with neighboring children.

"Perhaps the only way for me to actually describe my opinion —which I am more than sure is bizarre, though foundationally true in nature—about the situation in Stonyford is something just like Armageddon," she said, using her frail hands and arms to draw imaginary pictures in the air about Stonyford. "There are forces of both good and evil at battle. Sadly, the consequences between the two will be long lasting, and just about everything, for the king-dom of Lucifer, he is going to place his seal on it. This is going to be described as the mark of the beast."

Everybody should be wary and extremely skeptical of things and events not seen. False doctrines will be one of the means by which Lucifer operates. It will all intensify until this cycle of tribulations is completed.

"Sounds like... you know, something like a meltdown is going to happen in Stonyford," I said, murmuring my thoughts inten-tionally so she could hear me.

"Meltdown?" she said, surprised. "Uh-huh, I like that. Now you're beginning to catch on to what I'm saying, young man. A meltdown is exactly the concept I have been trying to explain about that old town."

*

Meanwhile, Brian continued calling Christine repeatedly, but there was no response. Silence filled the air, broken only by the soft sounds of dry twigs and tree stems burning around them.

"Where's Christine?" Melody asked, noticing Brian returning through the door by himself. "Oh my God, Brian. Where is Chris-tine?" She covered her mouth with her hands in shock.

"Man, Melody," he said, pushing past her toward the front and staring at the driver's seat. "You didn't find the keys?"

"No, I haven't checked yet," she said, her voice trembling at the thought of Brian not finding Christine. "But I think, Lori—just what the fuck is going on, Brian?" she demanded. "We gotta get outta here. I'm really scared. Oh my God!"

"Melody, try to get a hold of yourself," he told her, grabbing her by the shoulders and pulling her toward him. "Please, Melody. Try to get a grip. I need you to be strong right now—for all of us, you know?"

"She's back there trying to find a goddamn phone or some-thing."

"Lori!" Brian called out just loud enough for her to hear. "I think you should come up here for a minute. We gotta get our-selves together."

Without answering, Lori came rushing down the dimly lit hallway from the back of the Winnebago to see what he wanted.

"What?" she said, as if too busy to care. "I heard you."

"What were you doing back there?" he asked. "Did you find the key to this thing, or were you too busy to even look for them?"

"Well, for one thing," she began, one hand on her hip, "I was just about to drop number two in the toilet—for your information. And secondly, you didn't scare me peeping in that window. I fig-ured it was you."

"Lori, what are you talking about?" Melody asked.

"Just as I said," she replied, staring directly at Brian. "I was just about to, you know what, when I saw him looking at me—smiling. So when I jumped up to close the curtain I noticed was drawn back, Brian wasn't there anymore."

"I don't know what you're talking about, Lori," Brian told her.

"It couldn't have been Brian, Lori," Melody said, glancing out one of the side windows. "I mean, he was out there looking for Christine—"

Lori just stood there, staring slyly at Brian with a slight smile. "It was him, and he knows it," she insisted, still looking directly at Brian. "And by the way, where's Christine?"

"I was out there, and probably did walk past that bathroom window, but honestly, Lori, I didn't once look inside any window. If anything—and if that window was open—you should've heard me calling Christine's name."

"Well, if it wasn't you, then—"

"Okay, you guys," Brian said, heading for the door to lock it.

"Whatever it is that's happening, it's only the three of us left—unless Terry, Travis, Randy, and Christine showed up all of a sudden. But whatever's going on, it really doesn't look like that's going to happen."

"But where's Christine?" Lori asked, demanding to know. "She was just outside the door. Where is she? And where's Terry, Brian? You gotta know."

"Look, Lori," Brian said with a shrug, glancing around the room. "I'm as lost as you are. I just know we gotta do something to get the hell out of here."

"There's a rack full of keys hanging on one of the walls back there," Lori said, turning to head down the narrow hallway.

"What?" Brian asked quickly.

"Yeah, where?" Melody added.

"Follow me," Lori said. "I'll show you."

"Wait a minute," Brian said suddenly, stopping before entering the hallway. "You guys go ahead and check while I mess around with this driver's panel. Make sure to lock—and double lock—all the windows back there."

"And what about this door?" Melody asked him. "Is it locked?"

"Should be," he told her. "When I closed it, I think I remember using one of my fingers to switch the latch just above the knob. But why don't you guys check it to make sure?"

"Got it," said Melody. "Got it."

"See, that's the window I was talking about," Lori said, pointing at the small, square bathroom window, its light pink, blue, and white trimmings outlined with bright yellow flowers decorating the curtains.

"I know it was him, Melody," she again insisted. "And I am more than sure he got a chance to see—it! You know—just what he was trying to see."

"But what if it wasn't?" Melody tried to suggest, hinting that maybe she thought it was Brian. "Look, Lori, it could've been the shadow from all these trees around here or something. I mean, just think about that explosion. There are still a thousand pieces of that stuff falling from who knows where."

"But I know what I saw, Melody," she said, insisting it was Brian. "He's been after me like a serial stalker ever since we were in Stonyford."

"But why Stonyford?" Melody asked her. "I mean, you know, it's not like him to be sneaking around after what we've been through, and all of a sudden he's a freakin' stalker. Next you'll be accusing him of trying to rape you."

"I think that's what he wants to do, Melody," Lori said frantically. "That might be his next move—once he gets you out of the way."

"What are you talking about, Lori?"

"Everything that's been happening. I think he's in on it."

"Are you crazy? He isn't that type of person. Plus, I've known Brian ever since we were kids; and you have too, Lori."

"You don't believe me, do you, Melody? I thought you were my friend. You always told me I could trust you, that I could turn to you whenever I was in a jam or having problems. So now here I am, in a jam and having serious problems. But do you believe me? I don't think so, Melody. I'm having problems, and you don't want to listen. You don't even believe me."

"Oh yes I do, but—"

"Oh, I see. You have a crush on him, don't you, Melody? You're on his side against me. What? Am I next on your list?"

"Lori," Melody said softly, trying to calm her. "What are you talking about? There's no list. Nobody's next on anything. You're just being paranoid."

"Oh, what, Melody? You think I'm just imagining the whole thing? Like nothing is really happening? That all of this is just in my mind?"

"Look, Lori, we're all a bit stressed out. Just think about it—look at what we've been through! We're the only ones left. Who knows what's going to happen next? Do you? I sure don't. And neither do you or even Brian."

"What's the problem?" Brian said, coming down the hallway. "Where's the bathroom?"

"Like you don't remember," Lori said, slowly moving back.

"Lori!" Melody said, surprised. "It's right here, Brian."

"Are you guys all right?" he asked, staring at Lori. "Look, Lori, I really don't care what you think about me. I'm just trying to get us the fuck out of here—alive! So, you just keep saying what's on your mind about me. But see, somebody has to take charge and be responsible for all of us. And all I am trying to do is do everything I can to get help, and get us the fuck out of this crazy nightmare."

"I know you're frightened, and scared as hell about whatever it is that's been happening. But so is Melody, and I am too! Believe me, Lori, I haven't anything to do with any of it."

"This is a horrible dream that we didn't ask for. None of us. But here we are, distressing ourselves over shit that none of us have anything to do with."

Christine went out this door, trying to make sure this thing wasn't on fire. What happened after that? Your guess is as good as mine. But one thing's for sure: I wasn't looking in no goddamn window at you. It wasn't me. And sure, Lori, it's no secret how I feel about you, but I sure ain't gonna be waiting on you to go to the bathroom just to get a peep at you.

"Lori, why didn't you close the window?" Melody asked, squeezing past Brian, who was standing in the doorway to the bathroom.

"I thought I'd closed it," Lori murmured to herself.

"You closed the curtain, but you left this window wide open," Melody told her, shutting the window. "Now, it's closed and locked tight."

"I think we better do the same to all the windows," Brian suggested.

"What about the lights?" Lori said, looking up at the hallway lights.

"Yeah, I think you got a point, Lori," Brian told her. "Let's see if there's some way to dim them. All of them."

"You were up there messing around at the driver's panel," said Melody. "Didn't you see anything?"

"No, but I'll go check," he said. "But first, would you mind if I used the bathroom?"

"Oh, let me get out your way," Melody said, smiling slightly . "But that is unless, you know, you want us to stand here and watch you?"

"Well," he said, slightly grinning back, "after all that we've already gone through, closing this door just might not be a good idea for any of us, if you know what I mean."

"Mmm-mmm. I don't know," Lori said, mumbling.

"I got no problem with it," Melody said. "If it's the only way that we can keep an eye on each other without one of us disap-pearing, then I'll be first. You guys wanna watch me pee first? Or take a shit?"

"Hey! Hey! Hey!" Brian said, nodding his head while smiling. "I thought I was here first to use the bathroom?"

"Well, Lori. What do you think?" Melody asked her. "You wanna be by yourself and stand a chance of disappearing? Or are you going to join us?"

Lori just stood there for a minute, squinting her eyes at Brian, and then at Melody, who was acting as though she were about to unzip and unfasten all her clothing and get completely naked. *I know she isn't about to get naked, is she? In front of him? No way. But what if she does? I mean, then what? Am I to do the same, just because Melody's doing it? And what if Brian all of a sudden gets a hard-on? We'll all be in here walking around naked, and he'll be trying to fuck us. The both of us at the same time. NO! NO! NO! I don't believe this is really happening. Let me out of here—RIGHT FUCKIN' NOW!*

"Uh, Lori, what do you think?" Melody was still asking Lori, who was standing there as if in a daze, thinking to herself.

"Well?" Melody asked, shrugging.

"Okay!" Lori said, smiling. "I'm all for it. Let's all get buck naked."

CHAPTER FOUR

"AM I THE ONLY ONE WHO HEARD THAT OR WHAT?" Sheriff Blake said, looking around, trying to figure out where the loud, agonizing scream had come from. "Didn't you hear that?" he asked one of his flunkies. "Now don't tell me that I'm the only one who heard whatever that was."

"Uh, I think just about everybody heard it, Sheriff," his flunky told him. "But nobody can figure out where it came from. I think it's just some of these kids around here somewhere enjoying themselves."

"Yeah, with one of them, you know, goddamn bull-horns or a goddamn loudspeaker they'd probably swiped from one of our concession stands," Blake said, laughing to himself. "If that goddamn son-of-a-bitch keeps that noise up, one of y'all go find that bastard and lock his ass up for a while."

Everybody laughing.

"What?" the flunky asked. "For how long?"

"For as long as you want to," Blake told him. "Just make sure you keep his goddamn mouth away from that loudspeaker or whatever he's using."

"Whatever you say, Sheriff. I'm on it."

The flunky went on his way, big-headed from the thought of his mission. He was determined to find whoever had been making those loud, agonizing screams. The noise had been irritating Stonyford's thousands of festival-goers, all of whom were enjoying themselves with their usual malicious wickedness and illegal paraphernalia.

Yes indeed, Blake really knew how to rub elbows with the right people. There wasn't any question about it. The message was loud and clear: Stonyford was thought to be on a sure rebound, doing so with everything that would be considered forbidden by the law of the land.

Blake walked around like a man of supernatural power, with a few of his flunkies treating him as if he embodied ultimate importance. And he certainly thrived on this divinely imagined reverence, as if he were a deity, a supernatural presence foretelling the future of Stonyford.

At times, Sheriff Blake even found himself being addressed as a clergyman—despite never having performed a prayer in his life.

Yet, seeing so many bright smiles taking part in the festivity, with its long, winding procession, caused the sheriff to suddenly scream out loud, "You goddamn right! Stonyford is rebounding!" Then, in a quieter tone, he muttered, "You bunch of coward sons-of-Bitches!"

*

Incredibly, Sheriff Blake could still find himself utterly free of shame or guilt, yet remarkably, he remained knowledgeably and mathematically wrong about the rebound of Stonyford. His miscalculation about the town's resurgence was about to prove disastrously fatal, inevitably bringing deadly consequences for a vast number of proud, joyous festivity merrymakers—attacked by vicious, hollow fangs so poisonous that the victims would endure a long, agonizing death of internal bleeding, exacerbated by agents of Satan.

Innocent or not, submission was at hand, unmistakable and unconcealed.

Lucifer was about to reclaim his domain without difficulty. His brutal intimidation, enforced through confessions and long-established community practices throughout the Stonyford region, can best be comprehended by anyone visiting the area. Although somewhat difficult when interviewing elder residents, it appeared that the fulfillment of these dark designs had evaded crucial tests for decades, only to recur in the present with eerily similar, unique patterns.

However internalized the brutality, Lucifer's angels will appear in many forms. A primary example will be those in the form of ancient, historical birds and enormous brontosaurs emerging from the mountains on every side of Stonyford. This is also when you'll see the true imaginary chimera, with a lion's head, goat's body, and serpent's tail, ready to attack at will—devouring every living human being greedily and aggressively, while simultaneously violently attacking one another as if in combat, in a manner that humans would consider cannibalistic.

All so stunning, and yet, without concealment. The entire situation in the Stonyford region shall by all means come to pass, with every event geared toward the upcoming inauguration representing the submission on behalf of the fallen angels from heaven, now being released from the bottomless pit. Surrounded by thousands of basilisks—the legendary, lethal, lizardlike serpents with deadly breath and glance, extremely sharp teeth like those of a barracuda, and standing as tall as an anteater with wings like a guzzy lacewing insect—very large, oversized, carrion-eating vultures and various condors will appear like never before. Millions of vinegarroons will accompany them, though these scorpionlike arachnids are highly lethal, with a foul mastigoproctus giganteus that emits a strong, vinegary odor so disturbing it can paralyze.

This will be the beginning of the hateful behavior and the withholding animosity of Lucifer's belligerence. During this lengthy period in the development stages of this seemingly bloody outpouring, which represents a particular historical stage of events occurring throughout the northern California hemisphere, however intentionally concealed, the first inhabitants of the bottomless pit will emerge. They are desperate to once again take their place serving the deceiving trickster himself, Old Lucifer. His failed attempt to assert himself over the kingdom of heaven with false teachings, doctrines, and elaborate presentations is about to take place once more. Through careful manipulation, he can intimidate those ushered into his reign from all walks of life.

*

"Yeah, that's right," Blake said again to himself. "I got your back."

CHAPTER FIVE

"Uh, Lori. That's not what we're talking about," Melody said, turning toward Brian, surprised at Lori's statement. She thought about how not too long ago she'd accused Brian of peeping in the window at her, calling him a for-real serial stalker, and she was more than sure he had gotten a chance to see—*it!* Meaning her private parts. And now here she was talking about, *let's all get buck naked.*

"Are you all right, Lori? I mean—"

"Yeah! Why?"

"Just checking."

"Uh, you guys," Brian said, pointing at the door. "Leaving it open? Or are you going to close it?"

"Who gives a fuck?" Melody said, heading to the back of the Winnebago. "It's not like I haven't seen a naked man before."

"Yeah," said Lori. "Do what you wanna do, Brian. You won't be the first I've seen and definitely won't be the last."

"Easy for you to say, Lori," Brian shrugged. "Easy for you to say."

Entering the back area of the Winnebago, Melody noticed the large desk and immediately began searching through it for anything that could help them contact the Stonyford Sheriff Department.

"This closet door is stuck or something," Lori said, trying to open the sliding doors on both sides. "I can't get either of them to open."

"I'll help you in a minute," Melody said. "But first, let's find what we can in this desk, okay?"

"What about this big box over here?" Lori said, staring at a long, flat trunk lying on the floor. "The lock is open, so I guess I won't have any problem opening it."

"Do what you have to do, Lori," Melody told her, searching through every drawer and hidden sliding compartment. "Bingo!" she said. "I think I found something in this bag. Lots of money and a gun."

"And check this out, Melody," Lori said, holding up a True Navy Port Authority All Season II jacket. "There are also some Endeavor jackets in here, all for ladies. All colors and styles."

"Wait a minute," Melody said, staring at the closet. "Hurry up and get that stuff out of here. I'll get the guns and everything else."

"What's wrong, Melody?" Lori asked, looking toward the closet doors. "What'd you hear?"

"Just hurry up and get that stuff outta here," Melody told Lori again. "And tell Brian to get his freakin' ass back here right now. And to be quiet about it."

"What are you going to do?"

"Don't worry, I'll be all right. Just do what I told you, Lori."

"Okay, I'm hurrying up."

"Just go! Now! Don't worry about the rest of that stuff."

"But, Melody. I can't just leave you in here without knowing what's happening."

"Just please go, Lori," Melody insisted. "I promise you, I will be all right. Just make sure you tell Brian to come back here ASAP. Quick!"

*

An imaginary chimera? Could be, and especially after all they've gone through. Imagination can at times, tend to grant you your wish.

Melody stayed where she was until Brian could make it to the back of the Winnebago to see what was happening. Meanwhile, Lori, being a bit slow at times, could offer no help to Melody other than to make matters worse. And now Brian came to rescue Melody from what seemed to be a minor form of confinement and possible danger. Something was definitely hiding in the closet. But was it a chimera? How uncertain we can become when trying to guess. No matter how aggressively we focus our attention on any given subject, that very narrow mind of ours seems to miscalculate our judgment, leaving us scrambling to correct social embarrassment and frantically ward off basic defined identities.

As described in earlier chapters, the "Beast" or the "Manipulator" can only be identified as the "Dragon," in the likeness of Satan himself, manifested in internal forms throughout the meltdown of Stonyford.

*

"Brian!" Lori said in a low tone. "Something's back there. It's hiding in the closet, and Melody—she's still back there."

"What!" Brian shouted.

"Hold on for a minute," Lori said, covering his mouth.

"Man!" Brian yelled. "What're you doing?"

"I'm only tryin' to stop you from talking too loud."

"Like hell," he said. "You're trying to suffocate me doing that."

"No, I'm not, Brian," she said, shaking her head from side to side.

"Well—"

"Melody needs you back there right away. There's something hiding in the closet, and she said to tell you to get back there ASAP. But I don't know what ASAP means."

"Don't worry about it, Lori," he said. "It's just an abbreviation for words."

"Oh, that's it," she thought. "I've always wondered what ASAP meant."

"Just stay here and keep an eye on things, okay, Lori?" he said. "I'm going to see what's happening."

Entering the hallway, Brian could clearly see Melody seated at the odd-looking large desk, motionless but staring directly at something just a few feet away from the desk.

"What's the problem?" he asked, motioning to her with his hands.

"It's in there," she said, slowly raising one of her hands while whispering. "In there. It's in there. In the closet."

"What's in the closet?" he asked softly. "Can you move?"

"Yeah," she answered.

"Then why don't you get out from behind that desk?"

"Well, I want to, but you see, I think I'm in a bit of a jam."

"Melody, just what the fuck are you talking about?"

"Well, you see, I think I got my hand on one of those, you know, like a hand grenade or something."

"What the fuck!" Brian said doubtfully. "Are you sure it's a fuckin' grenade?"

"What, you want me to bring the thing up and show you?"

"No! Don't do anything like that. Just let me think for a minute."

"Think? Think about what?"

"Just let me figure this out. But are you really sure it's a grenade and not one of those, you know, fake ones? Like a little toy or something?"

"Well, I accidentally pulled the pin, and I can't seem to put it back inside this little hole. So I thought maybe you could do that for me instead of me trying to."

"And what about whatever it is in that closet?"

"What? You want me to ask it to come out here and do it?"

"No, that's not what I am saying, Melody. I just thought maybe if it's really something hiding in there, maybe you could, you know, probably, throw that thing at it or something?"

"Funny, Brian. Really funny. And what? Blow us the freak outta here?"

"It was just something—"

"Where's the other Jeep at, Brian?" Lori suddenly asked, coming up behind him. "I don't see it out there anymore."

"What?" Brian whispered. "You don't see it? It should be just where we parked it."

"Well, it's not! And I think you should go out there and find it, Brian, because we need it to get home."

"Where did you get her from?" Brian asked Melody, frowning and looking around the room. "I swear!"

"It's not out there, Brian," she said again, pointing at the window.

"Lori, please," he pleaded. "Please stay away from the windows. Really, there's no need for you to be pulling back the curtains or even opening them without us all being in the same room together. Okay, Lori?"

"Okay," she said, smiling weirdly. "But that's only if you say so."

"Where did you get her, Melody?"

"Never mind that, Dumb-Dumb," Melody said, upset and angry. "What are we going to do about this?" She held up the hand holding the grenade so Brian could see it. "What are we going to do about this thing?"

"Damn!" he said, almost yelling at the sight of the grenade in Melody's hand. "Oh, fuck. I ain't never seen one of them. I mean, a real one up close. Well, to be truthful. Not even close. But—"

"Here, why don't you take it," she said jokingly, stretching the hand holding the grenade toward him. "Here, take it."

"Okay, Melody!" he said, stepping slyly backward. "What if you trip on something and accidentally drop that thing?"

"Well, for one thing, I'm sure you'll catch me before I hit the floor. And the grenade—who knows? It'll probably end up being a dud and won't even detonate."

"Why am I really back here, anyway?" Brian asked, curious about whatever was supposed to be hiding in the closet. "I was busy trying to get everything together up front."

"It's still in there," Melody said, pointing toward the closet. "And whatever it is, it's listening to us talk about this grenade."

"And how do you know that?"

"Just like the trailer," she said. "They were in there too, just very quietly listening to our conversations and following us all over that thing. Sounding like a bunch of rats, crawling slowly in the ceiling."

"Excuse me, but these things really don't have ceilings. So whatever you guys were hearing, they had to be on top of the trailer. You know, like, outside up on top."

"Whatever, Brian," she said, frowning and wrinkling one of her brows. "Just what are we going to do about *this*?" Meaning the grenade.

"Let's see," Brian thought to himself. "Uh, is there any way you can stick that pin back inside that hole?"

"Um, probably," she told him. "But that's if I can find it."

"What do you mean, if you can find it? I thought you had it in your hand?"

"What? This hand?"

"No! Not that hand, stupid. The other hand."

"Oh, that hand? I did, but I guess I lost it somewhere."

"Somewhere? Melody, you haven't been anywhere except where you are."

"Well, it's over here somewhere."

"Where, Melody?"

"I don't know, Brian!" she said in an angry whisper. "Why don't you come over here and help me find it?"

"Hey, you guys," Lori called. "I think I just saw something."

"Fuck!" Brian muttered to himself. "She's still up in front looking out the goddamn windows. Melody!"

"Help me find the pin, and we can throw this thing out there."

"Hold on, Lori," Brian said in a low tone. "I'll be there in a minute; just hold on and keep an eye on whatever it is that you saw out there."

"Okay, whatever you say," Lori said, sounding like a child having fun.

The pin of the grenade was found just inches from where it had fallen and carefully placed back inside the clip.

*

Meanwhile, the thing hiding inside the closet remained completely quiet, not making a sound and diverting their attention from the unknown.

However, the facts remained.

The town of Stonyford was about to experience its worst nightmare as a huge gust of dangerous wind swept through the area. It was forceful and filled with the electrifying warmth of statically charged air, packed with deadly electricity that would startle the entire region for miles in every direction.

Lucifer was about to make his presence known throughout every northern California community.

The submission was at hand. But for those who refused to

submit to his authority, the accused were about to be judged severely and to the utmost extreme.

*

"You see?" Lori said, pointing out the window to the location where one of the Jeeps was supposed to have been parked. "You see? I told you it wasn't there. I think somebody stole it right out from under our noses."

"Did you find the keys to start this thing?" Melody asked Brian.

"I bet you don't even know how to drive it, Brian," Lori said, grinning.

"What? Can you?" Brian asked, frustrated.

"No," she answered. "But I saw a big thing that looked just like a bat fly right over there and land by that smashed-up Jeep. And then his wings just folded up behind him, and he looked at me, and then he just went walking that way."

"What?" Brian exclaimed loudly. "Just what the fuck is your problem, Lori? Everything you've been saying tonight just doesn't make any sense."

"See, Melody?" Lori said, nodding her head toward Brian. "See what I was telling you about him? He don't like me and wants to do something bad to me. I hope you're not thinking about killing me, Brian. Like what happened to Travis, and then Randy, and then Terry, and then Christine. That poor Christine. I thought you liked her, Brian. Is that why you want to kill me? Because I'm in the way? Then you can have Melody all to yourself."

"Where are the keys to this thing?" Brian mumbled.

"Did you check inside that thing on the back of the driver's seat with all them papers sticking out of it?" Melody asked. "Looks like something is down at the bottom, balled up."

"Good idea," Brian said, opening the thin cover on the back of the seat to get a better look at the contents. "Bingo, Melody. The keys are in here. Now, we're in business."

"Then, let's start this thing up and get out of here," Melody said, expressing her excitement. "And just make sure you run over anybody who gets in our way."

"But what if it's that man?" Lori asked. "You know—the one I was telling you guys about, the one landing over there by that smashed-up Jeep. He'll just fly away if you try running over him."

"Oh, boy," Brian mumbled again, looking up at the ceiling. "If I can just make it through this, I'll be able to make it all the way home tonight. But that's providing she doesn't drive me nuts by then."

"Is that the right key?" Melody asked Brian.

"Well, let's just put it in the ignition and find out," he said with a huge grin. "Come on, baby, start up for papa. We need you to take us far away from here."

"Oh, no," Melody said, frowning. "What's the problem, Brian?"

"Quick! Turn off all the lights and anything else that you think is on," he told them. "Hurry up!"

"What about that thing back there in that room?" Lori yelled frantically. "Is it still in that closet?"

"Damn!" Brian shouted. "Forgot all about it. What was it, anyway?"

"Don't know, and don't care," Melody said, reaching down and grabbing a rifle from inside the box that Lori found in the back room.

"What the fuck is that?" Brian asked, realizing what it was.

"Well, when Lori was searching through everything back there, she just happened to come across this box full of rifles, and a few other things that just might be what's going to save us from whatever is back there in that closet."

"You know how to use that thing?" Brian asked Melody, who

was holding a large .30-30 rifle in both hands.

"I think I do," she said, looking at its size. "This thing sure is a heavy motherfucker. Where are the bullets?"

"Right down there in front of you," Brian said, pointing at the .30-30 rifle shells still in the box. "That's got to be a goddamn fuckin' Remington you got there. Is it?"

"That's what it says," Melody agreed.

"Powerful motherfucker," Brian said brightly, smiling. "Are you sure you can handle that thing? 'Cause if not, you can drive while I wait for that thing to come out from back there and blow his freakin' ass away."

"I know how to use it," Lori suddenly said. "I used to hunt with two of my uncles. I always went hunting with them over the summer."

"Yeah, with what?" Brian said, frowning. "A freakin' BB gun?"

"I ain't never went hunting with my uncles with no BB gun, you stupid ass, Brian," she screamed at him. "We had real guns—I tell you. Real guns!"

"Lori! Lori!" Melody said, trying to whisper. "You don't have to be yelling like that. People probably heard you all the way up there in Oregon and Washington. And you probably even scared that thing back there so bad that it probably can't wait to get the hell away from us."

"Well, Brian thinks I'm stupid or something," she told Melody. "I ain't no dummy, you know."

"Ever used anything like this, Lori?" Melody asked her.

"We always went hunting with all kinds of rifles," Lori told Melody.

"One of these?"

"One of those and some shotguns too!"

"You know how to use this?"

"Yeah, I do. That's easy!"

"What do you think?" Melody said, looking at Brian.

"She said she knows how to use it," Brian shrugs. "Then let her use it and we'll know from there."

"Fully loaded?"

"It better be! Cause—"

"Well, nothing's come out from back there yet," Melody said to Lori, who was still angry after Brian's remark. "But we believe you know just how to hold this rifle. So do what you gotta do, Lori. Just make sure you aim it right."

"And please don't miss the target, Lori," Brian said. "I just want you to know that I trust you. OK?"

"Yeah," Lori said, smiling and blushing. "Okay!"

It happened to be a dream of Lori's to hold a rifle in her hands. Hunting with her uncles wasn't exactly true. In fact, she'd never actually gone hunting—not with any of her uncles. The only hunting she ever did was in the backyard of her home near the towns of Colusa and Williams. She used one of her older brother's broken slingshots to target old discarded pop cans and broken bottles that he sometimes collected to destroy during his leisure time.

At best, she'd pop an insect or two, just about killing the little invertebrate instantly, as she did the flies that rested on the Inky Cap mushroom plants by slinging those fast-moving rock-like boulders she'd used.

Hell, she'd even popped herself a few times when, after the slingshot's elastic rubber band broke, her forceful sling misfired and hit her.

If I were asked to bet on a hunter, you can surely believe I would waste no time finding someone more qualified and meeting the requirements to hold a firearm.

Lori being allowed to toy with a .30-.30? As powerful a rifle as the Remington?

I should say not!

"Tell me something, Lori," said Brian. "As dark as it is, how were you able to see whatever it was that you called a bat that somehow turned itself into a man?"

"Easy," she answered. "I was using that spotlight that I found hanging up over there on the hook by the weird-looking picture of President Barack Obama that's hanging up there on that wall."

"And you just started shining it out the window, pointed it at a bat that you said just happened to turn into a man. Oh, and then he walked away, but that was after he looked at you," Brian said, expressing embarrassment.

"You saw him too?" Lori asked Brian. "You know what, Melody? He looked just like one of those things I remembered studying in history class—a satyr, from ancient Greek mythology. They were creatures with heads, chests, and arms like a man, but with legs like a goat and huge horns sticking out from the front of their heads. I think they even had goat-like ears, if I remember correctly."

"And here we go again," Brian said, shrugging.

"No. Hold on for a minute, Brian," Melody told him, suggesting. "Now—what?" Brian asked, noticing Lori staring down the hallway strangely, as if she'd seen a ghost. "What's happening?"

"Sounds like that closet door back there sliding open," Melody told him, reaching for the rifle. "Let me see that for a minute, Lori."

"What!" Lori responded, not wanting to let go of the rifle. "I heard it too!"

"Wait a minute," Brian suddenly interrupted. "I didn't hear anything."

"Listen!" Melody told him. "Just be quiet and listen."

"I think it's coming out of the closet," Lori whispered, lowering the rifle and pointing it toward the back room. "I saw my brother—I mean, one of my uncles—hold it like this before. And then—"

Just as Lori was about to pull the trigger, an unusually large, pregnant raccoon came waddling slowly from the back room, searching for a place to deliver its litter.

Seeing the raccoon brought an immediate sigh of relief.

"Yeah, and just think about it, Lori," Brian said. "You were just about ready to slaughter an entire family of raccoons because you thought it was a monster in the closet."

"I never said anything about it being a monster in the closet, Brian," Lori said. "And for your information, that bat I saw that turned into a man—I know what I saw, and it really did happen."

"By the way, Lori," Melody asked. "Are you sure you know what you saw? I mean, next you'll be saying you saw a griffin."

"A griffin," Lori said. "What the heck is a griffin?"

"Yeah, man," Melody said, smiling at Brian. "Damn! Uh, it's like a sort of monster, but it's known as a fabhed, or something like that, with the head and wings of an eagle, and the body and long tail of a lion."

"Excuse me for interrupting your class," Brian said, pointing at the raccoon sniffing around in the kitchen area of the Winnebago. "I have to go outside this thing and check the engine to find out why this baby won't start. Plus, we need to get that raccoon out of here. Will somebody please try working on one of those CBs?"

"Excuse me for asking," Melody said. "But I just happen to be, you know, thinking about something."

"Oh, yeah? And what's that?" Brian asked, curious. "This I gotta hear."

"Well, don't take offense, Brian, but Lori thought you were, uh, I guess that raccoon."

"What!" Brian said, frowning. "No, she did not!"

"Well, she thought it was you staring in that window at her. When all the time it was the raccoon. I really wonder if she thinks the two of you look alike?"

"That's fucked-up, Melody," Brian said. "That's really fucked-up!"

"What's fucked-up?" Lori asked, as though she hadn't heard what they were talking about. "Now what'd you guys talking about?"

"Nothing!" Brian answered with attitude. "Nothing."

"No, we were just talking about the CBs," Melody said, throwing her off the subject. "I'll try the transmitter while you try one of those CB things, okay?"

"But what about this radio, or whatever it is?" Lori questioned.

"Where?" Melody asked.

"You say, what?" Brian asked, looking inside the box in front of Lori.

"Yeah. There're a few radios in this box here," Lori told them. "But there's a really big one over there in that other box."

"Bullshit!" Brian said. "You mean to tell me we've had these things with us all this time without knowing it? That's bullshit, Lori. Why didn't you tell us?"

"I thought I did," she said, shrugging and smiling. "Well, I remember trying to. I thought—"

"Melody, check and see if any of this stuff works," Brian said. "I'll be outside checking the engine and whatever else I can to get the fuck out of this place."

"Want me to still try those CB things?" Lori asked, confused.

"Yeah," Melody answered.

"I don't know how Brian can go outside in the dark," Lori said, peering out the door as Brian opened it. "I thought we were going to all stick together?"

"You know something, Lori?" Melody said, thinking about what they'd agreed to earlier. "Uh, wait a minute, Brian," she quickly called, trying to stop him from going outside the Winnebago by himself. "Wait a minute. Didn't we agree to stick together?"

"Yeah. But I guess I forgot," he told her. "Why?"

"You go out there, we're going with you," Lori said. "That's what we agreed to, isn't it?"

"Let's go," Brian said. "Time is passing, and the longer we stay, I don't want to know what's going to happen next."

"Hey, Melody," Lori asked, grabbing something from one of the boxes. "I'm gonna bring one of these weird binoculars with us."

"Binoculars?" Brian exclaimed. "Where?"

"Right here, Brian," Lori said, pointing inside the box. "See 'em?"

"Damn, man, Melody," he said, surprised at the brand of the binoculars. "These are the high-powered kind you use at night— the Bushnell kind. Uh, powerful G-Force rangefinders, and a few Legend HD type. I do believe we're now in business with all this stuff."

Outside the Winnebago, they stood within a few feet of each other. Lori stood closer to the steps while Melody kept an eye on Brian, standing just a few yards away. They turned off all the lights in hopes of preventing anyone—or anything—from seeing them, then returned to the Winnebago, hurrying inside and expressing how scared they were to check everything in the dark. Although they each had a pair of binoculars, using them offered very little comfort. Lori once again claimed to see something in the form of a chimera moving about the campground. She also claimed to have seen a babirusa, an East Indian swine with very sharp upper canine teeth that grow upward through the roof of its mouth, curving toward the eyes and lower canines, extending outside the upper jaw.

However, it was Melody who this time claimed to see a huge, tropical American boa constrictor moving throughout the campground, heading in the direction of Stonyford. She could only describe it as very large. "It was the size of a Volkswagen, extremely huge and round, sliding and moving slowly past the campground."

"And what about those ugly-looking spiders?" Lori asked,

checking to make sure none were on her clothing. "That was a big daddy longlegs. Don't tell me you didn't see it running across that big rock. That thing made that rock look small, didn't it?"

"I don't believe it," Melody said, shaking her head in disbelief. "You guys are going to think I am crazy if I told you what I saw when Brian was busy removing that plate covering the engine. I wanted to scream, but I couldn't."

"Oh, no," Brian said. "Please don't tell me you saw something too!"

"What I saw is what I am going to keep to myself," Melody said, clearly embarrassed to mention it.

"I think that giant mosquito was trying to get me or something," Lori said, still brushing her hands over her clothing. "It was so big, I think it wanted to pick me up, because it dived down at me, but it ended up, I think, being snatched by that other big thing that I believe is supposed to eat mosquitoes."

"All I know is," Brian said, "we gotta get the fuck outta here."

*

These sightings were no illusions or mistaken perceptions of reality. But the imagination can sometimes create false mental images of things that are actually absent, though resembling impressions of what is imagined.

Establishing and maintaining a relationship with Lucifer is an abomination and strongly condemned throughout Biblical scripture. Yet in the town of Stonyford, one can see the pride of its residents as they enjoy their own version of New Orleans Mardi Gras, with bright, colorful displays and exhibitions that seem to foreshadow something terrible yet foretold.

The Stonyford phenomena, a celebration of proof formulating the theory of evolution's accounts in sequence and numbers of forceful factors, are in direct configuration with Lucifer's deadly, forbidden structure. This connection is evident through accentuating circumstances put forth by both him and the people of northern California. This scenario marks the beginning of Lucifer's belligerent attempt to take captive the citizens of the region and conceal them in his privately structured bottomless pit, which will be filled with bitter animosity and the horse of Death.

*

"Is there anybody out there?" Melody yelled over the transmission. "Is anybody out there who can hear me? Please, we need help up here."

"Lori, try using those over there," Brian told her. "Keep trying until you get somebody. Keep trying."

"But what about all those cell phones and laptops?" Lori asked. "What about them? Can't we even try using any of them?"

"Yeah," Brian answered, looking around for the cell phones she described. "Where are they?"

"Hold on," she said. "I'll get them. They're back there in the back."

"Melody!" he called, signaling her to follow. "We're going back to the room to get a few more things."

"Okay, I'm coming," she said, rising from the chair and following behind Brian, who was following Lori. Lori immediately showed him the box containing the cell phones.

"Hold up! Wait a minute," Brian said in a low tone. "I thought we let that raccoon out."

"Oh, no," Melody said, glancing toward the closet, one of its doors slightly ajar.

"Look," Lori whispered. "One of the doors is partially open. I think something's hiding in there again."

"Man, I wonder if it's that raccoon again?" Melody said, staring at the desk across from the closet doors. "Check to see if it had

81

babies, Brian."

"Yeah," he said, refusing. "What? And get attacked? I heard one of these things can do serious damage, especially after having its litter. So why don't you check, Lori? You were first in the room."

"I wonder why it picked this RV," Melody questioned. "Out of all the others out there?"

"If only you knew what's in them," Brian said, discouraging. "If only you knew."

"What?" Melody asked. "You checked them?" "Believe me, Melody," he said. "You really don't even wanna know."

CLICK! CLICK! CLICK!

A loud static noise came from the front room.

CLICK! CLICK! CLICK!

CLICK! CLICK! CLICK!

"You guys hear that?" Melody asked, turning quickly toward the front room to see where the clicking noise was coming from. "Sounds like somebody's trying to open something."

CLICK! CLICK! CLICK!

CLICK! CLICK! CLICK!

"Wait a minute," Brian said. "You know what that is? It's somebody on one of those transmitters trying to make contact. Move out of the way—we gotta answer whoever that is."

Instead of moving aside, Melody rushed to the front room ahead of Brian to find which transmitter the clicking sounds were coming from. She left Lori alone with whatever was now making loud, startling hissing sounds as a warning to anyone who dared to come near.

"Where is it coming from?" Melody asked Brian, looking around the room.

"I got 'em," Lori said, coming out from the back room with a box in her hand containing the cell phones. "I think I got all of 'em. But I couldn't get anything else because whatever it is back there started hissing at me."

"That's good, Lori," Melody told her. "Now, please continue, Brian."

"How can you guys see anything with it being so dark in here?" Lori asked, listening to the constant clicking sound that still seemed as if someone were trying to make contact with them. "That's the noise I was trying to tell you about earlier."

"Lori," Brian said, scratching his head. "You told us about this?"

"Uh-huh," she answered, walking toward one of the transmitters. "This is where it's coming from. But I didn't know what to say, let alone how to use these things."

"Hell yeah!" Brian said out loud. "We got it now, dammit!"

"Ooh, yeah," Melody cried out. "Fuckin'-A, baby. Do it, Brian."

"Okay, everybody be completely quiet," he said. "Let me figure this out. What I wanna do is bring the sound close to us, you know, instead of it being all over the place. We need it to be right here with us—so if anybody or anything is outside trying to listen, it won't be able to."

"Want us to move out a little?" Melody asked, meaning if she and Lori should keep watch on the door and windows. "We've already double-checked the windows. And the door—I'll double-check it right now. Lori, you double-check the lights."

"What about that icebox over there?" Lori said, walking slowly toward it. "I wanna see if there's something left inside to eat. I'm hungry and need something to eat. I wanna see if there's some water in there or maybe something to drink."

"Now why didn't I think of that?" Brian said, licking his lips. "I could use a nice glass of cold water right about now."

"Hurry up, Lori," Melody told her, checking the latch on the door. "I do believe it's locked."

"Where're you going?" Lori asked Melody, who was on her way to the back room. "I'm closing this door back here so that thing can't get out."

"I'd bet anything it's that raccoon and her litter back there," Brian said, turning the knobs on the transmitter.

"Yeah, that's what I think too," Lori said, drinking from a glass of water. "Mmm, that tastes good."

"Where's mine?" Brian asked. "You forget about me?"

"I'll get it, Brian," Melody said, coming from the back area. "I could use some water myself."

"Hey, Melody," Brian said, smiling. "Check to see if there's any beer in there while you're at it."

"Sure," she said, slightly grinning. "What kind would you like?"

"Oh, I'd like a Coors or Bud Light," he told her jokingly. "Oh! And if possible, could you please add some pretzels and a bag of peanuts, and a nice cold RC Cola with that order. And—"

"Now wait a minute," Melody said, standing in front of the small compact refrigerator resting on a light brown cabinet. "Who's going to pay me for this?"

"Hey, what can I say?" he shrugged. "Just put it on the tab of the owner of this thing.

"You know what, Melody?" Lori said, laughing. "It's some of that stuff really inside that little icebox in front of you."

"You're kidding," Melody said, surprised that Lori knew what was inside the compact refrigerator. "Are you serious, Lori?"

"Let me show you," Lori said, opening the refrigerator. "See? What'd I tell you?"

"No, you gotta be kidding," Melody said, staring at all the cans and different sizes of bottles of alcohol. "Man! Just look at all this liquid in here, would you. The owner of this thing has to be a for-real, big-time, serious alcoholic to have a stash like this."

"What?" Brian said, laughing after hearing Melody's statement about the alcohol. "Let me see."

"And there's some more over there underneath that sink,"

Lori said.

"You gotta be kidding, Lori," Brian said, nodding his head after seeing what was in the compact refrigerator. "I can't believe this."

"Lori!" Melody said in a serious tone. "What else have you found that we don't know about?"

"Mmm, let me think," Lori said, mumbling to herself. "Oh, yeah. I found a safe over there in the bottom cabinet. And another one in the bottom one right there," she said, pointing toward the two bottom cabinets that were just inches apart.

"Gotta check this out, Melody," Brian told her. "Think we hit gold in here. Why would the owner of this thing need two safes?"

"More booze probably," Melody said. "I mean, come on, Brian. The owner is an alcoholic. These people—rich people—always hide stuff like this all over the place."

"But in a safe?" Brian said, trying to find a way to gain entrance to the safes. "I wonder if he wrote the number down anywhere?"

"It's some numbers on paper in one of those folders over there on top of that file cabinet," Lori said. "Want me to get it for you?"

Both Brian and Melody stared directly at each other, seemingly knowing what the other was thinking.

"Please get the folders, Lori," Brian suggested softly and politely, using extremely good manners toward her. "And if there is, you know, anything else that you know that we don't know about that'll be some help to us, please, Lori, feel free to let us know. You think you can do that, Lori? Huh?"

"What do you think I am?" Lori said, frowning. "Stupid or something? You can always count on me, Brian."

"Thank you, Lori," he said, trying not to yell from becoming a bit frustrated.

"I know. I know," Melody said, watching Lori reach upward for the folder or folders on top of the file cabinet. "You don't have to say it, Brian. I'm already fully aware of what you're thinking."

"Just... where did you guys find her anyway?" Brian questioned Melody.

"Believe it or not," Melody said, smiling. "The same place where, you know, we found you, Brian."

"Yeah, well, I do think I'll have myself one or maybe two of these few cans here," Brian said, reaching for a can of beer.

"Better get me one too!" Melody said.

"Hey, I want one too!" Lori said, handing Brian the folders. "Here you go, Brian. The one with all the numbers is on that paper I put on top."

Lori just stood there smiling in her cowgirl-tight Wrangler jeans and kid-style Ranchbaby "Show" Cowgirl Boots, with her light blue long-sleeve denim Wrangler shirt and matching cowgirl straw hat. Melody wore her tight "Naughty" light blue cowgirl jeans, revealing a clear view of her navel area. She also wore "Naughty" cowgirl thongs, paired with her Hyp Naughty cotton/spandex stretch cami, all Hawaiian blue hibiscus in color. And she had on an extremely nice pair of "Jaden's" calf suede boots by Step Up Comfort in taupe, with a pink solid bandana slightly covering her head.

Brian, as usual, wore his old-fashioned blue saggy cowboy jeans and dark blue denim shirt, Mariat work hog boots, and an old, worn, rusted beanie that was double-striped, organic, and natural.

"Are you sure you can handle drinking one of these, Lori?" Melody asked before passing the can to her.

"What kind is it?" Lori asked, not wanting them to know she really didn't drink liquor. "I only drink a certain kind."

"Lori, I really don't think you should be drinking any of this stuff," Brian told her. "You're just too nice of a girl to be drinking liquor."

"Yeah, that's right, Lori," Melody said, looking at the can of beer. "I really don't remember seeing you drink anything when we were on our way up here from Stonyford. But maybe you did have something, and I just can't seem to remember."

"Oh, you're right," Lori said. "I mean, it was a can of Coca-Cola."

"Bingo!" Brian said, opening one of the safes. "Got it—and man! Better look at this, Melody. And you too, Lori. Gold bars, diamonds, and gemstones everywhere."

"Just look at the shape of those things," Melody said excitedly. "There's a bunch of them in all these bags, sparkling like everything in here."

"Yeah," Lori said. "They look like a bunch of little flashlights with all the flashing and sparkling."

"Lori, quick," Brian said somewhat demandingly. "Get a flashlight. We need one without having to turn on any of the lights in here."

"It's one right there underneath that sink," she said. "But it's not too big like that spotlight up there."

"Just right," Brian said, grabbing the flashlight and opening the other safe, which contained not only diamonds but gold bars as well.

"Are we going to ever get out of this place?" Melody asked Brian. "Didn't you fix the engine?"

"Didn't need to be fixed," he said. "It wasn't broke."

"Well, what was wrong that it wouldn't start?"

"Modern times, Melody. Don't need keys anymore."

"What? Then how are you going to start the engine?"

"This Winnebago has a button you just push."

"That's it?"

"That's it."

"Then when are you going to push it?"

"Mmm. I really like the way you said that, Melody. Say it

again."

"I'll say it," Lori said, staring directly at Brian, smiling.

Everybody laughed in whispers.

"Want me to go push it?" Lori asked, not catching on to what Brian was insinuating.

"Maybe I will," Melody said, whispering so Lori wouldn't hear. "And I'm not talking about just pushing it, Brian. If you can read between the lines."

"You haven't answered my question, Brian," Lori exclaimed softly. "Am I going to push it or what?"

"That's right, Brian," Melody said, grinning. "Lori's waiting on you to answer her."

"Man, just look at this stuff," Brian said, avoiding answering what he knew Melody wanted to hear him say about Lori.

"Well?"

"Well, what?"

"Lori's waiting."

"Oh, excuse me, Lori," he said, standing upright. "You know what I really need you to do?"

"What?" she asked, hoping he would tell her to go ahead and push the button.

"Well, you know how you were holding that rifle?"

"Yeah," she said, smiling at the thought of Brian bringing up the subject of how she held the rifle.

"Well, you see," he began. "Once I start this thing up and let the engine warm up—let it idle for a while—I'm going to need you to hold that rifle tight so that if something tries getting in our way, I'll need you to start shooting at whatever it is. You know what I mean? Lori, me and Melody will be depending on you to do the job."

"But what if I miss and hit something else?" she asked, rubbing her face on both sides. "I mean, what if I get scared and drop the rifle, or it doesn't fire?"

"Just don't worry yourself about something like that, Lori," he told her, smiling. "We'll be long gone before anything like that happens."

"But what if the engine stops?" she said nervously, "and you gotta try starting it up again? Then what?"

"Well," he began, staring gleamishly and lustfully at Melody, "I guess that is when... uh... I guess I will just have to, uh, just have to, you know, just push it inside that juicy hole, nice and hard, and start pumping on the foot pedal, nice and slow at first, UNTIL—"

"Until what?" Melody asked. "Until what?"

CLICK! CLICK! CLICK!

CLICK! CLICK! CLICK!

"Oh, fuck!" Brian said, hurrying to sit down in front of the hand-held device constructed for talking through the transmitter. "Man, now this thing's gonna start clicking again—just when I was about to—"

CLICK! CLICK! CLICK!

CLICK! CLICK! CLICK!

"Who is it, Brian?" Melody asked, gripping his left shoulder.

"I don't know yet, Melody," he told her, sensing what she was doing.

"It's probably that guy who was trying to talk on there earlier," Lori said. "He kept saying something, but I couldn't understand what he was—"

"On here earlier?" Brian said slowly, looking upward. "Man! I swear!"

"Lori," Melody said, getting her attention. "Um, you know when we were talking about drinking beer, and I, you know, mentioned something about not thinking you should be drinking?"

"Yeah, and—"

"Yeah, well," Melody began, staring gleamishly back at Brian, "then just go ahead and grab a couple of those cans and... drink up, bitch!—oop! I mean, Lori."

"Hey!" Lori said, surprised by the remark, but started laughing as if she were already heavily intoxicated. "Bitch? I ain't no bitch! Not yet, anyway. Just wait till after I drink all of this," she said, grabbing as many cans as she could from the refrigerator.

"What are you doing, Lori?" Brian asked, looking at Melody, curious. "Don't tell me you're going to drink all of that—by yourself?"

"Yhrhuh," she uttered. "Yeah. All of 'em, too!"

"Hopefully, there might be a box of Tylenol in here somewhere," Brian said. "She's going to need some after this."

"Thought I saw a bottle in the bathroom cabinet," Melody told him. "I think."

"Who needs Tylenols?" Lori said, already downing one can of beer. "Quit being sissies!"

"Uh, excuse me, Miss about to become an alcoholic," Melody said. "You are up in here drinking like nobody else."

"Oh, well," Lori said, downing another can of beer. "I am also the only adult up in here—as you say."

"WHAT!" Melody exclaimed in a loud whisper. "Bitch!"

"Wait a minute," Brian suddenly said, snickering, listening to what was being said between Melody and Lori. "Just let her drink up, Melody."

"I'll beat that whore's ass up in here if she thinks I'm playin'," Melody said, leaning to one side and squinting her eyes at Lori.

"You're just jealous, Melody," Lori told her, holding another can of beer to her mouth.

"Jealous of what? Bitch!"

"You know I'm gonna fuck Brian before you do."

"What!"

CHAPTER SIX

Years Earlier:

Sheriff Blake and his crew, along with Flight Lieutenant Sherwin Taylor of the Twenty-Ninth Squadron, set out on an emergency search for whoever they'd heard crying and screaming over the Stonyford Ranger Station transmitter.

The light green-and-white, medium-sized building sat a short distance from the nearby supermarket, which they approached after landing in helicopters across from the Johnson estate, not long after their flight from the town of Willows.

After their brief conversation with Dan Eaton, better known as Uncle Dan, and his strange nephew, Chris Van Bebber, the entire crew once again found themselves airborne on another late-evening flight. They desperately searched for the person or persons who were urgently screaming over the transmitter for help.

Onboard the helicopter with Flight Lieutenant Taylor were Sheriff Blake and photographer Bedford, who were seated in back while Taylor and one of his men sat up front. Onboard the second helicopter was Detective Miller and Goldsby, accompanied by an armed uniformed pilot and a police officer.

"Think we gonna find 'em from up here?" Blake questioned

Taylor.

"We'll find 'em," Taylor answered. "Just as long as they keep yelling."

"Bedford," Blake said in a grumbling, discontented voice. "Now, you know it's not my intention to sound so goddamn grumpy. I really don't mean to come off that way, but sometimes I just do it without meaning to. You understand? My mood can get really cranky at times, and especially now. Up here in this god-damn helicopter just isn't where I wanna be. You should know that. Anybody who knows me, hell, they'll tell you that. But any-way, Bedford, I'm really irritable about this whole goddamn mess right now. Do you understand what I mean?"

"Okay with me," Bedford said, smiling and occasionally glancing out one of the windows.

"Well, all right then," Blake said, reaching for one of Bedford's hands to shake it. "Thank you, son. I appreciate that very much. You know, your understanding."

"Anytime, Sheriff," Bedford said, bobbing his head to a beat from the song he was listening to on his MP3 player.

"I think I oughta get me one of them goddamn things so I can just ignore everybody, too," Blake muttered to himself. "These kids today got just about everything at the touch of their hands. Why wasn't it like that for me?"

"Hey back there," the co-pilot said, grinning at Blake. "You all right?"

"Just where the hell are we right now?" Blake asked, looking out the window next to him. "So goddamn dark out there, I can't see anything."

"We'll be over the boys' ranch in just a few minutes," the co-pilot said.

"The boys' ranch?" Blake questioned. "What? You think maybe it was one of those kids playing around on the transmitter at this place?"

"No, I don't think so," he told Blake. "But the sounds are coming from somewhere in the immediate vicinity. Not particularly the boys' ranch."

"Well, then why are we up here hovering like this?" Blake asked. "Why don't you just land this thing so we can get out and walk?"

"Well, for one thing," he said, turning toward Blake while answering Taylor through the headset microphone built into his pilot helmet, "we are considering that hostile out there—or rather, should I say, down there. We aren't sure what we're up against at present."

"Hostile!" Blake said aloud. "Ain't none of them children down there hostile. They're just goddamn kids acting like real criminals. That's why they're there. Gotta teach 'em a lesson."

"I understand your point," he said to Blake. "But our job is to find out what's happening and whether we're being set up by the enemy."

"Enemy?" Blake said, astounded by the co-pilot's statement. "We're not at war here. Just somebody over the radio yelling for help."

"Sheriff Blake," he said, staring seriously at him, "in case you've been a bit too busy, you have a serial killer likely at large around here. Stonyford and every surrounding community are at extremely high risk. People are being murdered, bodies are being found everywhere, and the theory is that this area is in danger."

"But Stonyford is on the rebound," Blake told him. "What happened was an isolated matter, and we have Margaret being held accountable at this time."

"For your information, Blake," Taylor said over the noise from the helicopter engine, "your subject, we believe, is entirely innocent of that little girl's death. In other words, your boss, the Commissioner, and those people in Sacramento also believe that Margaret is innocent. And I tell you, Blake, you better, by all God's means, find another suspect, or you'll soon find yourself among those standing in the unemployment line—after those legislators in Sacramento have stripped away your retirement pension."

"Pension?" Blake said. "How are they going to do something like that?"

"Lawyers, Blake," the co-pilot said, smiling broadly. "Big-time lawyers, and they'll be all over you, stripping you of everything you got!"

"I think they found something over there," Taylor said, pointing toward the other helicopter hovering over a certain area with one of its emergency wide-angle spotlights on high beam, illuminating whatever had drawn their attention.

"Whatcha think?" Blake asked, watching the light move around in circles.

"Don't say it!" Bedford said, slightly grinning at Blake. "I already got it rolling," referring to his camera.

"No way, Taylor," the co-pilot said. "You gotta be kidding me."

"Hey, will you look at that," Blake uttered. "Goddamn pieces of a truck or something down there."

"I don't think that's a truck," Taylor said, maneuvering the helicopter with precise skill and dexterity.

"Think this is where the screaming is coming from?" the co-pilot asked, reaching down and activating the craft's emergency spotlight, setting it in motion.

"I was wondering the same," Taylor replied, making another sharp maneuver around an old barn. "See anything down there?"

"Negative," the co-pilot said. "See anything, Blake?"

"Not in there," Blake said, looking down at the old barn, a rusted white building with large doors, one of which was open. "I believe this place is still used by those goddamn kids over at the boys' ranch."

"I think they got something," Taylor said, maneuvering the

helicopter away from the barn and setting a direct course toward the other helicopter, which hovered in a small circle.

"Looks like a bunch of scrap down there," the co-pilot said, moving and readjusting the craft's emergency spotlight.

"I don't know," Taylor said, checking the instrument panel, which was brightly illuminated in yellow, orange, white, and light blue lights. "I see whatever it is down there in a bunch of seemingly discarded pieces. Is everything all right back there?" Taylor asked Blake, who was staring out the window as if trying to process the small broken fragments scattered along a hill full of brush.

"Hey, Blake," the co-pilot said out loud to get his attention.

"Uh, yeah?" Blake responded, troubled. "Uh-huh, yeah. I heard you the first time. What was it that you called me for?"

"Taylor wanted to know if you were all right."

"Am I all right?" Blake asked the co-pilot.

"Yeah! Are you all right?"

"Well, just what the heck do you think is down there?"

"I really don't know," the co-pilot said. "A lot of wreckage. Looks like a salvage yard. Or was a salvage yard."

"What about whoever was screaming and yelling for help?" Blake asked, reaching into his coat pocket for something to smoke.

"Uh, Blake," the co-pilot said, grinning at the sight of Blake placing a long, strange-looking cigar in his mouth, "you think you can just, you know, hold off on that thing, at least for right now?"

"What? This here?" Blake said, holding up the cigar. "You mean this?"

"Uh, yeah."

"Ah, now wait a minute. You see, this here thing is all I got to chew on to keep these nerves from jumping all over the goddamn scale."

"Oh, you're not intending to smoke it?"

"For Christ's sake, there, fellow, hell no! I was just pulling it out so I could chew on it. You know what I mean?"

They laughed.

"Damn!" Taylor said out loud. "What the—"

"Man, what was that?" the co-pilot exclaimed, looking aimlessly at the windshield.

"I saw it too," Blake told them. "It looked just like one of them, uh, I think it was one of them goddamn giant horseflies or something."

"No, I don't think that was any giant horsefly," Taylor said, staring intently out the front and side windows. "It looked more like a mosquito or something."

"Well, whatever it was," the co-pilot said aloud, "that thing had a head like a human. Didn't you see that?"

"Hey, we got something over here buzzing around us!" a cry came over the transmitter. "We got something over here. We're pulling out! I repeat, we're pulling out!"

"Roger that," Taylor said, responding to the pilot of the other crew in the helicopter. "Hurry up and get out of there as fast as you can. One of the unknowns buzzed us too!"

*

Giant horsefly? No way. Both helicopters were about to be attacked by giant mosquitoes, each with a human head, just as the co-pilot had described. These mosquitoes were driven by the works of Lucifer. Here again is the primary example of the submission.

Once again, the residents of this region were going to suffer a terrible crisis and deadly waves of prophetic fulfillment established by none other than Satan himself. Many of the residents would go undiscovered, while most—the spirit of Lucifer speaking loud and clear—would feel the physical presence of his becoming.

Stonyford would, by all means, suffer under the enforcement of the law of Satan.

No one should believe themselves incapable of this crisis. The entire region would become like open prey, hunted by every scavenger that feeds on the dead and decaying—those presently residing in this region who were already dead, though still breathing their last breath among the living, awaiting their turn to become prey of these scavengers.

So stunning would this event be in the Stonyford region. Furthermore, it is documented in the book of Revelation: the dynamic reinforcement of this brutal and unfortunate submission.

The human-head mosquito is a deadly parasite, ultimately establishing and revealing the manifestation of its predecessor, Satan. The wave of these aggressive parasites is described as fallen angels encoded in the new kingdom, escalating progressively and rapidly, intensifying the meltdown of Stonyford. While directing their undeniable power in repetitive patterns in cycles of fundamental degrees, each of these parasites, following its spiritual sequence, will undoubtedly begin the mobilization of the entire region.

*

"You getting' all of this?" Blake asked Bedford, who was aiming his camera at something on the ground below.

"Yeah, I'm getting everything."

"Then why the hell are you pointing that thing down there like that?"

"I know you ain't gonna believe what I just saw down there, but man, I got it all in here," Bedford said, nodding his head as though not wanting to tell Blake what he'd captured on his camera.

"What are you talking about, Bedford?" the co-pilot asked, looking out the right-side window. "I don't see anything but a bunch of big-headed mosquitos down there."

"Yeah, and what do you see them doing?" Bedford asked, snickering.

"Hold up! Wait a minute," Taylor said, banking the helicopter into a steep maneuver with extra dexterity to get a better view of what was happening on the ground. "Check that out," he told them. "Look!"

"What the?" the co-pilot uttered. "Can you believe this?"

"Better watch it," Blake shouted while slowly moving to one side of the window. "Looks like one of them things is headed this way."

"No, I don't think so," Taylor said. "Looks like it's headed in the direction of the other helicopter. But wait a minute. Hold up! No, that's not what it's doing. Can you get a good view of it?" he asked the co-pilot.

"Man, where is it?" the co-pilot muttered, looking aimlessly into the dark sky. "Anybody see it?"

"It was coming up this way," Bedford said, moving his camera from window to window. "It's out there somewhere."

"Hell, we already know that, goddammit," Blake said, trying not to spit the cigar out of his mouth.

"Hold up!" Taylor said in a loud whisper. "From what I'm hearing from the other helicopter, that motherfucker is hitching a ride on our butt. Hell no! Can't do that. I got something for you."

"What?" Blake yelled. "How the fuck is it doing that?"

"Don't worry," Taylor said, smiling furiously. "I got this! You guys, hold on! This motherfucking helicopter is mine, and nobody calls themselves hitching a ride on my craft without my permission."

"Buckle up, everybody," the co-pilot said, looking back at Blake and Bedford, grinning and revealing the huge gap between his upper front teeth. "Hold on tight and enjoy the ride."

"I sure in the hell hope you ain't gonna be trying to fly this thing, you know, like that Airwolf movie helicopter," Blake said, struggling to fasten the belt around his pop-belly stomach.

"Here, want me to help you with that?" Bedford asked, reaching to help him fasten the belt.

"Now, did I ask you for help?" Blake said, yanking the belt tighter so that he could fasten it. "I ain't helpless, you know."

"Didn't say you were," said Bedford, slightly smiling. "Just thought I'd help you out after—"

Taylor took the helicopter into a fast, steep 30° bank, and then into a quick 10°, spinning the craft around, maneuvering it in small circles, tossing the giant, human-headed mosquito off, severely disrupting its coordination and killing it instantly.

"We're coming in," a voice came over the transmitter. "I'll take that sucker out!"

"Hey, I think we got it off our backs," Taylor yelled into his mic. "I think we got that big-headed son of a bitch off our backs. Just keep a visual on the rest of them."

"Man, what the fuck is that crawling around down there?" the pilot of the other helicopter screamed over the transmitter. "You guys see that?"

"Jesus fuckin' Christ!" Blake yelled, grabbing onto one of Bedford's arms and pulling it as a child would do a rag doll. "Get that goddamn camera over here and get this—"

"Gotta be kiddin' me," the co-pilot said out loud. "Man, just look at that. It looks like a bunch of giant scorpions down there."

Just as the co-pilot was describing what looked like scorpions, the other helicopter suddenly sped below Taylor's helicopter at a high rate of speed, dropping into a fast 60° right bank while holding steady altitude with a quick spin at 200 feet, opening fire on anything and everything crawling around on the ground.

There was no doubt about it: the UH-72A Lakota was a dangerous piece of machinery to contend with. The defense armor proved operable with extreme, devastating effects, resulting in an overwhelming number of the scorpions being destroyed.

"Good job down there," Taylor said through his helmet mic. "Couldn't have done it any better myself."

"Just how in the hell are you guys seeing what you're doing?" Blake asked, either Taylor or the co-pilot. "The spotlight wasn't directly on most of those things, but they sure in hell took them out."

"Night lenses made just for the eyes," the co-pilot said. "A combination of soft lenses with transparent structures in the eyes that, I can say from my experience, seem to focus light rays through the pupil, giving you a perfect mental image of your intended target, which enters the retina like a photograph."

"What, you guys don't believe in using the old binoculars anymore?"

"We do, but not if we don't have to. I'd rather keep these little quips I'm wearing than jam a pair of binoculars in my face."

"Uh, okay, copy that, Ghetto Boy," Taylor responded in his mic to the pilot of the other helicopter.

"Ghetto Boy?" Blake questioned. "Is that his name?"

"Nah, it's the name we call him," the co-pilot said, snickering. "The truth about your real name is that nobody gives a fuck about your real name anymore."

"Ghetto Boy, uh," Blake uttered. "Sounds like a goddamn gangbanger or something, asks me."

"That's what he is," the co-pilot told him. "A for real freakin' crazy-ass gangbanger fresh out of the ghetto."

"Why don't you let old Blake listen to a little of what the Ghetto Boy is listening to?" Taylor said, grinning. "Who knows, he just might like what he's hearing."

"Think so?" the co-pilot asked.

"How you gonna let me hear what you're talking about?" Blake asked.

"Hit the switch, Mitch," Taylor told him. "And turn that shit up so both of them back there can hear what the Ghetto Boy is fuckin' with."

"Hell, ain't gonna bother me one bit," Blake said, trying to see what he could see out the side window. "Where are we going now? 'Cause ain't nothing happening anymore up here since you killed those things down there, or maybe back there."

"Let me tell you a thing or two about what it's like whenever we are on a mission," Taylor said to Blake in a slightly loud voice. "You should consider yourself blessed when flying with the best of the very best, 'cause baby, this shit has only begun."

While Taylor was explaining what it was about to be like on this mission, the co-pilot smiled and grinned again, revealing the huge gap between his upper front teeth. Turning up the transmitter to hear what the Ghetto Boy and his crew were listening to, a sudden sound blared loudly through the speakers—an old-school track by the late legendary musician Donny Hathaway. It was the long instrumental version of *The Ghetto*, raw and uncut.

"Oh, hell yeah," Blake said, looking at Bedford, who was still pointing his camera out the window, this time at Ghetto Boy's helicopter while listening to his MP3 player. "Hey, Bedford," Blake yelled, reaching over and waving a hand in front of him. "I just wanted to know if you listening to this?"

"I got my own style of music that I listen to, Blake," Bedford said. "Y'all listening to that old stuff from way back in the day. That's old. People don't listen to that stuff anymore. That's only for you old people."

"What the hell you talking about, Bedford?" Blake asked seriously. "Just what the goddamn hell are you trying to insinuate?"

"I'm trying to insinuate the fact that I'm up here flying around and fighting monsters with a bunch of old people who listen to music that's out of style for us younger folks," Bedford said, laughing out loud.

"Hey, uh, Bedford," the co-pilot began, carefully unwinding a shiny, light-gray extension cord. "Maybe you'd like to plug your

MP3 into this system. Just take this end right here and stick the jack into the headphone section of your unit."

"Now, isn't this just a bit ironic? You know, what you guys are doing," Blake said, referring to Bedford and the co-pilot. "I mean, hey. Here we are up here in a battle with God knows what, potentially in the development stage of a deadly crisis, and you guys are tinkering with the helicopter's wires, experimenting with Bedford's little gadget so everybody up here can hear some goddamn music."

"Sounds like you're a bit too nervous there, Blake," said the co-pilot. "Whatever Bedford is listening to might actually help you out."

"Geez," Blake muttered. "The only thing that can help me out is seeing Stonyford rebound like never before. You know what I'm sayin'? What that town needs is a big celebration or something— a ceremonial parade and ostentatious display with the townspeople wearing all kinds of elegant, colorful clothing to show every neighboring county how we can celebrate and commemorate, with respect, the town's rebound."

"There'll be all kinds of rejoicing at the celebration, with hundreds and hundreds of people joining in from miles around."

"Even the well-known and very famous celebrities will be invited from all across the country and around the globe."

"Hell, I just might even invite you guys."

"Hey, all right with me," the co-pilot said.

"All right with me too," Bedford said in agreement.

"Uh, what about me? Am I invited?" Taylor asked, not really knowing just what they were talking about.

"Everyone is invited," Blake told 'em. "Just as long as you bring your friends with you. And make sure you tell them to bring a friend."

"Damn!" said Bedford, rubbing the right side of his face. "I don't have that many friends."

"Uh, you don't have to worry yourself about that," the co-pilot told him, grinning. "I got plenty to go around for everybody. And some, I really don't need 'em."

"Does that include me?" Taylor asked him, arching one of his eyebrows.

"What," the co-pilot responded to Taylor in a long slur. "Me and you ain't never been friends. We just met earlier this evening, and now you wanna be my friend."

Everybody laughed at the co-pilot's joking remark toward Taylor.

"Have you forgot who's flying this thing?" Taylor said, smiling.

"Incoming!" a voice rang out over the transmitter. "Are you copying me over there? We've got hostile contacts approaching!"

"What the hell!" the co-pilot said, looking at Taylor. "Hostile contacts?"

"Where are they?" Taylor questioned back at Ghetto Boy.

"Three o'clock, downtown," Ghetto Boy responded. "Hold on. I think a group of them is coming up at us."

"I got a visual over here," the co-pilot said, activating the emergency spotlight to high beam. "Buckle up tight, ladies!"

"Ghetto Boy!" Taylor yelled through his mic. "Let's do this! Except this time, let's finish the job once and for all."

"Copy that!" Ghetto Boy yelled back, responding to Taylor. "Hell yeah! Let's do this, baby! Daddy's coming to get you, bitches!"

"Bedford!" the co-pilot said out loud, making sure he could hear him.

"Yeah, what's up?"

"You gonna just sit there holding the jack? Or are you going to plug that motherfucker into that bitch-ass unit?"

"Oh, I'm in here trippin'."

"And whatever that is you're listening to, it better be freakin' good!" Taylor told him. "Or you find yourself takin' a free-fall without a goddamn parachute. Isn't that right, Blake? You know, the goddamn part?"

"Goddamn right!" Blake said, laughing. "If I don't find anything on that goddamn camera of yours, you're a goner anyway you look at it."

"Wow!" a voice came over the transmitter. "I think we're being attacked by those ugly-ass horseflies."

"Tell 'em those things are giant mosquitoes, for God's sake," Blake said. "If they were horseflies, we'd all be able to just put our arms out the window and swat them bastards with our hands."

"Uh, Ghetto Boy," Taylor called out through his mic. "Ghetto Boy, are you copying?"

"Where the hell is he?" the co-pilot said sternly. "Where is he?"

"Ghetto Boy!" Taylor called again. "Do you copy?"

"Oh, gosh. Don't tell me," Blake said, looking around aimlessly. "Those things probably got 'em."

"Ghetto Boy! You copy?" Taylor continued.

"Hey, I got a reading and a clear visual on them," the co-pilot said, pointing toward the boys' ranch. "They've landed, and I believe they're having problems with their communication system."

"Thank God," Blake said, shaking his head. "I was just about ready to take hold of your helicopter's guns and start an all-out war up here."

"Uh, this isn't over," Taylor said angrily. "Once we find out what's happening on the ground, and the problem gets fixed, it'll be wartime like none other. Regardless!"

The mosquitoes, threatening enough on their own, had now pushed the entire team into a state of deep anger—irate and steaming mad at the thought of one of the helicopters being attacked, even though it had landed safely in a field at the boys' ranch.

After landing his craft, Taylor instructed everyone to take extra precautions.

"What about the boys' ranch?" the co-pilot asked. "Doesn't seem to be anybody here."

"First, see what's up with Ghetto Boy and his crew," Taylor said, scanning the area to see where the mosquitoes had gone.

"What's the problem?" Blake asked, curious.

"What?" Taylor snapped.

"Well, I mean, you know—"

"The boys' ranch? Our landing here? Or the mosquitoes watching us from who knows where they're hiding," Taylor clarified.

"Man, Blake," Detective Miller said as he approached. "It's so good to see you guys. You just don't know what it was like up there."

"I don't think I can take this anymore," Detective Goldsby said, walking alongside Miller. "Something really ugly was trying to grab the front of the helicopter, and—"

"I heard somebody over the radio calling them mosquitoes with human heads," Miller said. "But, Blake, man, you should've seen them."

"Hold up, hold up!" Blake said, trying to calm Miller down. "I already know what you guys saw. Hell, one of them things was buzzing around us too if you just quiet down and think about it. Goddamn thing had, I guess, a tight grip on our ass. Jesus, darn thing wouldn't let go. Well, not until the pilot spun us around a few times. You guys saw that."

"Hey, Reggie," Taylor called out to his co-pilot. "Make sure you keep your lenses focused around here. Don't want anything sneaking up on us, being that it's dark as hell out here."

"Way ahead of you," the co-pilot said. "Observing is my specialty, which I specialized in during training. Remember, Taylor, I'm a product of special distinction. Just like a pecan pie full of detail."

"Funny, Reggie," Taylor said. "Very funny."

"Think it'll be any problem if, you know, me and my guys take a walk over there to see if anybody's here?" Blake asked, suggesting that he and his crew walk over to the boys' ranch. "I'm sure you probably have a few extra flashlights—don't you?"

"Sounds good, Blake," Taylor said. "Only problem with that is that you gotta help me find a flashlight."

"Uh, I have a cigarette lighter if that'll help," one of the crew members said, holding up his lighter and flickering its small blaze.

"Hold up! Wait a minute," Taylor said, thinking seriously. "That little light—now, do you think those things can't see it from where they are? They're probably out there just waiting for the right moment, for an opportunity to snatch one of us. Has anyone out here heard any more screaming over the transmitter? Just think about it."

"Well, what about that wreckage and all that debris we saw over there scattered all over that hill?" one of the crew members asked. "I mean, it looked like those were also bits and pieces of somebody's remains, ask me."

"Exactly!" Taylor said. "That's just what I'm talking about— those things watching us as we speak."

"And how do we know it wasn't really them screaming over the radio just to get us out here?" Miller asked, hoping no one would agree with him.

"Now, you're takin' the words right out of my mouth," another crew member said, feeling he was the only one considering that everything could be a set-up.

"Now, you know what, Taylor," Blake said, taking the cigar out of his mouth and stretching his arm toward the person holding the lighter, hoping for a light. "They could possibly be right about that if you really think about it. Though."

"Anything's possible," the co-pilot said. "But why are we out here causing paranoia and delusions when all we have to do is go over and check the boys ranch, you know, see if anybody's home?"

"This boys ranch," Goldsby said, sounding confused. "I mean, all you keep calling it is a boys ranch. Does it have a name or something, other than 'boys ranch'? Is there a girls ranch out here too?"

"Hell, I'll answer that one for you, sweetie," Blake said, struggling to see in the dark. "It's Faust Springs Boys Ranch. And no, there's no ranch out here for girls—well, not this far anyway. This place was built so young boys would have somewhere to go after getting into all sorts of trouble. So the courts wouldn't have to put them in prison at a young age, they made this place for them to, you know, return home to their families without any problems."

"So, it's Faust Springs Boys Ranch," Goldsby said. "And where did those things come from?"

"Your guess is as good as mine," Blake told her. "Something isn't right in this neck of the woods anymore. Ever since that little girl was murdered, strange things have been happening and continue to happen."

"Isn't there a way we can just, you know, move the helicopters?" Miller asked Taylor. "Like, move them closer to those buildings over there?"

"I was thinking the same thing," Taylor said. "And I'm sure we can. But first, let's check and see if there's anybody over there or not."

"What about it, Blake?" the co-pilot asked, since he's the one who knows so much about the ranch. "Is there anyone still using this place?"

"I'd reckon so," Blake said, raising his head to see if he could spot a recognizable motor vehicle driven to the ranch by one of his acquaintances. "If they've moved out, hell, nobody said anything to me about it."

"Uh, Ghetto Boy," Taylor called out. "Can you still fly that thing?"

"Just give me another thirty minutes, and I'll let you know," he said. "Just gotta get some of this weird, nasty-looking, ugly sticky shit off my rotor that left on it."

"Want us to go on over there?" Blake asked, referring to his crew.

"Hey, that's up to you, Blake," Taylor told him. "All I can say is that it'll be at your own risk if something should start happening."

"Something like what?" Goldsby asked Taylor.

"Something like a gang of those ugly-looking giant mosquitoes swooping down on you in the dark, fast and very swiftly, and carrying you back to wherever they are breeding so they can feed you to their litter."

"Ah, hell no," Goldsby said. "Fuck that! Ain't nothing like that gonna happen to me. Fuck that."

"Well, you asked the question, and I answered it," the co-pilot said.

"Just look at what one of them things did to that helicopter," Taylor pointed out, reminding them. "Well, just think what it'll do to one of you."

"And, hey!" Ghetto Boy yelled out. "Just think what caused all that wreckage over there. And you know what I think? I think some of that debris wasn't only pieces of the wreckage of a crashed plane, or even a freakin' car or big truck, but, baby, let me tell you something. Honestly, I believe some of that was human remains scattered all over that fuckin' hill."

"That figures," Blake said, puffing hard on his cigar. "I could've bet anything that I saw somebody's legs and arms down there lying on the ground. I even think I saw a head or two with the torso ripped from it."

"Making me sick," Goldsby said, placing one of her hands

over the bottom section of her stomach.

"Making all of us sick," Miller said. "I thought I'd seen the same."

"Got it!" Ghetto Boy yelled. "I got this sucker ready to dance to some freakin' rock and roll now, motherfucker!"

"Got it, Ghetto Boy," Taylor yelled. "You got it, Baby Boy?"

"Goddamn skippy, Taylor," Ghetto Boy said with a stern, inflexible expression. "Let's move these motherfuckers to wherever you want them."

"Okay, everybody," Taylor said with determination. "Everybody back onboard for this short trip across this field so we can see what's really popping at the boys ranch."

"Ghetto Boy!" Taylor yelled.

"What's that?" he answered.

"Got plenty of ammo?"

"All the ammunition one man can handle. What about you, baby?"

"Packin', Baby Boy. Packin' too much Heat!"

"Then, let's do this."

"COPY," Taylor said, firing up his engine while observing Ghetto Boy do the same.

"Hey, Bedford," the co-pilot yelled over the engines from both of the helicopters. "You've been awfully quiet. What's on your mind?"

"Action," said Bedford. "Nothin' but action and more action."

"You got a girlfriend, Bedford?" he asked him.

"Gettin' a little personal, aren't you?"

"Just thought I'd ask you, 'cause when the action starts, providing we get any, just make sure you squeeze old Blake there. He's gonna need a hug."

"Yeah, try playin' that homo crap with me," Blake said, staring directly at Bedford. "My .357 will be the last thing you'll see."

Everybody laughed.

"Man, Blake," Bedford said, grinning. "Man, that wasn't even me who had suggested doing anything like that, and you know it."

Suddenly both helicopters were once again airborne for the short trip across the dark field to the nearby boys ranch. Taylor took his craft a few feet higher than Ghetto Boy's with a much wider angle. He positioned his craft in a different direction from which to go in for a landing in case of an emergency requiring him to fire upon any unidentified incoming.

"Why're you going way out here instead of following the others?" Blake asked Taylor. "Aren't we going to the boys ranch too?"

"Remember what I said about taking extra precautions," Taylor said in his attempt to remind Blake about the danger of being watched by the giant mosquitoes. "Well, these helicopters should never get in a bind together as to where the enemy can take both of us out. We're back here so that we can keep an eye on each other if danger arises from anywhere around us. One will inform the other."

"And then what?" asked Bedford. "I already know, but I just wanna hear you tell Blake."

Taylor turned his head from side to side before answering, as though he were looking out the windows, and then he said very adamantly, "Let me remind you that once the both of us ever have to open up fire on anything, you'll think it's the beginning of the goddamn Armageddon!"

*

Precisely and accurately stated and particularly highly distinctive from other forms of observance in terms described as important prophecy with few scenarios and timelines.

"It's so incredible how Taylor's understanding of the Armageddon shows how he so systematically demonstrates it to the crew. The amazing point, which by all means effectively—and without him realizing it—became a vital part of the final prophecy, fulfilled the final days of the town of Stonyford and the surrounding region."

Lucifer's deadly reign of power and terror prevails, widespread. It is slowly creeping into the region to transform those whom he recognizes as his own, which will undoubtedly symbolize his spiritual creation and signify lasting consequences for those who fail to submit to his authority.

In this final prophecy, which Margaret so candidly described, the entire region becomes subjected to the lawlessness of Sheriff Blake and his group of flunkies. The calculation of the transition is at hand. Lucifer and his false prophets are obviously about to execute and will indeed accomplish the primary goal once again against the teachings of God.

Margaret is desperately revealing through me the new theological works and deadly potentials of Satan himself in all true forms, as he promised would occur.

But why in the quiet community of Stonyford?

As she deeply described with observances, and certainly not for other purposes, Stonyford and the surrounding region must by all means fess up and face this circumcision—a castration like none other.

"The entire region is definitely going to be held accountable for this spiritual literary work against Lucifer," Margaret said. "But not from that of Almighty God, but from that of old Lucifer himself. Those living in these communities shall be removed from the face of this earth for their conscious willingness. After careful consideration of their personal and collective moral principles, they prohibit their collective participation in Lucifer's march against heaven. This, by all means, is a deliberate act believed to have been conscripted by heavenly angels. This region shall indeed suffer a very slow, agonizing death with intense physical pain, so enormously great, and to an immense degree, until Lucifer finds himself completely satisfied with pure gratification."

"Some will be simply caught in the crossfire, though, unfortunately, it will be too late for them to retreat to any form of seclusion.

"The retribution and the punishment of Stonyford will begin the return of the resurrection of Satan's army, bringing death to everyone, retaliation with evil for evil, as an eye for an eye, as a retainer would do when he's collecting his portion of his household, retaining that which belongs to him.

"Lucifer is about to collect his property with violating vengeance."

Margaret can best be described as a watchman with viewpoints and clarifications professing the truth about the events that are going to take place throughout the Stonyford region. Her cooperation hasn't been easy, but rests as the only testament thus far when questioning the validity in relationship to both past and present events throughout the vast majority of this region. Her testaments bear truth, regardless of whether you believe in her plight or not.

During the lengthy retribution, it is how Margaret used such a symbolic means to describe the return of these fallen angels, who are themselves under the direct influence of Satan after the collapse of their challenge against heaven. The entire encounter will bring an astounding amount of familiarity and knowledge, remembering those angels who were themselves severely wounded, as some were also destroyed during the battle.

"Familiarize yourself with these events," said Margaret. "Don't let this encounter happen without you recognizing and understanding its purpose. Take notes, for then you'll be able to recognize the things I'm telling you."

Once again, Margaret has spoken in great parables of redemption and a time for celebration throughout this region. "No one will be isolated to himself" during this terrible time of tribulation.

It is so important, intentionally, that the reason for this event be put into perspective is the presentation and power of Lucifer, which for many years was said to have been completely stripped of such power.

Nonsense!

Such foolish thinking by the behavior of many people, and mainly by that of the "Church" is the reason why most believers who once believed in God find themselves doomed today! False doctrines have been and are being taught as a principle by false preachers calling themselves "Prophets" of faith, professing to be the only connection to God. And of course, it may seem at times that these "Prophets" might mystically describe recognizable events. Legitimate inquiry should be quickly established to withstand faulty beliefs.

"Again, and please try to understand what I am trying to tell you—that is important for you to know," Margaret said in her attempt to describe what had been encoded in patterns of events to take place. "The entire region, which is inhabited by virtually the unintended leadership of manipulators and failed supervisory leaders whose deception was generated, and by all means designed to deceive God's creation."

This is quite a phenomenon, which Lucifer has used to torment the born-again anticipation of those who favored God instead of him. There is no mystical resonance to unfold to reveal this truth. However, regardless of the misery of this region, the people living in these communities shall forever have their hearts and eyes blinded without mercy. And although quite stunning when put into perspective, it is still remarkable to think how manipulative Lucifer can be.

The unbelievers are the unsaved and are doomed to hell. The Submission? Many shall bow in prayer to submit to Satan, who will blind them instantly and with no form of compassion. God shall cut them off for denying him. And Lucifer, he will open his ears to their cry and immediately toss them deep into the bottomless pit forever.

Blessed are the ones who are saved from this form of rapture, which is also a form of Satan's delusional entrapment for those who genuinely make and attain a spiritual covenant with him. He manipulates them to believe he is trustworthy to them, canonizing and glorifying them as saints against the will of God, our Heavenly Father.

"But Stonyford is no delusion, though, indeed an entrapment operated by and orchestrated by the will and method of Lucifer himself. The entire region, and mainly Stonyford and the surrounding communities, are going to be severely punished for deliberately refusing to obey the authority of Lucifer and for disorganizing this region's structure and disorienting every living creature's sense of direction, dispelling one's thoughts and separating each individual from Lucifer's reign."

*

"The Armageddon?" Blake said loudly. "Hell! We don't have enough, you know, uh, ammunition in this thing for a battle like that, do we?"

"You wanna bet?" the co-pilot asked him, grinning.

"Well, I was just thinking about all that firepower that kid you guys call Ghetto Boy used when we were over there," said Blake. "He should be on empty by now. Wouldn't you think?"

"Not hardly," Taylor yelled back at Blake while hovering at a distance from the other helicopter. "Push come to shove, we just might have to leave you guys here at the boys ranch."

"Push come to shove?" Blake said, confused. "Don't look like anybody is at home. Whatcha mean, leave you guys? What's that about?"

"What he's sayin' is that," the co-pilot began, "if any of those things should come after us right now, we'll ditch only to let you guys take cover, and then, we'll go after 'em."

"Looks like they've landed and ready to go in," Taylor said. "I'mma take us over on the other side."

"Don't look like anybody's home," Ghetto Boy said over the transmitter. "We're going inside."

"Hold up for a minute," Taylor told him. "We'll be coming in from the other side."

"Uh, Ghetto Boy," the co-pilot called. "Looks like lights on inside. Am I mistaken?"

"Lights on inside," said Ghetto Boy. "Plenty lights, but no movement."

"Okay, we've touched down, Ghetto Boy," Taylor told him, shutting down the engine. "No movement on this side from our view. Keep in mind, it's dark, and the mosquitoes, scorpions, and horseflies are most likely watching us."

"Jesus Christ, Taylor," Blake said, turning around and staring off into the dark sky that surrounded them. "You just had to re-mind me."

"Just didn't want any of them things creeping up on you, Blake," the co-pilot said, pointing his handheld flashlight in the direction of an area where a few mobile homes sat, apparently used for the staff who worked at the boys ranch when needing to stay overnight.

"Looks like somebody just might be at home over there," Bedford said, pointing his camera. "Thought I saw something moving out there, somewhere."

"Where?" the co-pilot asked, moving the light around.

"No, I'm talking about over there in that direction," Bedford said.

"Where?"

"To your left," Bedford said again, pointing in the direction of what the light beam reflected on—a reddish-looking house that sat by itself.

"Oh, yeah," said the co-pilot. "Now I see what you're talking about out there. Thought I saw something too."

"Uh, Blake and Bedford," Taylor said. "Why don't you guys come in with me, and Reggie, why don't you stay out here for now and keep vigil."

"What about Ghetto Boy and his crew?" the co-pilot asked.

"Well, now that you've mentioned it, I was thinking that maybe we could get you up onto the roof."

"Got you," the co-pilot said, comprehending what Taylor needed him to do.

"But wait a minute," said Taylor, pulling out his radio. "Need to contact Ghetto Boy."

"Just hoist me up on this thing, and I'll give him the information."

"Come on, Bedford," said Blake. "Help me push him up there."

"Hold up, Blake," Taylor told him. "Man, tell me you didn't forget how we did stuff like this in the military."

"What?" Blake said, snickering. "Climb up on my back and break it? It's not my intention to be walking around all bent over for the rest of my life at my age."

CLICK—CLICK—CLICK

"I'll do it," Taylor told 'em. "Come on, let's go, Reggie."

CLICK—CLICK—CLICK

"Sounds like that might be Ghetto Boy calling you, Taylor," Blake said while looking inside one of the windows. "Something isn't right about this."

"You took the words right out of my mouth," Bedford told him. "I was just about to say the same thing, until—"

"Go ahead, Ghetto Boy," Taylor said over the radio.

"Everything all right round there?" he asked.

"Roger that," Taylor answered. "Reggie on the roof—prowling."

"Need any extra?"

"One is enough."

"Waiting on you."

"Any unlock?"

"Negative."

"On the count of three!"

"Let's do this."

"One—then there was—three!"

Upon saying the number three, Taylor and his group immediately burst into the large-style dormitory building that provided long, narrow sleeping quarters for quite a number of people. Ghetto Boy and his group entered through the main entrance, while the co-pilot, Reggie, moved slowly on the roof keeping vigil.

The building was built somewhat like a starfish, except it had only three arms that extended from a central counter with a desk where staff sat for supervisory purposes. In front of this building sat an office building for admitting clients. Alongside this building, within a few feet, was the huge cafeteria, which looked more like a restaurant at best. Next to it sat the education department.

Not far from where the helicopters hovered when Ghetto Boy opened fire on the mosquitoes, scorpions, and horseflies, there was a runway built for private airplanes and helicopters. It was used to deliver clients to the Boys Ranch whenever the drive was excessively long.

The road traveling to this area ran between the location of the barn and the airstrip. Past this area and the boys ranch, there sat a small campground about half a mile into the hills.

"Anything?" Taylor shouted.

"Negative!" said Ghetto Boy.

"Somebody check the bathroom area," Taylor yelled. "Blake,

make sure your guy, Bedford, is recording everything."

"I'm already on it," Bedford yelled back.

"Reggie, you copy?" Taylor asked over his radio.

"Copy!" Reggie answered.

"Fire on anything," Taylor told him.

"Gotcha!" Reggie responded.

"What about us?" Miller asked Taylor, referring to himself and Goldsby.

"Just do what you do best," said Taylor. "Investigate what you see."

"I wonder where everybody is?" Blake said, questioning himself. "I was just talking to one of the guys who works up here just yesterday."

"Here today and gone tomorrow," Bedford said. "This place is empty."

"Not hardly," Blake told him, staring out one of the windows. "Look at that house. Do you see anything moving past one of the windows?"

"Uh, I really can't tell that much from here," Bedford said. "What I'm seeing just might be a branch from a tree moving over there."

"Well, is it moving or blowing around?" Miller asked.

"Hell, I think it's just the wind blowing it around near that one window," Blake said, staring intently at the house.

"Mmmm," Miller mumbled. "Now that's really something, and this is really strange."

"What's that?" Taylor asked Miller seriously. "What's on your mind?"

"Well, I really can't seem to recall the wind blowing," Miller said.

"Reggie, you copy?" said Taylor in a low voice.

"Copy!"

"Feel any wind blowing from up there?"

"Strangely negative."

"Everybody up front!" Taylor called out to the crew. "Immediately!"

"What's happening?" Ghetto Boy asked with a stern expression.

"OK, you guys. Listen up," Taylor said, somewhat unsure of what he was about to say. "And this isn't any bullshit. But I think we have some really strange phenomena jumping off around here."

"Oh, damn," Blake muttered to himself. "Uh, you guys mind if I fire up this cigar?"

"I think I need a cigarette myself," said Miller, reaching into one of his shirt pockets.

"Phenomena?" Ghetto Boy repeated, confused. "What are you talking about?"

"Well, what I'm talking about is that I think I know why those ugly-looking motherfuckers haven't come this way," Taylor said, referring to the creatures crawling around the outer boundary between where they were and the area seemingly conditioned for them to remain.

"So, in other words," said Goldsby, "what you're saying is that those things out there can't cross some kind of borderline or something."

"That's exactly what I'm saying," Taylor told her.

"How'd you figure that one out?" Miller asked. "I mean, it's like you're saying there's a line they can't cross."

"Okay then," Taylor said, pointing at Blake's cigar. "Go ahead, Blake, fire it up. And Miller, you do the same with yours—your cigarette. Go ahead."

"You guys know what?" Miller said, unable to light his cigarette. "Uh, this kinda reminds me of a movie I remember watching once. It was about some people traveling through a time zone or something. And after landing at an airport, they found out they couldn't do what they needed to do because of the air. There were also some weird-looking monsters chasing one of the guys around."

"Oh, yeah," Bedford said, agreeing with what Miller was talking about. "Man, I think I saw that movie too. It was called *Langa* something. They finally got that big-ass plane off the ground and back into the air, and made it back through that time zone that was lit up in all kinds of colors, if I'm not mistaken."

"Well, you guys," said Taylor, "this isn't that movie. This is some for-real shit going on out there. Reggie's up top keeping watch."

"And why can't I light my cigar?" Blake asked, still busy trying to get the lighter to fire up. "Damn thing won't light."

"That's because there isn't any air for that thing, Blake," Bedford told him. "That's what we were talking about. Those things can't seem to cross some kind of boundary, or they'll prob-ably suffocate from the lack of oxygen."

"There's still quite a bit of oxygen here," said Taylor. "But it's not enough for them, seeing that they need lots of oxygen to fly. And some of them use quite a bit just to survive—you know, to live longer."

"Yeah," Goldsby said. "Like before I squash them."

"Not hardly," Ghetto Boy told her. "The size of those things isn't any small matter to be calling yourself attempting to squash. If anything, those things gotta be destroyed by guns. Big guns."

"Hey, Ghetto Boy," said Taylor, curious. "Where's your co-pilot?"

"Stayed in the helicopter in case an emergency should arise."

"Does he know Reggie's up top?"

"Think so. I mean, I sure hope so."

"Make contact and find out," Taylor told him. "They'd bump into each other in the dark, and all hell would break out. And knowing them, with all the firepower they each have, they'd end up clashing at best and reducing everything out there into pieces —even us. Hurry up, make contact, and advise them of each other's position and location."

"Damn!" Blake said. "Y'all done left the poor guy out there all by himself without letting him know what's happening?"

"Oh, he knows," said Ghetto Boy. "And he can handle being out there, even if it really was by himself."

"Yeah?" Blake said, looking out one of the windows.

"Being by himself is one of his specialties," Taylor told him. "Just don't need those two killing all of us, which is another of their specialties when the moment arises—especially during times like what we are experiencing."

"What's that guy's name anyway?" Blake asked.

"It's Chad," Ghetto Boy told Blake. "Chad Osbern. One of the best of the best co-pilots I have had in quite a while."

"Mmmm," Taylor mumbled. "Don't need him and Reggie clashing out there."

"Chad, you copy?" Ghetto Boy said over his radio transmitter.

CLICK—CLICK—CLICK

"Copy!" Chad responded. "Be aware that Reggie's up top."

"Copy!" Chad added, staring through his night lenses. "Got a visual."

"Reggie, you copy?" Ghetto Boy asked over the transmitter.

CLICK—CLICK—CLICK

"Copy!" Reggie said. "Got a visual."

"Everything seems to be secured here," said Taylor. "Think we should advance to that house first. Any objections?"

Silence.

"Uh, Reggie,Chad, you copy?" Taylor called out.

CLICK—CLICK—CLICK

"Copy!" Reggie.

"Copy!" Chad.

"Taking it to the streets," Taylor told them.

CLICK—CLICK—CLICK

"Roger that," a voice said. "How?"

"Just follow the Yellow Brick Road," Taylor responded.

"Yellow brick road?"

"Yellow brick road," Taylor responded again.

CLICK—CLICK—CLICK

"Make sure to watch out for the Wiz," another voice said, snickering.

CLICK—CLICK—CLICK

"Sure you wanna walk the yellow brick road?" the first voice asked.

"Copy," Taylor answered.

CLICK—CLICK—CLICK

"What if I hover?"

"Don't wanna wake up the GOATS," Taylor told him.

CLICK—CLICK—CLICK

"Quiet! Can hear G's on the prowl," said Chad.

"COPY!" Taylor said, listening after opening one of the windows.

CLICK—CLICK—CLICK

"Roger that," Reggie said, already hearing the noises.

"Uh, why don't we double-check this place before heading out," Taylor suggested. "And then we might wanna lock this back door, so that Chad and Reggie can spot anything suspiciously moving about."

"What about the lights?" Miller asked. "Think they should be shut off?"

"No," said Ghetto Boy. "Let's leave 'em on, so those things will keep focus on this place instead of where we'll be headed."

"Damn, that's right," Miller said, staring at all the empty beds. "Man, I wonder where everybody went? I mean those kids who were supposed to be here?"

"I was just wondering the same thing myself," Goldsby said,

looking at an empty pair of boots under one of the beds. "Where could they be?"

"Who knows," Blake shrugged. "Just hope they're nowhere around here."

"Hey, uh, Bedford," Taylor called. "You been getting this, haven't you? Wouldn't want to leave footage like this without capturing it on film."

"I'm doing good for now," Bedford told Taylor. "But I might have to, I think, get my other bag out of the helicopter."

"Then let's get it," Taylor said, heading to the back door. "Come on, I'll help you."

"Isn't, uh, what's his name, still up there on the roof?" Bedford asked.

"Uh, yeah," Taylor responded. "Why?"

"I'm cool then," Bedford said, attempting to go out the door without anyone with him.

"No, I don't think so, Bedford," Taylor told him, opening the door and peering into the darkness. "Hold up. Let me make Reggie aware of us being down here first. Uh, Reggie, you copy?"

CLICK—CLICK—CLICK

"Copy!" said Reggie, walking slowly on the roof.

"Uh, we'll be getting something out the bird," Taylor told him. "You copy?"

CLICK—CLICK—CLICK

"Copy!"

"Let's go," Taylor told Bedford.

"You guys gonna need any help?" Blake asked.

"No, we got it," said Taylor.

"Man, it's black out here," Bedford said, straining his eyes to see. "I could never live out here in the wild. If Kansas City ever got like this, I might have to move to another city, like New York, where lights are just about everywhere you go."

"Hold up for a minute, Bedford," Taylor said, listening to the noises in the distance. "Sounds like they're right over there some-where."

"I've been up here listening to that too," Reggie said, surpris-ing both Taylor and Bedford.

"Man!" Taylor said, shocked. "What are you trying to do? You scared the everything out of us. Damn! I was already thinking about those body parts over there, scattered about with that wreckage, and here you come with that deep voice talking to us out of nowhere."

"Didn't mean to startle you guys," Reggie said, giggling. "But I just wanted you to know that I've been hearing those noises too. They're out there quite a ways, like at the bottom of that huge hill. I think it's the hill everybody calls Snow Mountain. That's where the noise seems to be coming from."

"How's he seeing that from here, as dark as it is?" Bedford asked Taylor.

"Remember our conversation about special lenses," Taylor said. "Well, that's what he's using. They make the darkness turn into light just as if it were daytime out here."

"Got any more of them?" Bedford asked.

"Nah, Bedford," Taylor said, quietly laughing. "But come on, man, I'll help you find your way around in the dark, 'cause this type of darkness can really make you paranoid if you're not careful."

"Hey, you guys all right out here?" Blake said, slowly opening the door.

"Yeah, Blake," Taylor told him, inching his way through the doorway.

"Why?" Bedford asked Blake.

"Just thought I heard you guys out here having a little too much fun without me," Blake said, looking around in the dark.

"Just kicking it with Reggie," Bedford added, squeezing past Blake.

"Gonna stay out here and keep me company, Blake," Reggie

said, whispering somewhat.

"Goddamn it, you son of a bitch," Blake yelled in a low, rugged tone. "Just what the hell are you trying to do? Give me a goddamn heart attack? You crazy bastard!"

"Didn't mean to scare you, buddy," Reggie told him, giggling. "You must've forgotten that I was up here."

"No, I didn't forget. I just didn't expect you to be sneaking up on me like this, that's all."

"Sorry, man. But it really wasn't my intention to sneak up on you. I mean, hey, I was already out here before you came out that door."

"Blake!" a voice called from inside the building. "We need you to bear this."

"Gotta go, Reggie. Gotta see what's happening."

"all right, Blake. Talk to you later."

"The reason I need to talk to you guys before we head out into the open is because I want you to remember our purpose for being here in the first place," Taylor began. "As you guys know, our mission up here was to find whoever it was that we heard screaming for help over the transmitter. But was it just a prank? Or was it really somebody needing help? We don't know, and yet we have to find out."

"You think those things out there have anything to do with it?" Miller asked. "They sure seem to be waiting on us."

"Anything's possible," Taylor said, rubbing his hands together. "Really can't say."

"I wonder where they came from?" Bedford asked again, staring out one of the windows into the darkness. "It's like they're all over this place."

"Maybe Blake can answer that question," Taylor said. "He's the one in charge of these parts."

"Yeah, that's right," said Ghetto Boy. "You're the sheriff around here, Blake. How long have these things been crawling around up here?"

"Now, wait a minute, you guys," Blake said. "I ain't never heard a single word out of nobody about them things. Ain't nobody ever said nothing to me about this. They must've just come here."

"Well, just where is everybody?" Goldsby asked Blake. "I'm talking about the kids. Where are they?"

"Your guess is as good as mine," Blake told her.

"I think those things—" Bedford began.

"Okay," Taylor said, picking up a few large shoulder bags from the floor. "Get everything together, and let's head on out."

"The lights?" Ghetto Boy said, ready to hit a switch.

"Let's leave them on," Taylor told him. "Remember, they'll think we're still here."

"Damn!" Bedford said, smiling. "Doing it like that, you might as well turn on some music."

"Not a bad idea, Bedford," Miller told him. "Now why didn't I think of that?"

"Do it!" Taylor said, smiling. "Just make sure they'll, you know, be listening to whatever it is that you are listening to. That way, if any of them motherfuckers make it past that barrier, they'll know who to come after."

"Yeah," said Ghetto Boy, trying to hold in his laughter. "You'll be the one playing that funky music that they'll be tired of hearing. Those things will be trying to find you to kick your motherfuckin' ass, Bedford."

"Man, you full of shit," Bedford said, turning up the volume on his MP3 player.

"Wait a minute," Taylor said, waving his hand to get Bedford's attention.

"Now, what?" Bedford asked Taylor, removing the head-phones from over his ears. "Man, my joint is playing."

"I think Ghetto Boy has a point, Bedford," Taylor said, rubbing a few fingers on his chin. "Plug your MP3 into that entertainment system, and let that motherfucker play the same song over and over. Repeatedly."

"Yeah," Miller said in agreement. "Just put it on repeat. Or whatever it is. And let it play. Loud!"

"And who's gonna save you from getting your ass kicked? Loud, Miller?" Bedford asked, grinning. "Cause right after those things are done stampeding and smashing up my MP3, I'mma make sure they rush your dumbass and stampede the shit outta you."

Snickering.

"But he does have a point, Bedford," Ghetto Boy said. "We gotta make sure they think we're still in here, when really, we'll be over there."

"And what kind of music have you been listening to, anyway, Bedford?" Blake asked. "I've really been meaning to hear some of it since we were over there by that barn."

"Man," Bedford said, turning down the volume on his MP3. "Why don't you guys just turn on a radio station or something? Or play one of those CDs?"

"Still wanna hear what you've been listening to," Blake said, smiling.

"Yeah, Bedford," Taylor added. "I'm curious too."

"Well, I guess I'd better join in before we leave," Goldsby said. "I wanna hear it too!"

"And I guess you're waiting too?" Bedford said, looking at Miller. "And you too, Ghetto Boy?"

"Wouldn't mind if you let me hear it," Ghetto Boy said, smiling.

"Okay with me, Bedford. I mean, if that's all right with you. But that's only if you don't mind," Miller said.

"all right!" Bedford exclaimed. "You want it? Then you got it!"

"Plug it in for them, Ghetto Boy," Taylor told him.

"I bet it's some DMX," Ghetto Boy said.

"Nah. It's probably some Lil Wayne or Cee-Lo Green," Goldsby said.

"Uh, what about, uh, what's his name," Miller said, trying to remember who he was thinking about. "Uh, it's, what's his face... uh, 50 Cent, I think."

"Nobody mentioned anything about Chris Brown or Usher," Taylor said.

"Well, here we go," Ghetto Boy said, extending a cable from the entertainment center to Bedford so he could plug it into the side of his MP3 player's headphone jack.

Reggie sang loudly from the MP3, "Do you really wanna hurt me? Do you really wanna make me cry?"

"Oh, hell no!" Ghetto Boy shouted.

"Man, Bedford," Taylor yelled. "What the fuck?"

Confused, hysterical laughter from everyone.

"What?" Bedford said, surprised. "What's so funny?"

"Jesus Christ, Bedford," Blake said, grinning embarrassingly. "You're really off your rocker."

CLICK—CLICK—CLICK

CLICK—CLICK—CLICK

"Yeah, go ahead," Taylor said, responding to the clicking sound from his radio.

Chad called over the transmitter, "Please don't play that song. If you value that MP3 player, you'll never play that song again."

Reggie added over the transmitter, "I would have to agree. I'd rather be at war with these things out here than hear Bedford's music."

"You guys just don't know," Bedford said, unplugging the extension.

"Think we're sane enough to leave after hearing that?" Ghetto Boy said, shaking his head and shrugging his shoulders.

"Yeah," Miller said. "Them things might be able to catch up with us now."

"And what about you, Goldsby?" Taylor asked her. "Anything you want to add to what just happened?"

"I think I'm getting sick," Goldsby said, frowning and raising one of her eyebrows. "But I really don't think it has anything to do with Bedford or anything, though..."

"All right," Taylor exclaimed. "I think we're crazy enough to head on out, and especially after that experience. But please don't get me wrong. I really liked that song. But—"

"Man," Ghetto Boy said, "can you guys just imagine us at war with those things while listening to that song?"

"What?" Bedford said seriously. "Why y'all staring at me like that?"

CHAPTER SEVEN

"EVERYBODY FALL BACK A LITTLE," Taylor said, checking the clip on his Glock. "Put some space in between each other. A few feet or more. Like maybe five to ten, or more."

"What?" asked Miller. "Like scatter out?"

"No," Ghetto Boy said, tightening the night vision scope on his rifle. "Single file, Miller. Single file everybody."

"Try being as quiet as you possibly can," said Taylor. "Make no sounds that'll cause those things to come searching for you."

"Blake, you gonna use your gun?" Bedford asked him.

"If I have to, why?" Blake asked.

"Well, I thought—"

"Reggie, you copy?" Taylor called out through his radio.

CLICK–CLICK–CLICK

"Copy!" Reggie answered.

"Chad, you copy?" Taylor again asked.

CLICK–CLICK–CLICK

"Copy!" Chad answered.

"Okay, it's time," Taylor said, meaning it was time for the group to move out.

"Hey, uh, you guys know the three of us don't have anything

to use if those things come after us, don't you?" Bedford said nervously.

"Well, looks like you guys will be the ones carrying the supplies. But that's if you don't mind," Taylor asked.

"What?" Goldsby said, frowning. "Them bags look too heavy for me to be trying to carry all the way over there."

"You mean over there," Ghetto Boy said, correcting her. "All we're doing is moving from here to there, Goldsby. That's all."

"Damn," Bedford mumbled. "Just give me a gun or something, and I'll be glad to climb Snow Mountain."

"Well, you sure can't use mine," Blake told him, rubbing his holster.

"Hold on, Bedford," Taylor told him, walking back to the back door. "I think we just might have something for you."

"Oh, yeah," said Bedford. "Where is it?"

"Mounted," Taylor said, smiling generously. "On the side of the helicopter."

"Mounted on the side of the helicopter?" Bedford questioned. "What is that? A big-ass machine gun?"

"You guessed it," Ghetto Boy said, grinning. "Got two of 'em. Can you carry one too, Miller?"

"Wow! Hold on a minute," Bedford cried out. "Man, I ain't said nothing about being a freakin' bodybuilder to be trying to lug one of them things up there. Let alone on my shoulder."

"Well, you said that if you had a gun or something, you'd climb Snow Mountain," Taylor said, opening the back door. "I'm only trying to help you out so that you can make it to the top."

"Yeah, but not like—"

"Reggie, you copy?"

"Copy!" Reggie responded. "Beware, on your doorstep down below."

"Copy!"

"Before we move out, thought I'd get that Fifty-caliber,"

Taylor told Reggie, who happened to be standing on that side of the roof. "Gotta give Bedford an opportunity to feel like he's part of the team, or something. You feel me?"

"I feel you, but is he capable? Correction! I mean, qualified in terms of being able to operate such a weapon along with its artillery and everything else?"

"Well, let's say not as artistic and skilled as ourselves. But let's allow him this chance in his short lifetime to finally do something that we would consider worthwhile."

"Worthwhile indeed, but for how long?"

"Well, from the looks of things, that'll be until he runs out of, let's say, ammunition," Taylor said, snickering quietly.

"Uh, now, you know there is definitely going to be an explosive, wary type of situation tonight?" said Reggie. "And is it safe for me to say that he'll be the one who'll start it?"

"Uh-huh!"

"Damn! Let's get this thing started!"

"Uh, Bedford," Taylor called. "Help me unmount this sucker."

"Unmount it?" Bedford said, staring into the dark curiously at what Taylor was talking about. "What are we unmounting?"

"This, right under here," Taylor said, pointing underneath the left side of the helicopter.

"Man, what the fuck is that?" Bedford asked. "A freakin' bazooka? Man, I was thinking about something that fires bullets, not rockets and missiles."

"We're on a serious mission, Bedford," Taylor told him. "Now help me unhook this thing."

"Damn!" Bedford exclaimed. "A freakin' bazooka!"

"This isn't a bazooka, Bedford," Taylor said, unfastening two clamps. "Inside this container is a .50-caliber machine gun that you'll be using in case—"

"A .50-caliber machine gun?" Bedford yelled in surprise. "Man, what in the hell am I gonna do with something like this?"

"Use it," Taylor told him with a stern expression that Bedford could see in the dark. "And when that time comes, I advise you, Bedford, please don't blink, or—"

"And what am I supposed to put in it?"

"You'll be carrying the straps that are at the bottom, right there underneath your weapon."

"Damn, man," Bedford exclaimed. "How come you don't carry it and use it?"

"Because I have a dangerous assault rifle that's been my friend for so many missions," Taylor told him. "It's the only one I know. But just around on the other side, we do have a bad-ass, ugly-looking bazooka!"

"And that'll definitely go on Miller's shoulder," said Reggie.

"Ah, man. What the fuck!" Bedford said, startled by Reggie's voice.

"Didn't mean to scare you," Reggie told Bedford. "You forgot so quick that I was up here?"

"Man, I had these bazookas, and machine guns, and everything else on my mind," Bedford told him. "Next, you guys will be talking about cannonballs and who knows what."

"Hey, Miller?" Taylor called quietly. "You want to come out here for a minute?"

"Yeah, what's that?" he answered.

"Got something for you."

"Something for me?"

"Yeah," Taylor told him, stooping down and removing two more clamps. "I need you to grab hold of this thing with me and lower it slowly to the ground."

"Want me to help you guys?" Bedford asked.

"Naw, we got it," said Taylor.

"Well, in case you forgot, Miller," said Bedford, "remember, Reggie is up on the roof keeping watch. So if you hear him say something, just don't let him surprise you like he did me."

"Is that right?" Miller said slyly, looking upward. "Where?"

"Right here in front of you, Miller," Reggie told him, snickering in a mumbling sound.

"Luckily I wasn't out here by myself," Miller told Reggie. "I probably would've run off and gone far out there somewhere."

"And been lost as hell," Reggie said. "Cause as dark as it is, those things out there would have come after you. And the only thing we would've heard was you screaming for help."

"Grab that, will you?" Taylor told Miller.

"Just what, the?" Miller started to say.

"It's a Bazooka!" Taylor told him in a grungy voice.

"A Bazooka?" Miller exclaimed, raising his voice slightly.

"Yeah, you heard him right," Bedford said, laughing while trying to hold it in. "I couldn't believe it either at first, but—"

"Chad, what's up?" Reggie asked into his radio, which could be heard by everyone else.

"Got movement around nine o'clock," Chad replied, meaning something was moving about a quarter mile away toward the entrance to the ranch.

"Copy!" Reggie said, turning and focusing in that direction with his night vision lenses. "Got 'em!"

"How many?" Taylor asked, removing the Bazooka from underneath the right side of the helicopter.

"Five to ten, or so," Reggie said. "Looks like different species in the same classification category, or maybe they interbred, creating an entirely new generation in a new category."

"Just what are you talking about?" Taylor asked, curious.

"Never seen anything like this," Reggie said. "In all my training, I never heard of anything like this happening."

"Chad, you copy?" Taylor called over his radio.

"Copy!" Chad responded.

"Be ready to move," Taylor said sternly.

"Copy!"

"Reggie, what are they doing?" Taylor asked.

"Man, Taylor," Reggie said. "I know you won't believe this. But what I'm about to tell you is something I wouldn't believe if I hadn't seen it myself. They are out there communicating the same way we do."

"Just what the hell are you talking about, Reggie?" Taylor asked. "I don't quite understand."

"Man," Reggie said, bending down to explain, "those things are communicating just like we do. It's like they're human or something."

"But what are they doing?" Taylor asked, frustration creeping into his voice. "Describe what you've seen, dammit!"

"Look, Taylor," Reggie said, attempting to describe what he saw. "Those things are out there talking to each other just like I'm up here talking to you. All of them have something like large fruit bats clinging onto them as if guiding them and telling them where to go. All of them talking to each other just as we are talking."

"How's that?" Taylor asked. "How do you know they're talking to each other like we do?"

"Because they have human heads on them," Reggie told him. "And they are really out there talking and moving those long, skinny-looking legs just as if they were arms and hands."

"Hold up," Taylor said, stooping upward from removing the Bazooka from underneath the helicopter and laying it flat on the ground. "Help me get up there, Miller."

"Come on," Reggie told him, reaching for one of his hands.

"Gotta see this for myself," Taylor said, curious as to what Reggie was talking about. "Man!"

"Want me to come up there too?" Bedford asked while rotating one of his cameras around in circles to film both Reggie and Taylor's reactions.

"Think we need him up here?" Reggie asked Taylor.

"We do," Taylor answered. "But before you know it, everybody'll be up here instead of heading over to that house over there."

"Yeah, but see what I mean?" Reggie said, pointing at the movement. "I told you."

Taylor shouted, "Motherfuckers! Would you—"

"What's happening, Chad?" Reggie asked.

"I think I need a little help turning my craft around without having to gear up my engine," Chad said, wanting to point the helicopter away from the building.

"Taylor," Reggie was about to suggest.

"Do it!" Taylor quickly said. "Tell 'em to hurry."

"Hey, Miller," Reggie called. "Check this out."

"We already know," Bedford told Reggie. "As quiet as it is out here, everybody could hear what Chad needed help to do. We're on it."

"I'll pull you up from the other side, Bedford," Reggie told him. "And what about the rest of us?" Miller said, looking around. "Need us up there too?"

*

Everything is geared toward the unknown. The monsters, the things crawling around in the hills, the amazing creation of the giant mosquitoes, scorpions, and horseflies—all part of Lucifer's creation. But unfortunately, the system commonly referred to as the "Stonyford Submission" is still in its beginning process and comes at the expense of the examples set in place by Sheriff Blake and the entire community of the Stonyford region.

This battle is on a much broader scale, distinctive from that described in certain chapters of the Bible. The scale described by Margaret will undoubtedly prove incredible, with Satan at the helm and incomplete control, steering this deadly, unveiled parable into the worst conclusion ever engineered during a tribulation.

Still, the egregious element will be the turning to a false redemption, so elaborate it resembles a counterfeit bill, employing scarlet principles during this period of persecution.

Lucifer is indeed anticipating the inclusion of the entire Stonyford region into his family during the tribulation.

The theme will be that Lucifer created the world and all things; in him, the people of this region will return, live therein, and at that time live forevermore.

This type of interaction with Lucifer is a testament within itself.

Quite frequently there are references throughout the history of Stonyford's alternative and so-called legitimate inquiries, which have been repeatedly documented, mystically describing the presence of Satan among the people of this region.

"Have mercy on us, our God in Hell, and quickly rise up, speedily, from the bottomless pit."

"This reference depicts the people of Stonyford praying to Lucifer for mercy, acknowledging their bond with him, and awaiting his return from the bottomless pit to begin the New Covenant, a belief widely documented throughout northern California."

For the sake of universally documenting the submission, virtually at the period when Margaret became completely dominated by the deadly, eager embrace of Satan, the question remains: why? Why is the small community of Stonyford the subject? Only the people residing in this town are able to provide these facts.

The younger members—the relatively obvious allusion being that the elders are, after all, responsible—though however unfair it might seem, this theology could in itself never be refuted in any way, since the facts about Stonyford have been completely unveiled and are evident to be reproof as elaborate truth.

*

"No, that's all right," Reggie told him. "You guys be headed out in a few. Just help Chad get that helicopter turned around so that if he has to open fire, he'll already be facing the right direction."

"Sure must be one hell of a helicopter," Miller mumbled, staring at the one in front of him. "Whoever designed this thing had a lot in mind."

The UH-72A Lakota Light Utility Helicopter is a craft designed for law enforcement missions. Its high-tech equipment lets the pilot and crew see things up to five miles away while simultaneously relaying images of the target to people on the ground at another location. This helicopter is a must-have during any emergency mission, according to a National Guard news release. "We're able to see things that people on the streets can't," co-pilot Chad Osbern said at a Task Force news conference on the newly equipped helicopter.

Other high-tech equipment built into this unit includes a moving map with three screens that can pinpoint the helicopter and its crew's location at various stages and speeds.

"I wonder what's over there by Snow Mountain," Taylor questioned. "I keep hearing something like water running."

"Sounds like a creek or something," Reggie said. "I've been hearing the same thing myself, but I just thought nothing of it."

"Ghetto Boy, you copy?" Taylor called through his radio.

CLICK—CLICK—CLICK

"Copy!" said Ghetto Boy. "What's your progress?" Taylor asked.

"One hundred percent," Ghetto Boy responded.

"I know you have one of those Long-Range Sniper Optics on that rifle, don't you?" Taylor asked Reggie.

"The best," Reggie answered. "Why?"

"Uh, why don't you just let me check it out for a minute,"

Taylor said, taking the rifle and aiming it in the direction of the creatures moving about on the outer perimeters of the boys' ranch. "And what type is this?"

"It's a Mark 4, ER/T 6.5-20x M5 Auto-Locking Adjustment. ITAR," Reggie said with a stern expression. "Got a Mark 8, Cobbs 1.1-8x, which is really a designated marksman and battle rifle optic. And then I have this real pretty little thing here that's a Mark 4, HAMR, fixed 4x Reflex Red Dot, Service Rifle and Carbine Optic."

"Mmm," Taylor mumbled to himself. "Wonder why I don't have any of these here that you have?"

"Your guess is as good as mine," said Reggie. "What are you looking at?"

"I wonder if them things know just how relentless we can be?" Taylor said. "Feel like I can use one of Blake's cigars right about now."

"I think you mean how unyielding and harsh we all can be, and want to be, right about now," said Reggie. "Why don't you just go ahead and do what's on your mind?"

"Mmmm," Taylor again mumbled to himself. "You shouldn't tempt me to do such a thing to our creepy crawling neighbors out there. But—"

"Hold up," Reggie said, mounting a rifle underneath one of his arms.

"Now, just where in the heck did that come from?" Taylor questioned.

"Oh, it was just something that I had Chad toss up here to me," Reggie said, snickering in a whisper. "Thought I'd need something extra up here."

"Yeah, and what is it?" Taylor asked, wanting to know the type.

"Just the kind I use around the house," said Reggie. "30-30, baby."

"Yeah, well, don't be calling yourself babying me up here,"

Taylor told him. "The things out there just might possibly have a sense of hearing, and I would hate for them to start thinking that we ain't nothing but a bunch of queers over here."

"You really think they can understand our language?"

"That, and a combination of other things," Taylor said.

"Well, push come to shove, you think we should try communicating with them first?" Reggie suggested. "I mean, you just might have a point, and I wouldn't mind giving it a try."

"Oh, like what," Taylor said, still peering through the sniper optic at the creatures moving about in the distance. "What? Now you want to be like that guy in that movie who tried to be friends with the Abominable Snowman? I think you should keep in mind the fact that this is not the Himalayas, and those things out there are in no way big, hairy humanoid creatures for you to be calling yourself wanting to plan a date with. Goddammit, Reggie, I thought you were more intelligent than that?"

"Nice for you to recognize my intelligence," Reggie said with a huge grin on his face. "Because I am, but it was just that I was thinking, you know, that maybe—"

"Man, those things are like some for real motherfuckin' monsters out there," Taylor told him firmly. "And not something you wanna be playing that tune 'What's Up Pussy Cat' with—"

CLICK—CLICK—CLICK

"Taylor, you copy?" said Chad over the transmitter.

"Copy," Taylor answered. "What's up?"

"Nine o'clock," Chad told him, looking to the left. "One attemting to scale the boundary!"

"Copy!" said Taylor. "Subject in sight."

"There's your shot," Reggie told Taylor. "Or you want me to take it?"

"Thought you had a softness for these motherfuckers, Reggie?" Taylor said, staring intently into the sniper lens.

"Naw," said Reggie. "It was just that, from the way those

things were communicating with each other, just like we do, I was just thinking that maybe it was possible to try communicating with them first."

"Like the old saying goes," Taylor draws a mental description. "Once that snake bites you, unable to inject its deadly poisonous venom because you just happen to grab its head, pulling it away from you just in the nick of time, are you then going to attempt picking it up again?"

"Hell, no!" Reggie responded. "I'm killing it."

"Why?" Taylor asked him.

"Isn't that obvious?" Reggie said. "Motherfucker tried to bite me, so I'mma kill it."

"So what about these things out there?" Taylor asked. "You've forgotten the wreckage and mutilated corpses and scattered remains we saw on that hill? But okay, Reggie. If you really wanna try communicating first, I am sure you know that I'll support your decision. Just don't be foolish. If anything, put a message in a bottle or something and throw it as far as you can. Let's see if they'll answer."

"And what if they do?" Reggie asked Taylor. "I mean, what if they send the bottle back, and that's providing it's not broken, but what if they actually answer? Then what?"

"We'll kill 'em anyway," Bedford said in an angry tone. "I hate bugs."

"Man," Reggie said, astounded at the thought of Bedford listening to what he and Taylor had been talking about. "Where'd you come from jumping in on this conversation?"

"Who, me?" said Bedford. "Oh, I was already here, filming you guys. I just happened to hear what you were talking about, and it's pretty interesting. But what if that bottle comes flying back at you? Then what?"

"How they gonna throw it, Bedford?" Reggie asked him. "Things don't have arms and hands like humans, though."

"Well, then," said Bedford, wondering, "what if those things are smart enough to act like helicopters, you know, like fly over here and start dropping stuff on us?"

"What about this, flash muzzle?" Taylor asked Reggie. "You like 'em?"

"Can't do without 'em," said Reggie. "Although it adds another 2.75 inches to my rifle. But I'm good."

"I know one thing," said Taylor. "Sure don't bog down your weapon."

"Oh, I see what's happening," Bedford said. "You guys—"

"You hear anything?" Taylor said, ignoring Bedford intentionally.

"Uh, not me," Reggie said in agreement with Taylor. "I don't seem to be able to hear anything for some reason."

"Fuck, y'all," Bedford said, slowly inching his way toward another section of the roof, still filming everything.

"Now, all I need is a bottle or something," Reggie said. "Is it still out there at nine o'clock?"

"It and a few more," Taylor told him. "Looks like his buddies are out there trying to figure out how to help him."

"What's he trying to do?"

"I would guess, climb the fence."

"Well, I mean. What's it trying to do?"

"You don't know if it's a it or the other," said Taylor. "All of them look alike, you ask me. I can't tell any difference between 'em."

"Now, you know that tactical rifle is going to probably blow 'IT' to kingdom come!" Reggie told Taylor humorously.

"You know, you're probably right," Taylor said, aiming the rifle while again staring intently through the sniper lens.

"Just hold on for a minute, Taylor," Reggie told him. "Let me get one of the guys to find a bottle or something so that, you know, I can, at least put something in it, you know, just to see what'll happen."

"OK, then tell me something," said Taylor, pulling away from the sniper lens. "Once you get your message in the bottle, or whatever you find, just how in the fuck are you going to get the thing out there?"

"Just leave it up to me," Reggie told him, smiling in the dark. "Got a pretty good idea in mind that I'm sure is going to work."

"Oh, damn," Taylor mumbled. "Next thing you'll be talking about is wanting me to guess who you'll be bringing back for us to meet for dinner."

"Just hold up," said Reggie. "And don't get too trigger happy yet. But just keep an eye on them things, you know, until I find something. Just give me a few minutes."

"Hey, Ghetto Boy," Reggie called out in a low whisper. "Ghetto Boy!"

"Yeah, man. What's up?" answered Ghetto Boy. "What's up?"

"Uh, check this out," Reggie began. "I need you to come up here for a few minutes, so that, you know, I can come down there and find a bottle or something."

"A bottle?" Ghetto Boy questioned. "For what? So you can piss in?"

"Mmmm," Reggie mumbled. "Never thought about that one. But no, man. I need something like a bottle or something so that I can, you know, put, uh, a little note or something in."

"A note?" Ghetto Boy said, curious as to what Reggie was up to. "And what's that for?"

"Damn, man, Ghetto Boy," Reggie said. "What's with all this third-degree stuff?"

"Just wondering," Ghetto Boy said. "You're up to something, and I'm just trying to figure it out. That's all."

"What he wanna do is write a love letter to them things out there in hope that one of 'em will be willing to go out on a date with his dumb ass," Taylor said suddenly, adding to the conversation.

"What the fuck!" Ghetto Boy said, startled by the thought of what he'd just heard Taylor saying about Reggie's intentions. "Man, are you crazy?"

"Just come on up here and let me come down there," Reggie told him.

"What'd you think, Taylor?" Ghetto Boy asked. "Gonna let him?"

"He's his own man," said Taylor. "Man gotta do what he gotta do."

"On my way," Ghetto Boy said, going back inside the building, heading to the back entrance where he would meet Reggie.

"Whatever you're up to, Reggie," Taylor said, "be careful. I'll be on you all the way."

"Thanks," Reggie said, walking over to Taylor and embracing him. "Just get the fuck outta here before you end up finding me objecting to what I think you have in mind. It's crazy, but I know it's what you want to do."

"Be back before you know it," Reggie said, walking over to the edge of the building and climbing down with Ghetto Boy coming up.

"How'd you get up here so easily?" Taylor asked Ghetto Boy. "I know you couldn't have used Miller's or Blake's backside that quick."

"Found a little something like a stool," Ghetto Boy said. "Except it was really like a ladder, tall enough to reach the top of this building."

"Is it still there?" Bedford asked.

"Yeah," Ghetto Boy answered. "Why?"

"In case I have to get down in a hurry," Bedford said, looking around.

"What? Scared of something?" Ghetto Boy asked. "Afraid those things are going to start flying over here?"

"You know, that's a possibility," Bedford said. "Anything's

possible."

"You know something, Bedford?" Taylor said, also looking around. "Think you have a point. And for some strange reason, I do believe we need to tell everybody to take cover and get ready."

"Ready for what?" Ghetto Boy asked Taylor.

"For what Reggie is about to do once he gets out there," Taylor said.

"Out where?" Ghetto Boy said, staring into the dark in the direction both Taylor and Bedford were looking. "Man, I know he isn't calling himself going out there, if those things are at, let alone probably by now all around us."

"We know," Taylor said. "That's why I want everybody to take cover if anything jumps off. We'll have his back so he can make it back safely."

"And you guys are just going to let him do it?" Ghetto Boy asked.

"Uh, it's like Taylor said," Bedford reminded him. "Man gotta do what a man gotta do."

"Chad, you copy?" Taylor said over the transmitter.

CLICK CLICK CLICK

"Copy!" Chad said.

"Get everybody inside," Taylor told him. "And get ready."

"Copy!" Chad said.

"Ghetto Boy?" Taylor said.

"Yeah? What's up?" Ghetto Boy answered, still confused as to why Reggie would want to try whatever he was about to try.

"How many radios do we have?" Taylor asked.

"I would say roughly a dozen or so," he answered.

"Good," Taylor said. "Chad, you copy?"

CLICK CLICK CLICK

"Copy!"

"Reggie anywhere near?"

"Copy!"

"What's up?" Reggie asked.

"Make sure everybody has a transmitter," Taylor said.

"Roger that," Reggie responded.

"Now, what if those things really do come flying this way?" Bedford questioned. "Then what?"

"Duck down," Ghetto Boy told him. "Maybe they won't see you."

"What about that house?" Bedford asked again. "Don't you think we'd be better off over there?"

"Yeah," Taylor said. "That's if we ever make it there. But from the looks of things, don't count on it being anytime soon, if that's what you're thinking."

"But what about that building right there?" Bedford asked again, referring to the building just a few feet from the one they were on. "I think it might be better than this. I mean, it looks like a kitchen or something."

"Yeah, now what?" Taylor said, laughing in a low hush. "Oh, now I think I know what's on your mind, Bedford. Reggie wants to introduce himself to the monsters, and now you—you wanna prepare something for them to eat. But the real irony of what'll probably happen is that one of you guys will most likely end up their meal on the table."

"Bullshit!" Bedford said, somewhat out loud, snickering at the thought of Taylor's statement. "That's bullshit. Maybe Reggie or one of you guys, but not me. But if anything, I'll be blasting those motherfuckers all over that kitchen."

"Are you sure that's a kitchen?" Ghetto Boy asked Taylor. "I mean, it does resemble a mess hall or something like that."

"It's a kitchen, all right," Taylor said. "Looking at the similarities in the building structure and all those windows, I bet that's where they had their meals. And probably still do, provided they ever return."

"Ah, man, you guys," Bedford said, as if he'd seen something.

"Man, you guys just made me think about something regarding that kitchen. I mean, if that's really the kitchen for this place, well, then there should be, you know, some huge freezers in there, right?"

"And Bedford," Taylor said, "what's your point? You want something like frozen pork chops and baby back ribs, or what? Or maybe some of those big, fat, juicy, country-style pork BBQ Boston Butt roast steaks."

"And some of those lean pork tenderloins," Ghetto Boy added. "With a freshly prepared dip spread. You know, the assorted variety kind. And definitely don't forget dessert—like that delicious, big 12-inch, four-layer deluxe Oreo cookies and cream cake, with a side of Blue Bell ice cream. Your choice of flavors."

"And don't forget something to drink," Taylor said, acting as if he were tasting everything they were talking about. "I'd like to see you and your friends sitting there at one of those tables, enjoying some refreshing sodas—maybe a Coke or two. Or maybe even some 7-Up."

"Or what about a Pepsi?" Ghetto Boy said, snickering.

"Or some green Lipton tea," Taylor said.

"Mmm," Ghetto Boy mumbled. "Hey, or some cool Budweiser, like a refreshing Bud Light. Or Miller's."

"What?" Bedford tried to add to the conversation. "No chips?"

"Hell no!" Taylor said firmly. "You and your ugly friends get one frozen roll, just like those people serve the inmates at the Lansing Correctional Facility in Lansing, Kansas."

"And the roll won't even be done!" Ghetto Boy said. "That company they use to prepare their food, ARAMARK, well, from my understanding, they don't ever prepare the food right."

"And that's how you and your ugly friends will be served here at the boys' ranch," Taylor told Bedford.

"Man, y'all on something," Bedford said. "Y'all done went way off the subject."

"Wasn't it food you were talking about?" Taylor asked Bedford.

"You see?" Bedford said. "That's just what I'm talking about."

"Well, wasn't it?" Taylor asked again.

"Hell no!" Bedford answered.

"Then what was it?" Ghetto Boy asked him.

"Man, I was thinking that, since we don't see anybody here... You know, I mean. It's the wrong thing to think, but—"

"OK," Taylor said. "I think I already know where this is going."

"Where?" Ghetto Boy asked, curious. "'Cause I know you're not—"

"You're on point, Ghetto Boy," Taylor told him about what Bedford was thinking.

"I think maybe Bedford just might have a point, too!" Ghetto Boy said, looking in the direction of the kitchen.

"I mean, if you guys just think about it," Bedford began, suggesting the absence of the people who were supposed to be at the boys' ranch. "I mean, where are they?"

"Locked in the freezer?" Taylor said, hoping he was wrong.

"But just how could that be?" Ghetto Boy said, scratching the top of his head. "Isn't that what we saw over there on that hill?"

"Don't really know," Taylor said, staring directly at Bedford.

"Then just who in the hell was that screaming over the transmitters?" Ghetto Boy whispered.

"Reggie, Chad, you copy?" Taylor called over the radio.

CLICK CLICK CLICK

"Copy!" Chad said.

CLICK CLICK CLICK

"Copy!" Reggie said.

"Stand down for a minute," Taylor told them. "Got something important to check out first."

"Thank God," Blake could be heard saying out loud. "Holy

shit, got all of us scared as hell."

"What the fuck!" Bedford said, looking around. "Y'all hear that?"

"I'm sure everybody heard it, Bedford," Taylor said, nodding his head in disbelief after hearing Blake's confession of being terrified.

"Fucken guy might not even be able to handle this, Taylor," Ghetto Boy said, commenting on Blake's fearful statement.

CLICK CLICK CLICK

"Taylor, you copy?" Chad asked over the transmitter.

"COPY!" Taylor answered.

"What's happening?" Chad questioned.

"Uh, hold up for a minute," Taylor told him. "Coming down."

"Want me to stay up here?" Ghetto Boy asked Taylor.

"Yeah," Taylor said. "That way, you can keep a visual on the back while Chad keeps a visual on the front."

"And what about me?" Bedford asked Taylor. "Need me to come with you?"

"Wasn't it you who thought of the possibility that friendlies could be locked in the freezer?" Taylor asked.

"Yeah, but—"

"Then, enough said," Taylor told him. "You'll be leading the way with your camera in full function."

"So long, Bedford," Ghetto Boy said, smiling. "Been nice knowing a guy like you. I'll make sure the world hears all about you."

"Fuck you, Ghetto Boy," Bedford said. "It'll be me telling the world how, when we came from the kitchen, those things were eating your ass."

"In your dreams, Bedford," Ghetto Boy said, giggling. "In your ugly dreams, with those things all around you, clawing the living shit out of you. That's what I'll be telling the world was the last thing I saw happening to you, Bedford. And when really thinking about it, maybe you should just leave your camera up here with me, so I can show the world the actual scene and footage of those things chasing you all over this place. You'd be running your ass off, screaming and hollering for help."

"You know something, Ghetto Boy?" Bedford said. "You's a sick bastard, aren't you?"

"Yeah," Ghetto Boy answered. "But you know what else you can add to me being a sick bastard? I got your back, baby. Ghetto Boy got your back."

Everybody laughed in a whisper.

CHAPTER EIGHT

"Be careful how you open that door," Taylor told Reggie. "Them things could already be in here as far as we know."

"What about any side door?" Blake said, trying to look through the blackness that prevented anyone from seeing the full structure of the side of the building.

"Go ahead and check it out, Blake," Taylor told him. "Just make sure you don't get lost."

"Want me to come with you?" Miller asked.

"What? You gonna protect me or something?" Blake said, slowly moving in the direction of a side door.

"Hate to see them things grab hold of you, Blake," Miller told him.

"Better yet," Blake said. "Why don't we just wait right here on them?"

"I think that'll be much better, 'cause then—"

"What's wrong?" Goldsby asked Miller. "Thought you guys were checking to see something about a side door?"

"No," Miller told her. "Blake decided to wait on everybody."

"You guys coming?" Bedford asked Miller.

"Yeah, but where's Blake?" Miller asked Bedford, looking

around.

"Man," Bedford said, somewhat startled. "That scary moth-erfucker just about knocked me down getting past me to get inside this building."

"Who?" Goldsby asked Bedford.

"You're kidding," Miller said, giggling. "He really did that?"

"Who are you guys talking about?" Goldsby asked Bedford again.

"Blake," Miller told her.

"So that's why he shot past me like that," said Goldsby. "I thought he was the sheriff around here? You know, the big man in charge?"

"Okay, you guys," Taylor said, holding the door open. "Let's go inside and see what we can find."

"What is it that we're looking for in here?" Miller asked Tay-lor.

"Anything we can find," Taylor answered. "But mainly, the freezer area."

"Sure is a nice-looking dining hall," Goldsby said, looking around in the dark. "I really like the way they built this fireplace. And just look at the chimney. Sure like to have something like this in my house. One day."

"That's not a fireplace, Goldsby," Taylor told her. "It's more like a barbecue pit. And that thing you've called a chimney, it's re-ally called a smokestack, you know, just like what you'll see on a ship standing vertical. These things are what smoke and other combustion gases are emitted through."

"Well, whatever this thing is," Goldsby said, "it sure need to be in my future home one day."

"Nothing in this part of the kitchen," Reggie said. "But what-ever is on the other side of those two doors right there, I do believe that's where we'll find our answer."

*

What Reggie was referring to were the two doors that obviously led to the storage room where all the supplies were kept for the boys' ranch. But curiosity and inquisitiveness had become eager anticipation for everyone.

Once again, if you were, for instance, in charge, just what would your decision be as an obligation to your team?

Establishing and maintaining their relationship with Taylor was, on many occasions, employed by fear, making it difficult for the group to question the validity of Taylor's leadership. But I would also guess that you could say his authority over them was more like a malicious vandal—though without in any way being maliciously destructive to their performance.

Beyond the doors, the natural man receiveth not the things of God, and neither can he know them. And even when we are inhabited by such words, our entire perspective is, as always, significantly foolish.

Everything is geared toward the spirit of Lucifer, ultimately paving the way for his manipulation and inauguration to once again inhabit trinity doctrines, proving himself God of the earth.

The rapture, as written, is proof enough, voicing its final interpretations aloud, confirming the primary assertions with arrogant voices in doctrines that Lucifer is indeed our God, and that we shall by all means serve him.

How awful it would be to suffer his double-headed blade.

But many will turn away, unresponsive to his spoken words, and the time of judgment will await them. For in this realm, death will surely see to it that this prophetic fulfillment is documented in the courts of law, as an entitlement furnished by the enslavement of a people within the entire Stonyford Region. Many of these regions will expose the truth about those associated with the realm of Lucifer repeatedly, for the beast of this deceptive kingdom shall destroy them all. Death will see to it.

As prophesied during this awful tribulational cycle, it is un-deniable that Lucifer shall prevail, predominantly through the bizarre uneducation and eerie recapitulation of the people of the surrounding towns north of Stonyford, and mainly in Garberville and Hayfork.

*

"Really, Taylor, man," Miller asked again. "Man, what's so important about this particular building? Just what is it that we're searching for?"

"Do you really want to know?" Reggie asked Miller. "Do you really want that question answered?"

"Damn, man!" Miller responded angrily. "Wouldn't you?"

"Bodies!" Taylor told him, also angry at the fact that he kept questioning. "Bodies and more bodies, and most likely those kids that are supposed to be here. Little kids, Miller. Little kids. Kids that could possibly be related to you."

"We think that maybe there's a possible chance that they could all be on the other side of those freakin' doors," Reggie said in a much calmer voice.

"Think they could still be alive?" Blake asked Reggie.

"Possibly," Reggie told him. "But who knows."

"Sorry, guys," Miller said, apologizing. "Didn't mean to sound rude. But I was just—"

"No need to apologize, Miller," Taylor told him. "We're all on edge. I am just as curious as you are, especially knowing we are about to make our way to the storage room."

"Guys," Blake said, nervous at the thought of what they were about to do. "I really don't know about this. I mean, you know. It's my job, but I just don't think I can handle going back there."

"It's all right, Blake," Taylor told him. "No one is going to force any of you guys to do this. But it gotta be done regardless of our feelings about the situation at hand. Plus, we really don't even know for sure that those kids are back there. It's just a hunch that it might be possible."

"Well, isn't there a window or something that we can look through, you know, like around the back of this building?" Goldsby asked Taylor.

"Mentioning the back of the building," Reggie said, "that's what Blake was supposed to be doing, wasn't it?"

"It was," Blake said. "But man, I guess you can say, with all of them things running around out there, I just didn't want to be taking any stupid chances."

"Mmm," Bedford mumbled. "I feel you on that one."

"Think any of these light switches work?" Reggie asked, just as a suggestion.

"Really don't think we need to be turning anything on if they do work at this point," Taylor said. "But if you just wanna see if they're working, flick the switch really fast without lighting us up in here."

Reggie flipped a switch as quickly as he possibly could, which made a slight illumination of the room without adding any light that would give away their position.

CLICK—CLICK—CLICK

"Taylor, you copy?" Chad asked over the radio.

"Copy!" Taylor said.

"Wouldn't want to do that if I were you," shouted Chad.

"See anything?" Taylor asked.

"Any longer would've been like Christmas," yelled Chad.

"Copy!" Taylor said while turning toward the two doors. "All right, people, it's time. Let's do this. Blake, you stay here with Goldsby. Bedford, yeah, that's right. You're coming with us."

"And make sure you keep that camera rolling," Reggie told him.

"Keep your back to the wall," Taylor told Blake and Goldsby. "And, by all means, please keep a constant visual out these windows."

"But not in them," Reggie added.

"Everybody be completely quiet," Taylor said. "Remember, don't speak a word unless it's me speaking to you. All right? Enough said. Then let's move. I'll take the lead."

Taylor then looked directly at Reggie, who was moving toward the two doors. He carefully opened one of the doors very slowly, as if disengaging the switch on an electrical device, allowing Taylor to peer into an even darker area of the building. He could see a long, narrow hallway that led to the back entrance of the building, where the storage room was located.

Using his night-vision lenses, he could see three doors to his left. The first door was at the end of a short half-hallway that led to a side entrance. The second door was obviously a bathroom for the boys. The third door was a bathroom designated for staff members only. At the very end of the hallway were two more doors that led to a back area of the building used as an emergency exit.

At the very end of the long, eerie hallway on the right side were the two doors that led directly into the storage room. A terrible stench of death filled the air, emitting the foulest, most offensive odor imaginable. These were the only doors on that side of the hallway and the only way to enter the storage room.

The only other person with night-vision lenses was Reggie. Miller and Bedford had to follow closely behind each other, using their hands to feel around in the dark, as well as relying on their humanlike sensors—the photoelectric cells of the human body, which respond to the slightest stimuli and transmit signals to the brain. Both Miller and Bedford used this instinct to keep track of each other's movements.

Suddenly, Taylor and Reggie stopped. Without saying a word or making any movement, they could hear the sounds of Miller's and Bedford's hearts pumping blood through their veins in the quiet, still darkness of the hallway. Both Taylor and Reggie very slowly and quietly signaled to each other through sign language to forcefully burst through the two doors as quickly as they could and destroy anything that didn't appear to be human.

A quick flash, and the doors were blown open by the force of their specially made military combat boots. They moved in with their guns fully ready to eliminate the fortified enemy.Reggie's fully loaded AK-47, using the muzzle flash to suppress the sound that might have been heard by the creatures crawling around the outer perimeter of the boys' ranch, shattered the doors into pieces, exposing the dreaded remains of the young children's rotting, decaying corpses.

The terrible stench of the badly decomposing bodies began to fill the dark hallway, making Bedford and Miller cough and gag.

"Man, what the fuck is that in there?" Miller cried.

"Ah, hell no," Bedford said. "I can't deal with this!"

"Quick, everybody back to the front," Taylor told them. "Let's go!"

"Damn! Motherfucker!" Reggie shouted.

"Everybody out of the building!" Taylor exclaimed loudly as they entered the dining area where Blake and Goldsby waited. "Let's go! Now!"

"What the—?" Blake started.

"What happened back there?" Goldsby asked.

"Look!" Taylor said, slamming the kitchen doors closed behind him. "We gotta get as far away from here as we possibly can."

"What did you guys see back there?" Blake asked. "And just what the heck is that odor I smell on you guys?"

"Death, goddammit!" Reggie yelled. "It's death!"

"Hurry up, you guys," Taylor said roughly. "Get all the guns and every piece of artillery you can carry. They want war, we're gonna give it to 'em. Them motherfuckin' bastards."

"Ghetto Boy, you copy?" Reggie called over the transmitter.

"Copy!" said Ghetto Boy, watching all the commotion from the roof.

"Chad, you copy?" Reggie called.

Click—click—click.

"Copy!" said Chad.

"Get ready," Taylor added. "Our friends want a birthday party."

"Everybody inside," Reggie said. "Get everything you can and prepare to move out."

"Ghetto Boy," Taylor said, standing at the front entrance to the boys' living quarters. "You and Chad just stand down for right now. For some odd reason, those things can't seem to cross over the fence. But that's not to say it'll last for long. So for now, the rest of us are heading up to that house. Hope what we found in that kitchen isn't like what we'll find over there."

"Taylor!" Ghetto Boy said. "What'd you guys find?"

"Bodies, Ghetto Boy," Taylor told him, his voice heavy with sadness. "Nothin' but a bunch of bodies scattered all over that storage area back there. The kids—all of them. Bunched together. Body parts everywhere."

"Need me to come down?" Ghetto Boy asked Taylor. "That's a negative for now," Taylor told him. "I need you up there to con-tinue keeping vigil. But, Chad, I'm gonna need you to blast the mess out of the kitchen. I want that entire mess hall completely flattened." "Don't you think we should notify others about this?" Chad said. "I'm sure they'll get more people up here right away." "Thanks for reminding me, Chad," Taylor said. "With everything that's been going on, I just about forgot there are other people in the world."

"Hey! Hey! Hey!" Ghetto Boy yelled. "Man, what the fuck is going on out there?"

Startled, both Taylor and Chad turned as Reggie came rushing over to find out what all the yelling was about. "What's happening?" Reggie asked Taylor. "What's all the yelling about out here?"

"Don't really know," Taylor told him, staring up at Ghetto Boy, who was looking outward over the boys' ranch in the direction of the creatures still moving near the fence. "What's the problem, Ghetto Boy?"

"Man, you guys ain't gonna believe what I think I just saw happening. I don't believe it myself," Ghetto Boy said, still looking as though something on the outer perimeter had deeply frightened him.

"Ghetto Boy," Reggie called out, "man, get a grip on yourself. What is it that you saw happening out there?"

"What is it, Ghetto Boy?" Taylor asked. "What is it you're seeing?"

"Whatever it is," Chad said, "I'm ready to fire. Just say the word and whatever he's looking at will be history."

"Miller," Taylor called out.

"Yeah," he answered. "What's happening?"

"Uh, I need you to keep watch out back," Taylor told him. "I need Ghetto Boy right here where he's at."

"What's going on, Taylor?" Miller asked slyly, looking toward the kitchen. "Oh, shit!"

"What?" Taylor asked.

"Thought I just saw something moving around in that kitchen," Miller said, still staring in that direction.

"Just give the word, Taylor," Chad said. "That building will be just another part of history."

"Ghetto Boy," Taylor called up to him. "What did you see out there?"

"Those things," Ghetto Boy said, looking through his sniper lens. "One of them, I think, turned itself into one of us."

"Man, what the hell are you talking about?" Reggie asked.

"What did he just say?" Chad asked Taylor.

"Ghetto Boy, get a grip on yourself," Taylor told him. "Repeat what you thought you saw."

"I think I did see something moving around in that building," Miller said again.

"I said, I think I saw one of them things turn itself into a human. I think something that looked like one of us," Ghetto Boy repeated. "That goddamn thing turned into a human being. I know what I saw."

"Uh... I'm gonna get a flashlight," Miller said. "I know I just saw somebody standing in one of those windows. Looked like a little kid, or something."

"Want me to go back down there and turn on the lights?" Reggie asked Taylor.

"Wait a minute," Taylor said. "Blake, I need you for a minute. Both of you come here for a minute."

"Both of who?" Blake asked.

"Damn, I plum forgot about Bedford," Taylor said. "I was thinking just of you and Goldsby. But why don't all three of you come out here for just a few minutes."

"Still want me to watch out back?" Miller asked Taylor.

"Uh, no," Taylor said. "What I need is for Blake and Goldsby to do that, for then everybody'll be in place."

"And what about me?" Bedford asked. "Camera still ready to roll?"

"Uh, yeah," Taylor said. "I need you to climb back on top of this—you know, the roof—and continue rolling everything from up there. Okay?"

"On my way," Bedford said, heading through the building to climb back up on the roof where Ghetto Boy was.

"OK, Reggie," Taylor said, placing an AK-47 under his arm. "Let's move on down there again. Anything moves, you already know what to do."

"Gotcha," Reggie said, placing a pair of night vision binoculars specially made for the facial area over his eyes.

"What do you think about wearing them things?" Taylor asked Reggie about the new experimental night vision binoculars.

"Just like daylight right about now," Reggie said. "And whoever it was in one of those windows watching us, they just went through the two doors leading to the hallway."

"Told you," Miller said anxiously, as though he were waiting for his sighting to be confirmed by someone other than himself.

"Think some of them things are turning into human beings just so they can be like us," Ghetto Boy said. "Cause those inside that kitchen were supposed to be dead. Shouldn't they be?"

"What did you see, Reggie?" Taylor asked. "Could they have possibly been any of those kids?"

"Think so," Reggie said. "Sure wasn't adults, now that I think about it."

"Miller, where's that flashlight?" Taylor asked.

"Oh, hell," Miller said. "Gotta go get it."

"Well, get more than just one," Reggie said, checking the light on his sniper lens. "I think I'm good with this baby here."

"You got any flashlights up there, Ghetto Boy?" Taylor asked.

"Got a nice-looking spotlight," Ghetto Boy said. "You know, like the type you plug into your car's cigarette lighter, except this thing can be hooked up to a battery."

"And there is only one?" Taylor asked.

"Only one of me, isn't it?" Ghetto Boy said humorously.

"Well, shine that goddamn thing at that building," Taylor told him.

"And it better light somebody up so I can blast 'em to Hell," Reggie said, laughing. "Or I'm firing up at you just for the hell of it."

Everybody snickered.

"And it'll just be a whole bunch of firing going on," Ghetto Boy said. "'Cause I'll make sure you join those things—whatever they are."

"I think we got some for real dangerous Zulu Zombies out there just waiting their turn to attack us," Chad said. "And you guys are just having a ball right here."

"Better check on Blake and Goldsby," Miller said. "Awful quiet around here, don't you think?"

"Uh, yeah. That's right," Taylor said. "Bedford, you up there?"

"No," Ghetto Boy said. "He's up here, but just not right here where I am."

"Where is he?" Taylor asked him.

"Over there on the other side of this roof talkin' to Blake and Goldsby, I would think," Ghetto Boy told Taylor. "I mean, I hope that's him, 'cause—"

"Damn!" said Taylor. "Now I can't remember what it was that I wanted him for. But oh well, must not have been that important."

"It was to see if everything was all right," Chad said. "If all of 'em was all right."

"Mmm," Taylor mumbled to himself. "Old age must be getting to me."

"What's happening on the light?" Reggie asked Ghetto Boy.

"Just hold your horses," Ghetto Boy said. "It's right here. I was just waiting on you guys before I turned it on."

"Well, go ahead," Reggie told him, walking slowly down the pathway to the kitchen.

"Not too fast, Reggie," Taylor said, arming himself with some more high-powered ammunition. "Not too fast."

"Man, Taylor," Chad said in a surprising voice. "Sure hope you don't trip on anything and fall down with all that stuff you're wearing. Blow this whole goddamn place to kingdom come."

"Oh, what?" said Taylor. "You're puttin' a jinx on me or something?"

"No," Chad told him. "I was just—"

"Maybe this is the one you need to be shinin' that light on

instead of that building," Taylor said to Ghetto Boy, giggling to himself. "Man wants me to trip on something and fall down just so that he can see us all get blown to Hell."

"Hey!" Chad said, laughing. "Now, that's not a very nice thing for you to be saying about me!"

"Keep moving, Reggie," Taylor said. "Don't pay him no mind."

"You know something, Taylor," Reggie said, slowing down. "Uh, Chad just might be on point about zombies. I'm really thinking about what he said."

"Zombies or no zombies," Taylor said. "Whatever comes our way is going to wish it had been a zombie."

"And what if it's one of those kids?" Reggie asked Taylor. "Are you still going to draw down on it?"

"Zombies don't die," said Taylor. "They just keep coming back at you until they kill you, and then you become one of them."

"That's what people say," Reggie said, watching the beam from Ghetto Boy's spotlight illuminate the dining area in the building. "That's what all them people be saying in them zombie movies."

"Reggie," Taylor said in a firm voice. "This is no freakin' movie. What all of us are going through isn't some freakin' movie! This fuckin' shit is for real! Can't you see that for yourself? It's really happening."

"Well, I'm also wondering what I would do if, so happen, a young kid just happened to come at me in a hostile manner," Reggie said. "I mean, I just don't know, Taylor. I'd be afraid to, you know—"

"Put 'em down?" Taylor questioned Reggie. "You mean to tell me that if the kid came toward you in an aggressive manner, you'd be afraid to put him or her down?"

"Quite frankly," Reggie said, hesitating. "I'd probably attempt trying to communicate first. And then—"

"And then you'll be dead in a matter of seconds," Taylor told him.

"How you figure that?"

"Because every goddamn time I turn around, you're trying to, I guess, call yourself trying to communicate with the devil. You just can't always be trying to do that, Reggie. It's insane, and apparently, you're not thinking logically when dealing with your opponent."

"Now, see what I mean? Just hold up for a minute, and pull on that door very slowly."

"I got it, Taylor," Reggie said, slowly inching the door open.

"Go ahead and hit that switch," Taylor told him. "I'll cover you while I check behind this counter by the sink."

Reggie flipped the light switch, illuminating the entire area of the mess hall. Taylor very quietly advanced toward the kitchen counter to check underneath the sink area. There, he could visibly see that there was slight movement in one of the large storage cabinets, where a utility drawer up top was slowly closing, being controlled by something underneath it.

Something, or someone, was hiding inside the large, wide cabinet and was pulling the wide drawer up top closed very slowly.

Taylor waved and quickly got Reggie's attention. He motioned for him to keep a visual on the two doors leading to the storage area. They had secured it earlier after finding the remains of the children living at the boys' ranch bunched up together in the storage room.

Slowly and carefully preparing to open fire, Taylor just happened to notice a silver, narrow spray can, which he knew contained a deadly chemical substance described as Reagent—a chemical that detects other deadly substances. The can had a straw-like device protruding outward from its spray cap. Taylor knew it could be used like a portable flaming torch when a match, coated on one end with a compound easily ignitable by friction, or even a cigarette lighter, is lit and held underneath the substance sprayed. It is then that the chemical can produce a firing spray like a torch when welding, applying heat, and sometimes very strong pressure.

"I know what you're thinking," Reggie told him in a low tone, smiling.

But Taylor said nothing except stare intently at the spray can, and then back at the large storage cabinets underneath the utility drawer. He knew he couldn't hesitate much longer. Whatever was hiding in the cabinet, Taylor knew he had to take action immediately.

Tightening up the muzzle on his weapon to suppress the sound, Taylor found himself thinking about Reggie and what he kept saying about trying to communicate. "But why in the hell would anyone want to attempt communicating with monsters? And mainly, like the ones that are out here trying to take us out?" he questioned himself. "Should I give it a try? Hell no! Fuck this shit Reggie's been talking about. I'mma take whatever is in this cabinet down! All the way, down!"

Signaling to Reggie to get ready, Taylor coded him to open fire with everything he had—which Reggie knew wasn't out of the ordinary for marksmen as skilled as both he and Taylor, trained as professional assassins.

They were trained to assassinate for political purposes, determined to resolve their target with results unlike even those of specially trained Navy SEALs.

But each time Taylor inched his finger to pull the trigger, Reggie's words haunted him like an imaginary ghost, patronizing him in his mind.

How pathetic Taylor must have felt, carrying this ponderous, unwieldy tenderness deep in his consciousness at a moment when split-second decisions had to be made.

The can of deadly spray, his tactical rifle—a machine so relentless when fired—and now the decision to incapacitate whatever was hiding in the cabinet weighed on him, the creature beneath the sink unaware of its disadvantage in the circumstance.

Once again, Taylor checked and squeezed the muzzle to make sure that the sounds from his weapon during firing, as when engaging in a brutal battle, were suppressed.

Once again signaling to Reggie to get ready, he also coded him to open fire with everything he had, which Reggie already knew wasn't out of the ordinary for someone like Taylor under such circumstances.

But for reasons unknown to Reggie, Taylor hesitated, staring at the cabinet. It was as if he had begun to relax, studying certain areas around the cabinet as though drawing a mental map.

Reggie, watching Taylor's every move, wanted to question him about his actions but decided to remain silent after observing him slowly rotating the tip of his rifle along the same path he had traced mentally.

Though relaxed, Reggie could still sense Taylor's unyielding determination to take down anything that threatened the mission. Religiously.

Suddenly, Taylor reached outward and squeezed the muzzle while turning it at the same time. He looked at Reggie, raised his hand, nodded, then quickly dropped his hand, squeezed the trigger, and began firing nonstop.

Signaled by Taylor, Reggie muttered a low, distinct, "Yeah!" and, without seeing any movement at the doors or in the dark hallway, began to open fire, spraying the entire corridor with deadly bullets and highly powerful projectiles that demolished everything in their wake as if executed by a professional demolition team.

The intense destruction caused both doors at the end of the hallway to be blown completely off their frames and hinges, scattering debris over one hundred feet across the field behind the now-smoldering hallway and back entrance of the building.

Even with the dining room lights on, the rapid fire from the rifles was visible to the crew as both Reggie and Taylor targeted everything in the building.

Suddenly, the firing ceased as quickly as it had started. The only sound was the crying of a child, coming from underneath the sink where Taylor had been firing. It became apparent that Taylor, during all his rapid fire, had formed a mental image of the cabinet and had fired around the exact location of the movement without harming the target—which he and Reggie soon realized was a small eight-year-old child, hiding and likely thinking they were the monsters who had destroyed his friends at the boys' ranch.

The entire cabinet was demolished, leaving the child exposed.

At that moment, the fatherly instincts of both Taylor and Reggie kicked in as they stared in silence. Quickly, Taylor reached down with his right hand, grabbed the child, and lifted him to his shoulder, embracing him as though he were his own. Reggie smiled and headed toward the front entrance, opening the doors so Taylor, carrying the child, could exit without worry.

Waiting outside was Chad, surprised at the sight of the child —resting and still somewhat crying—while Taylor held him tightly in one arm and carried his weapon in the other.

"I wonder what's in that building?" Taylor asked Reggie. "We gotta find out where they kept all the medication and everything else in this place."

"Chad, let's check it out," Reggie said, referring to the small building-like office area between the kitchen and the boys' living quarters. "Ghetto Boy," he called out, "keep watch."

"Gotcha," Ghetto Boy answered from on top of the roof. "What's that you got there, Taylor?"

"Something we've just adopted as a new member of this team," Taylor told him.

"Oh yeah? Is that right?" Ghetto Boy said, shaking his head

while looking toward the building. "Man, after all the flashing from your weapons, I'm really surprised—"

"Know what you mean," Taylor said, slowly lowering the kid onto the ground.

"What's his name?" Ghetto Boy asked.

Before the kid could say anything, Taylor answered, "Bud. We're gonna call him Bud for now, until we can get a grip on things."

"You took the words right out of my mouth," Bedford said, pointing his camera down to film Taylor and Bud. "That's a cool name for a kid like you."

"Never envisioned this type of result coming from that building," Taylor said. "This was completely unexpected, given the circumstances. I mean, I just knew we'd bring something out of that place, but not—"

"Quite unusual, isn't it?" Ghetto Boy said, staring intently at the human-like figures near the fence. "I think we got some serious movement going on, Taylor. Somebody's moving precariously next to the gate, trying to come this way."

"How many?" Taylor asked.

"More than just one," said Ghetto Boy. "Hesitating, and I guess they seem to be debating and having a long discussion about something."

"Chad, Reggie, you copy?" Taylor said over his radio.

CLICK—CLICK—CLICK

"COPY!" Reggie answered.

"Let's go. We're moving up the Yellow Brick Road," Taylor told him. "We got movement ready to attempt coming this way."

"Think the movement can cross?" Reggie asked.

"With proper instructions," Taylor answered.

"On our way with that—and much more," Reggie told him.

"Ghetto Boy, Bedford," Taylor called out.

"Yeah, what's up?" Ghetto Boy asked.

"What are they doing?" Taylor asked, wanting to know what the figures on the outer boundaries of the fence were doing.

"Looks like they're studying their chances or something," Ghetto Boy said. "I even think that those things just might be trying to listen in on our, you know, conversation or something. I mean, it's the way they're standing in one place. It's like they are just waiting for something. Like the perfect timing to come this way."

"What's happening?" Reggie said, looking around in the dark. "Where are they?"

"Hold up," Ghetto Boy said, as if trying not to talk too loud. "Man, I think those motherfuckers are trying to, uh, listen in on our conversations or something. Yeah, that's what they're trying to do, 'cause every time I, you know, say something, they suddenly freeze and stop what they were doing."

"Are you sure?" Taylor asked.

"Affirmative!" Ghetto Boy said sternly.

"Chad," said Taylor. "Get this baby ready. I'mma do the same. Okay, you guys, it's time to move out. Reggie, take charge on the ground. Ghetto Boy, you and Bedford come on down and get ready to head up the Yellow Brick Road. Miller, you, Blake, and Goldsby, gear up and get ready to move out."

"Looks like we got somebody traveling on that road up there," Ghetto Boy said out loud. "And whoever it is, they're headed this way, and right in the path of those goddamn things."

"Any way to try stopping them?" Reggie asked Ghetto Boy. "Anything that we can do to stop whoever it is from coming this way?"

"Damn! I mean, with what? And how?" Ghetto Boy asked. "Maybe I can take a shot and hit something in front of them. Maybe that'll get whoever it is to stop and turn around."

CLICK—CLICK—CLICK

"What the fuck!" Chad shouted, hearing the clicking noise

coming from his helicopter's transmitter. "Is that one of you guys on my radio?"

CLICK—CLICK—CLICK

CLICK—CLICK—CLICK

CLICK—CLICK—CLICK

"Uh, Taylor," Chad said into the transmitter. "You copy?"

"Copy!" Taylor replied.

"Is that you clicking?"

"No!" Taylor shouted. "I thought that was you, Reggie, or maybe even Ghetto Boy."

"That's a negative, Taylor," Chad said.

CLICK—CLICK—CLICK

CLICK—CLICK—CLICK

"There it goes again," Reggie said.

"Who the fuck is that?" Chad asked.

"Chad, you copy?" Taylor called over the transmitter.

"Copy!" Chad replied.

"Uh, that's not any of you?" Taylor asked.

"That's a negative," Chad said.

"See if you can get a reading and location," Taylor instructed.

"Copy!" Chad said, attempting to lock in on whoever it was.

"Hey, you guys," Ghetto Boy said, getting their attention. "You know what I'm thinking? I think that's coming from whoever it is coming down that hill in our direction."

"Man, I hope not," Reggie said. "But we gotta find out."

After both Ghetto Boy and Bedford made it down to the ground from the building, they immediately started gathering everything they could.

By the time Reggie decided to assist Taylor, he could hear the engine from Taylor's helicopter idling on the other side of the building. He hurried through the building to try to reach him before he began to hover.

Chad had also begun the rotation of his craft's blades, the

strong, powerful helicopter rotors spinning in a wide circle, moving faster and faster as the engine grew louder.

Reggie reached the other side of the building before Taylor had taken off. Sitting in the co-pilot's seat of Taylor's craft was the young child rescued from his horrific ordeal—after witnessing the brutal slaying of his friends—and now adopted by the crew. He had been given the nickname Bud. He sat quietly and motionless, securely strapped in the co-pilot's seat, staring out the front window. His wide, observant eyes occasionally moved from side to side and sometimes vertically.

"Hey, Taylor," Reggie called over the noisy idling engine. "Think that clicking might be coming from whoever's coming down that road? I don't think they know about those things out there."

"Didn't Ghetto Boy take that shot?" Taylor asked.

"Maybe I should do it," Reggie said. "I could probably take it from a different angle, use a little trickery."

"Oh yeah? Meaning what?" Taylor asked.

"Like knocking those things off if we can't get whoever it is to stop and turn around."

"Don't you think time's passing?"

"On my way," Reggie said, heading back inside the building to retrieve his rifle.

"What's happening?" Ghetto Boy asked while gathering a few things.

"Whatever happened to that shot you were supposed to take?" Reggie asked him.

"Didn't wanna cause too much attention," Ghetto Boy said. "Plus, those things out there—far too many to stop. I thought whoever that is would have a better chance coming this way than trying to stop them, only to slow their own chances of getting away by turning around. The only chance to get away is for them to continue on as they are, and hopefully, whoever it is might just be coming here."

"And if not?" Reggie questioned. "Then what?"

"Hell if I know," Ghetto Boy shrugged. "Hell if I know."

"You guys go ahead and start moving out," Reggie told him. "And make sure to put at least a ten- to fifteen-meter interval between you."

"And what about you?" Ghetto Boy asked Reggie. "Aren't you coming?"

"Yeah, after I take this shot," Reggie said.

"From where?"

"Back up top."

Silence.

CLICK—CLICK—CLICK

CLICK—CLICK—CLICK

The clicking noise could be heard on all the transmitters.

CLICK—CLICK—CLICK

CLICK—CLICK—CLICK

"Taylor, you copy?" Ghetto Boy asked, wondering what was happening.

"Copy," Taylor responded. "ID," meaning for Ghetto Boy to identify who he was when transmitting.

"Ghetto Boy."

"Copy!" Taylor answered. "Your point?"

"The clicking."

"Chad, you copy?" Taylor called.

"Copy!" said Chad.

"Did you lock in the subject?"

"Traveling," Chad said about the subject.

"Everybody on the Yellow Brick Road," Taylor said, telling everyone to head up to the house. "Reggie, go ahead and take that shot."

"You gonna do it?" Ghetto Boy asked Reggie, who was about to head toward the ladder used to climb onto the roof.

"Get ready," Reggie said. "I got this."

"Chad, you copy?" Taylor asked over the transmitter.

"Copy!" Chad responded.

"It's time," Taylor told him, opening the throttle on the helicopter and accelerating its power. "Anything heads our way, you know what to do."

"Copy that," said Chad, opening up his throttle.

"Keep vigil. Reggie's on the roof," Taylor told Chad. "I'll swing over and pick him up."

Suddenly, just as Taylor ended his sentence, a bright yellow-and-reddish flash lit up the roof from the firing of Reggie's rifle.

"Taylor, you copy?" Reggie called over the transmitter.

"Copy!" Taylor said.

"Mission established, and mission complete," Reggie told him. "Need a taxi. Our subject refused to take heed."

"Copy!" Taylor said, slowly hovering in his direction. "Chad, do you copy?"

"Copy!" Chad responded.

"Keep watch on our subject," Taylor told him. "Make sure they get a safe passage."

"Copy!" Chad said, hovering slowly in the direction of the road outside the fence where the vehicle would have to travel. "Taylor, you copy?"

"Copy!" said Taylor. "What's the problem?"

"I believe our subject is the guy from the ranger station," Chad told him, directing the bright beam from his spotlight toward the now spun-out-of-control vehicle. "Our subject just lost control of his vehicle."

"What?" Taylor yelled over the transmitter in disbelief. "Can you in any way rescue him?"

"Can attempt to," Chad told him. "But that's only if you can cover me over here."

"Copy!" Taylor told Chad while hovering over Reggie so he

could reach up and grab one of the legs of the helicopter to airlift him to the ground.

Inside Taylor's helicopter, Bud sat quietly, observing everything that was happening, with an excited expression from the thought of flying in a helicopter—something he'd always wanted to do. But this was an experience he would never forget.

During the slow hovering flight in the direction of the house, Goldsby, who was walking a short distance behind Miller, happened to look up after hearing the loud engine of the helicopter overhead and noticed Bud staring down at her. She quickly waved at him, and he did the same, without stopping. Even as the helicopter veered to the left in a 45° bank, he could still be seen waving persistently at her, looking back until they could no longer see each other.

As a mother's instincts would be toward her child—with strong impulses by the laws of nature—Goldsby began to sense those same motivating factors in Bud. The longing for the attention of a mother-type figure in his life. Wanting it to not be in any way restrictive, as it had been for a child at the boys' ranch, where parents were not allowed to spend quality time with their children. But for this child, who had now been adopted by the crew, she could sense Bud's desire to attach to her willingness to become the mother he longed to have in his life.

"But how is it that this is happening at a time like this?" Goldsby thought to herself. "Here I am, a detective working on the gruesome slaughter of no telling how many people, out in the middle of these mountains, in practically nowhere, in the dead of night, where there are speculations of deadly monsters possibly taking on human form, and I feel the need to nurture this young child who has captured my attention."

Although the thought of what was happening puzzled Goldsby, here once again was the work of Satan's unique multitudes of great manipulations, which were so interesting and amazing—how he so cleverly and intelligently revealed his skills, suitable for one of his ultimate confrontations through such an appealing presentation.

Notoriously known to appear, revealing himself as someone else.

In this scenario, it was amazing how Bud could have actually been the only surviving pupil of the boys' ranch, where young kids were taught rules of law and instructed by teachers to become law-abiding citizens. But just like a punt played in a game of football, Satan had dropped a deadly ball on the entire crew, which they so generously named Bud.

"I wonder just who in the hell named these things walkie-talkies?" Blake said.

"Got me on that one," Miller said, examining the radio he carried.

"Got me feeling like a little kid or something," Blake said. "Isn't there a different name for these things?"

"In our department in Sacramento, we call 'em receivers, or just plain old radio transmitters," Goldsby told Blake.

"This thing is something like the one I got for my son at Christmas a long time ago," Blake said.

"Are you sure it was a long time ago?" Miller asked him. "Isn't your son still quite young?"

"Well, it seems like a long time ago," Blake said. "Being up here with you guys in these hills has me feeling old and run down."

"And just think about it, Blake," Goldsby said. "One day your son is going to be up here doing the exact same thing you're doing."

All of a sudden, there was a very loud, violent explosion, followed by waves of thunderous rumbling and flashes of lightning, like thunderbolts from electrically charged clouds—producing swells of abnormal pressure, exploding as during a heavy rainstorm. Except there was no rain, and this wasn't any storm. The sound carried throughout the entire region, shaking the ground like a wall of violent tidal waves and whipping strong winds violently across the area.

"Everybody take cover!" Reggie yelled. "Hit the ground now!"

"Man, what the fuck was that?" Ghetto Boy exclaimed demandingly.

"Jesus fuckin' Christ," Blake cried out. "Somebody help us all. I can't take no goddamn more of this. Somebody help me."

"Oh, no!" Goldsby screamed. "God, help me. Somebody help me. It's pulling me away."

"I knew something like this was going to happen," Miller cried out. "I knew it! I knew it!"

"Goldsby, where are you?" Ghetto Boy called out, crawling on the ground to avoid the falling debris from the explosion. "Goldsby, where are you?"

"Goddamn snakes all over the fuckin' place," Blake said, breathing hard. "I—I—I think I'm having a heart attack or something. I can't breathe, and my chest... it's killing me. Somebody help me."

"Just hang in there, Blake," Reggie called out in the dark. "I know Taylor and Chad will be back in a few minutes to get us out of here. So just hang in there, buddy. All of you hang in there and try moving over here toward me. That house shouldn't be too far from us."

"I don't think that house is there anymore, Reggie," Ghetto Boy yelled from the intense pain coming from one of his legs. "Man, I can't seem to move one of my legs."

"Holy fuckin' Christ," Blake cried out. "Bedford's laying here, and I think he's dead. Goddamn snakes all over 'em."

"Snakes?" Miller asked, crawling slowly in Blake's direction.

"Everybody be careful," Reggie said, pulling Ghetto Boy to him. "Just about every freakin' creature out here is crawling around. They're just as we are—scared as hell. Don't know what's happening or where to go."

"I think I got bit by a rattlesnake or something," Ghetto Boy said to Reggie, trying to pull up the pant leg on his left leg. "I'm sure it's a snake bite. It's really stinging something awful. Can you see it?"

"Goldsby, you hear me?" Miller called out to Goldsby in the distance. "Where are you?"

"Think they're coming?" Ghetto Boy asked Reggie. "I don't hear the helicopters anymore."

"They're coming, Ghetto Boy," Reggie told him, looking out into the darkness that seemed even darker. "They've probably landed and are helping whoever that was coming our way. They'll be back before we know it, and you can count on that. We just gotta hang in there. All of us."

In the distance, Miller could still be heard calling out to Goldsby.

Large amounts of deadly debris continued to fall from the dark sky after the explosion, with thick pieces still ablaze, glowing brightly and emitting waves of heat that could be felt throughout the region.

Steam hissed from the ground, and at times large pieces and chunks of burning twigs from the thick brush littered the ground around them, sometimes falling within inches of the crew.

"Oh God, no," Blake cried out. "Please no!"

"Blake, come this way," Reggie called. "Just come to my voice."

"They're coming, Ghetto Boy," Reggie told him, looking out into the darkness that seemed even darker. "They've probably landed and are helping whoever that was coming our way. They'll be back before we know it, and you can count on that. We just gotta hang in there. All of us."

In the distance, Miller could still be heard calling out to Goldsby.

"My leg is really killing me, man," Ghetto Boy said to Reggie. "I think I need something to tie around it."

What Reggie didn't want to tell Ghetto Boy was that the entire bottom section of his left leg was missing.

"You'll be all right, Ghetto Boy. Just hang in there. They'll be back to get us soon, buddy. Gotta hang in there."

"Where is everybody, goddamn it?" Blake yelled. "Where are you guys at?"

"Blake, come to the sound of my voice," Reggie shouted in frustration. "We're over here. Over here. Just come to the sound of my voice and you'll find us."

"Oh, God," Blake said. "I think a goddamn giant bat just crawled on my back. I think it just bit my shoulder."

"Oh, gosh no," Miller screamed. "Somebody help me. I think I just saw a giant frogman walk past me. I think it was carrying Goldsby."

"Miller, get a grip on yourself," Reggie told him. "Come to the sound of my voice. We'll find Goldsby later."

"Last time I heard her, she was yelling about something dragging her," Ghetto Boy said. "I'm sure she's out there just waiting for us to come get her. She has to be. And where the hell is Bedford? Shouldn't he be here too?"

Just as Reggie was about to say something, an enormous chunk of fiery debris came crashing to the ground directly on top of Blake, burying him and killing him instantly. The heatwave from the debris could be felt by everyone still clinging to life as the ground they lay on shook violently.

"Just hold on, Ghetto Boy," Reggie told him, squeezing him tight in his arms. "Hold on, man. We'll make it through this. Just hold on. Are you still with me?"

"I'm with you, Reggie," Ghetto Boy cried out from the pain in his leg. "I'm with you to the end."

"All right then," Reggie said with encouragement. "That's

what I want to hear from you. Do you hear me, comrade?"

"Yes, sir!" Ghetto Boy yelled. "I hear you loud and clear, sir!"

"Well then, buddy," Reggie said firmly. "We're going to stop acting like sissies, pick ourselves up, and get the fuck to that house. Do you hear me, Ghetto Boy?"

"Let's do this, Reggie," Ghetto Boy said, trying to get to his feet.

"Hold up, brave buddy," Reggie said, placing one of his arms underneath Ghetto Boy's left shoulder. "Lean every bit of your weight on me, okay?"

"But I can do this on my own," Ghetto Boy told him, still try-ing to get to his feet. "Just let me get a little blood circulation to my leg here."

"Hey!" Reggie snapped at him. "Am I your friend or what?"

"Comrades to the end," Ghetto Boy said, trying to balance himself.

"Then lean your freakin' ass my way," Reggie said sternly. "Or I'm going to have to just pick you up and carry your freakin' ass."

By this time, Miller finally made his way to the sound of their voices in the dark.

"Glad you could join us, Miller," Reggie said as he embraced him.

"I think I just saw Blake back over there somewhere about fifteen or twenty minutes ago," Miller said. "And then, I don't know where he went. But that was right before whatever that was came crashing to the ground. Really shook bad out there."

"It's all right, Miller," Reggie said. "It's all right, man. We felt it too."

"Couldn't find Goldsby," Miller said, staring out into the darkness. "But I know she's out there somewhere. That frogman-looking thing had her, carrying her in its arms. It took her, Reggie. It took her somewhere over there."

"Miller, I need you to pull yourself together," Reggie told him.

"Let's get to that house, and hopefully we'll find something in there to help us—at least for now."

"Man, Reggie," Ghetto Boy exclaimed painfully. "I think something's wrong with my eyesight. I can't seem to see my left foot. Everything is all bloodshot red when I look down. I can't see my left foot."

"Just hang in there, Ghetto Boy," Reggie said again, trying to move in the direction of the house as quickly as he could. "There, right over there. I think we're almost there, buddy. You still with us, Miller?"

"I'm right here beside you, Reggie," Miller said. "Just need to find Goldsby. I know she's out there somewhere waiting for us to help her."

"We're almost there," Reggie said. "Just a few more yards, and we'll be there, you guys."

"Where the heck is Bedford?" Ghetto Boy asked. "Wasn't he just with us a few minutes ago?"

"He's out there somewhere," Miller told Ghetto Boy. "I think I heard Blake saying something about Bedford being dead and that he had snakes all over him. Or something like that."

"And what about Blake?" Ghetto Boy asked. "Is he with us?"

"The last thing I think I heard him screaming about was something about a giant bat on his shoulder, biting him," Miller said. "And then, that was it. Don't exactly know where he is. But he's out there somewhere in the dark."

"Okay, you guys," Reggie said. "We made it. Think the front entrance is on the other side."

"Thought the lights were on?" Ghetto Boy questioned. "Could've sworn it looked like lights were on."

"I think that explosion knocked everything out around here," Miller said, staring at the house. "It knocked all the power out. Guess that's why it's so goddamn black out here. And if it wasn't for these fires burning, we probably wouldn't be able to see each other."

"Well, this sure is good to see," Reggie said. "Looks like this van still has the keys stuck inside the ignition."

"Yeah, but what about fuel?" Ghetto Boy asked.

"Damn," Miller exclaimed. "And with the way things have been happening to us, it might not even have an engine."

"Only one way to find out," Reggie said, opening the door and inspecting everything inside. "Am I the only one with a flashlight?"

"No. Mine is, I think, right here, hooked to my infantry belt," Ghetto Boy said, reaching for his military flashlight. "Man, Reggie. My leg is really killing me."

"See anything?" Miller asked Reggie.

"Not worth removing," Reggie said, turning the key just enough to see if the panel would light up. "Oh yeah, you guys. Looks like we've got power."

"What about the helicopters?" Ghetto Boy asked. "Think Taylor and Chad made it out okay?"

"Man, Ghetto Boy," Reggie said in a lost tone, "your guess is as good as mine. I just don't want to be, you know, speculating anything yet. I mean, the possibilities either way. We saw the same thing. It was like the revolution was jumping off or something. A sudden, mad, radical change in both he and Chad."

"The last time I saw Taylor's helicopter was when he came over us as we were headed this way," Miller said. "Just as we looked up, I saw that kid, Bud, staring down at us, waving, and Goldsby started waving back at him. It was like they knew each other or something. Then, instead of flying over us and hovering like I thought he was going to, Taylor suddenly turned and went in the other direction. The only thing we could see was that young kid still looking down, waving. It was like he was saying goodbye or something."

"Well, everything in this van seems to be working," Reggie said, turning off the ignition switch.

"You not gonna check and see if the engine works or anything?" Ghetto Boy asked Reggie.

"I thought about it," Reggie told him. "But I didn't want to attract any attention to us. Maybe I can do it really fast and quick enough so it won't be a concern."

Reggie then turned the key to start the engine, and immediately it roared to life. He quickly turned it back to the off position.

"Wasn't too loud, was it?" Reggie asked both Ghetto Boy and Miller.

"Man, Reggie," Ghetto Boy said. "Right now, with all this pain I'm in, I am the last person you want to ask something like that."

"Sounded good to me," Miller said. "But my only worry is how much gas is in this thing."

Once again, Reggie positioned the key and turned it so the meter on the gas gauge would register the amount of fuel in the van's tank.

"See that?" Reggie said, snickering. "Now would you believe it? Baby is on full."

"Are you sure, Reggie?" Ghetto Boy asked. "Why would anyone leave, you know, a full tank of gas just sitting there?"

"We haven't made it inside that house yet, Ghetto Boy," Miller said, staring at the house. "Possible they could be inside, just like those kids down there in that kitchen."

"Well, we still got these duffel bags and everything else," Reggie said, referring to the bags they were carrying and pulling alongside them. "You know they hold out for a while. And once we're inside, and every area of this house is fully searched and secured, we'll do something about that leg of yours, Ghetto Boy."

"Oh man, Reggie," Ghetto Boy said. "I just don't know. This leg is really killing me. The pain is driving me nuts."

"Miller?" Reggie said. "Uh, why don't you assist him while I go ahead of you guys and check to see if that door is unlocked? Might have to climb through a window, or maybe even bust through the door."

"Anybody thought about contacting Taylor or Chad on your transmitter?" Miller asked.

"To be truthful," Reggie said, "I've been waiting to hear from them."

"Want me to try?" Miller said, somewhat in doubt that anyone after the explosion would answer. "You know, once we're inside."

"That'll be cool if you want to," Reggie said. "Maybe we'll find a few land-line phones in there, or a cell phone or two. Hopefully."

"Everything I had, I left it onboard the helicopter," Miller said. "I wasn't looking forward to anything like this happening."

"Tell you the truth," Reggie said, pushing open the door. "None of us had anything like this in mind, Miller. Things sometimes happen unexpectedly."

"I see you got it," Ghetto Boy said. "But what the fuck is that odor? You guys smell that?"

"All too familiar, isn't it, Miller?" Reggie said, referring to the foul stench they had smelled in the storage area of the mess hall. "Just stay here with Ghetto Boy while I check out these rooms. Oh, and by the way, do close that door and lock it for now. Also, keep watch out the windows."

"And I already know," Ghetto Boy said. "Anything that comes this way that is not showing signs of friendly, take it down."

"You're still wearing your night lenses, aren't you?" Reggie asked Ghetto Boy.

"Thought you knew?" Ghetto Boy answered. "I can see that small leg back there lying on the floor by the door. Personally, we should just toss all of 'em outside. That's what I think."

"What leg?" Miller asked, curious as to what they were referring to.

"Don't worry yourself, Miller," Ghetto Boy told him. "The job gotta be done."

"Oh, I forgot about those things you guys are wearing in your eyes that make it possible for you to see in the dark," Miller said. "Wouldn't, by chance, you know, have an extra pair?"

"Should be in one of the bags," Reggie told him, pointing to his bag. "I usually pack an extra pair or two just for such an occasion. Go ahead and see if you can find a pair while I snoop down this hallway to see what I can come up with."

"You know something, Reggie?" Ghetto Boy said. "This must be where the warden lived with his family."

"I think you mean the director of the boys ranch," Reggie said, slowly walking down the hallway with his AK-47 assault rifle ready to fire on anything that moved offensively.

"Uh, what about this?" Miller asked Ghetto Boy, holding a tactical optic sniper scope in one of his hands.

"Yeah, well. Just look through it and tell me what you think," Ghetto Boy said. "You should be able to see exactly what we see. But there's also, I think, a pair of high-powered military binoculars in one of these bags. Might be more than one if I'm correct."

"All clear from what I could see," Reggie said, coming out of the hallway.

"All clear?" Ghetto Boy said, looking down the hallway. "What about that leg that was lying on the floor back there?"

"That was some little girl's doll's leg," Reggie told him. "Looks like she left it behind without realizing it."

"Sounds like she was in a hurry," Miller said. "I mean, for a child to leave something like that behind. She had to be in a hurry."

"Anyway, that's all there was back there," Reggie said. "Other than the fact that all the power is out around here. Has anybody checked to see if you can make contact with Taylor or Chad?"

"What if those things can listen?" Ghetto Boy asked. "What if they are just waiting to see if anyone is still alive?"

"Hold up, you guys," Reggie said, whispering. "You hear that?"

"What?" Ghetto Boy asked. "What'd you hear?"

"What is it?" Miller asked in a low voice.

"Ghetto Boy, get your AK ready," Reggie told him. "Miller, help me check to make sure all the windows are locked."

"Man, what did you hear?" Ghetto Boy asked again, tighten-ing the long-range sniper optic on his rifle. "And by the way, I'm fully aware of my leg being missing, Reggie. So, saying that, why don't you help me tie something around it to ease the pain?"

"What? Like a tourniquet or something?" Miller asked. "I know there's a sling in this place somewhere. There has to be, when living in this neck of the woods with all these creepy little giant critters crawling around."

"Just get something," Ghetto Boy told him. "Anything for right now."

"What did you hear, Reggie?" Ghetto Boy asked again, strip-ping away the rest of his pant leg that had been shredded into pieces and strips by the explosion.

"Thought I heard something moving around underneath us," Reggie said in a low voice. "Something's under this house, clawing at something. Sounds like it's trying to get out."

"Or maybe trying to come in," Miller added.

"Miller," Reggie said, "let's start checking these windows. We might end up having to hang tight right here for a while until we can find out what's going on around here."

"I think I'm gonna still need that tourniquet or something," Ghetto Boy said. "Gotta tie something around the rest of my leg before I end up losing it too."

"Here you go, Ghetto Boy," Miller said, tossing a black, nar-row-looking necktie designed to be worn around the neck at him. "Think you can tie it by yourself? Or do you need help?"

"I'll get it," Reggie said, picking up the tie. "Now, let me see—"

"Hey man, Reggie," Ghetto Boy said, looking up at him from the living room couch, which was actually a sofa bed. "You know what you're doing?"

"Well, if I don't," Reggie said, "just scream out loud. That'll let me know I'm doing it wrong."

"All secured," Miller said, coming from the hallway. "You know, I could hear you guys. Thought you wanted to be quiet?"

"You hear that?" Ghetto Boy said, placing one of his hands in front of Reggie to stop him from making any noise. "You hear that? I think it's coming from down underneath us."

"Yeah, I hear it now," Miller said, slowly moving backward. "Sounds like it's coming from under the house. Whatever it is, it's scratching or clawing on something. Like a piece of wood, or maybe this floor. Like it's trying to come up in here or something."

"Think it's one of those things?" Ghetto Boy asked Reggie.

"Don't know," Reggie said. "Those things know how to get quiet when they're trying to listen to us. But whatever that is, it's continuing to scratch and claw without any fear of us being here."

"I think it's something trying to get out from under this house," Miller said. "Like a giant rodent or something. You know, like a mouse. Except it must be huge, like a big rat that's been down there eating just about everything it can. And now that thing is clawing its way out, probably to try getting at one of us."

"You know what, Miller?" Ghetto Boy said. "You're full of shit, man. It's like Reggie was telling you about that frogman shit you were crying about, saying you saw it carrying Goldsby somewhere. You really gotta do something about your paranoia. You're starting to get delusional."

"I know what I saw out there, Ghetto Boy," Miller said sternly. "I saw that frogman-looking thing carrying her."

"Or somebody that looked like her," Reggie said, stooping upward after kneeling on the floor to wrap the tie-looking tourni-quet around Ghetto Boy's upper leg near his kneecap. "You should start to feel much better now."

"Wonder what that could be under this house making that

noise," Miller muttered to himself. "Sounds like somebody trying to scratch their way out. Could that be coming from the basement?"

"Don't think it has a basement from the looks of the foundation," Reggie said, quietly kneeling again, then suddenly laying flat on the floor. He pressed one ear against the thin floor paneling to get a mental picture of whatever was making the scratching noises underneath. "Sounds like it's digging a hole in the ground."

"That gotta be a dog down there," Ghetto Boy said. "Damn thing's trying its best to get out. They must've locked it in there and forgot to let it out when they left."

"Here boy! Here boy," Reggie whispered, hoping the noises were really coming from a dog. "Come on, boy! Come on!"

Suddenly, the noises ceased. Then a hard bark from a dog could be heard, panting loudly as if having difficulty breathing.

"It's a dog, all right," Reggie said. "It's down there gasping for air."

"Want me to go out there and find the entrance to let it out?" Miller asked.

"I think maybe we could pull one of these wooden planks up or something," Reggie said. "They're not that thick from the way they feel. Really shouldn't have any problem removing a few of them."

"Hey, Miller," Ghetto Boy said. "Why don't you check under the sink in the kitchen? Might be a hammer or something Reggie can use in there that'll do the job."

"But what about the noise?" Miller said. "Don't you think it'll be a bit too loud?"

"Well, if that's the case," Reggie said, "then what about the dog and all his barking? That's if he starts."

"Tell you what," Ghetto Boy began. "Why don't Miller go ahead and head outside to see if he can find a door or something to get under this house, and you, Reggie, start pulling up this floor."

"And what will you be doing?" Reggie asked Ghetto Boy.

"Me? Oh. I'll keep watch with this fully loaded AR-15," Ghetto Boy said, grinning. "Plus, I got this AK-47 standing by."

"Hold up for a minute, Miller," Reggie said, reaching for his rifle. "I think we should stick together. We'll get that dog out from in here, instead of you going outside trying to find a door in the dark. And especially after all that we've gone through."

"Might be a trap door in here somewhere," Ghetto Boy said, attempting to stand by using his rifle for balance. "Gotta be a movable door somewhere in this floor."

"I think I can see something that looks like a door in the ceil-ing," Miller said, looking up. "I mean, that's what it looks like."

"Good eyes," Reggie said, using his rifle to push up on the ceiling paneling to find the door. "Think that's really it, Miller. You got some good eyes, no doubt about that, man."

"Doctor told me when I was a kid that I had the eyes of an eagle, and that one day, I would end up flying away," Miller said, chuckling.

"And have you flown yet?" Ghetto Boy asked him.

"Yeah, I'd like to know myself," Reggie added.

"I've fallen off the garage roof twice thinking I could really do some for-real flying," Miller said. "That was when all the other kids had to remind me I didn't have any wings."

Quiet snickering.

"Man, Miller," Reggie said. "Seriously, you really thought you could actually fly?"

"You know how kids are," Miller said. "They'll try just about anything to see if it can really happen."

"What a freakin' dummy," Ghetto Boy said, hopping toward the dining room window and peering out. "Looks like everything's on fire out there. From the looks of things, the biggest part of the fire seems to be burning exactly where our guys were supposed to have been at the time of that blast and massive explosion."

"Uh, Ghetto Boy," Reggie said. "You know you just hopped over there and left both of these rifles on the couch?"

"Oh yeah, I know," Ghetto Boy said. "And I'mma hop my butt right back over there in a minute. Guess I'm still hoping that I see them coming back this way. Guess I'm not ready to face the grim reality that our guys might really have become victims. I mean, as good as they were."

"Pull yourself together, Ghetto Boy," Reggie said in a harsh but respectful tone. "I need the both of you to keep it together."

"What about that van?" Miller said. "Maybe we should just get the hell out of here while we have a chance."

"And say we did try it," Reggie began. "And all of a sudden, we find out the road is blocked and can't get through. Then what? And those things are still out there and start coming after us. Then what?"

"But what if they went up in the explosion?" Miller said. "I mean, what if that explosion killed them things?"

"Now, just think about it, Miller," Reggie said. "Just think where that took place. Wasn't that at the front entrance? Or was it in the back?"

"No, Miller. It was at one of the main entrances, meaning the rest of those things are still very much alive and all around this place."

"And just probably out there in the dark waiting on us to make that one final mistake," Ghetto Boy said, grabbing a pair of night vision binoculars to get a better view of the situation after the explosion.

"Sounds like we're in a tough jam," Miller said, slowly pulling the thin white and light bluish curtains covering one of the windows back so he could get a view of what was happening. "Man, looks like everything is on fire out there."

"Probably is," Reggie said, lifting one of the planks on the floor, hoping to free the dog from underneath the house. "Whatever caused that explosion, you guys saw it for yourselves. Freakin' thing was huge."

"I'm just surprised we haven't heard anyone trying to contact us," Ghetto Boy said. "It's like nobody heard it or saw it except for us."

"But you guys know what would really be fucked up?" Reggie said. "Is if there was somebody else on the way up here, you know, besides those two guys from the ranger station."

"And?" Ghetto Boy said. "What's the point?"

"They got them too," Miller said. "Them things got 'em. All of 'em."

"Yeah, you took the words right out of my mouth," Reggie said, still trying to pull upward on the plank. "Got it! I think I got at least one of these suckers. But damn, where's the dog?"

"You know what I'm thinking?" Miller said, looking down at the narrow empty space in the floor where the plank had been re-moved.

"Oh no," Ghetto Boy said. "Don't say it, Miller. We've had enough of your superstitiousness already."

"That dog just might be one of them, if you know what I mean," Miller said, backing away from the open space in the floor that Reggie was now about to shine his flashlight through. "Strange he ain't making any more noises."

Hearing this, even Ghetto Boy turned around and stared at the open space in the floor. "You're right about that, Miller," Ghetto Boy said while hopping back to the couch and getting one of the rifles. "I'm not taking any chances."

"Just keep an eye out the window, Ghetto Boy," Reggie told him. "We got this."

*

The fact that they were each describing the process everyone knows firsthand—the quietness of the dogs, Miller's superstitiousness, and details directly related to Satan's calculated cycle of truth—revealed a complete sequence of events. The creation of these events at the boys ranch was symbolized by the perfection of Lucifer's guided prophecy, wielded repeatedly throughout the unfolding occurrences. The components were at hand with brutal, lasting consequences, and the fall of Stonyford was, in every aspect, completely sealed and could never be changed.

As Margaret would say, "It's so important to recognize the fall of this entire region, and that's without being far too skeptical of false doctrines. Everyone in this region who believes that Satan is truly the one and only God will not realize their mistake until they are embedded deep within the bottomless pit. Unfortunately, the region will at best become filled with immense hateful animosity, functioning in a higher existence than the neighboring communities can comprehend, though in much greater depth, inhabited by the physical appearance of Satan himself, after which time all obligations by this region will undoubtedly be met."

Reggie was indeed worried and had every reason to be, realizing that he had placed himself in a situation that required assuming a greater role in life through his willingness to accept the responsibility of leadership.

The isolation of the three was another brutally intimidating course of action, obviously brought about by Lucifer, however unfair the situation might seem. The entire region would suffer the deadly, ongoing consequences for their failure to prove themselves worthy of Lucifer's outset, which began this belligerent scenario.

Suddenly, a loud crash came from underneath the house, and the entire narrow opening in the floor burst upward, sending fragments and debris of various sizes throughout the room, sputtering as each piece shattered into even smaller shards—sharp, distinct, and abrupt.

Shrill and intensely felt, the pain echoed the severity described in Margaret's account of each event.

*

"Oh, fuck, man," Miller cried out loud. "My eyes. I can't see anything in here. My eyes. The pain is killing me. Somebody help me."

"Ghetto Boy, where are you?" Reggie called out. "Ghetto Boy, where the fuck are you, man? Answer me, goddamn it!"

CHAPTER NINE

Years Later:

"Just let her go ahead and drink it," Brian told Melody. "The more she drinks that stuff, the better off we'll be."

"Fuck that bitch!" Melody said angrily. "Ooh, I can't stand her when she gets like this."

"Yeah, I hear you talking 'bout me, you stinky cunt," Lori said while still drinking from the can of beer. "Brian, you ready to fuck me? Let's do it right here in front of the stinky cunt right there."

"Lori, why don't you chill out," Brian said, trying to get her to calm down. "We need you to help us get out of this problem we're having."

"Oh yeah," Lori said, speaking somewhat in riddles. "For what? So that you and that nasty cunt can turn me into a chimera puppy? Ha! Ha!"

"Just forget about her, Brian," Melody told him while closing the door to one of the safes after grabbing a medium-size bag of diamonds, crystals, and gemstones. "We don't really need her. We can do this without a drunk like that. Really wish we could just throw that bitch outside where she belongs and let them things have her."

"Hey, wait a minute, hold up, Melody," Brian quickly whispered. "Uh, you didn't close that all the way, did you?"

"No, I don't think I closed it all the way," she said. "Why?"

"Think I'll get a bag or two for myself," he said, reaching down to open the door while using his flashlight.

"Get enough for the both of us, Brian," Lori told him, staggering unsteadily toward him. "'Cause when this is all over—me and you, you and me—we're gonna buy a speedboat and go over to the Bahamas. But that fuckin' cunt there won't be allowed on our island. Only Bahamians allowed," they shouted.

"Fuck you, you whore," Melody said, turning to slap Lori, only to be stopped by Brian, who grabbed her hand before she could strike. "Ooh, you bitch, you better be—"

"Hey, you guys," Brian suddenly said. "Looks like somebody's coming this way. Isn't that a car headed in our direction?"

"Where?" asked Lori. "I don't see nothin'."

"I think it is," Brian said, looking at Melody. "You see it? Isn't that a car coming this way? Or maybe a pickup."

"Where?" Lori said, slowly staggering to the front of the Winnebago, trying to look out the windshield. "Where is it? I don't see—"

"Oh no. Please don't," Brian began pleading to himself.

"Yeah, I think whoever it is, they're turning around and going back the other way," Melody said, staring at Brian. "What's your reason for not moving this thing, Brian?"

CLICK! CLICK! CLICK!
CLICK! CLICK! CLICK!

"Hold up!" Brian yelled. "Just hold up, everybody. Think I'm on to whoever it is."

"Well, who is it, Brian?" Lori screamed. "Fuckin' who is it?"

"Lori, hold it down so he can find out," Melody yelled. "You're making all kinds of noises. How'd you think he's gonna find out?"

"Fuck you, you rotten cunt bitch," Lori yelled back, still

screaming for Brian to answer her. "Who the fuck is it, Brian?"

"No, fuck you, you tramp, bitch!" Melody shouted back at Lori. "You really don't wanna know just who the fuck you're messin' with."

"We're out here not too far from, I guess, the boys' ranch," Brian said to the person on the other end of the clicking. "I just started up this thing, and it's warming up. We'll be headed that way in a minute."

"Okay, just be careful, young man," the voice told him from the speaker system constructed throughout the Winnebago, they shouted. "We're having problems just about everywhere down here. Something bad is happening all around us, and mainly over there in places like Garberville and all the surrounding communities near that town. Y'all just try and be very careful on your way down. I'll be surely praying for ya," they added.

"Wait a minute, hold on for a minute," Brian said through the handheld mic. "Wait a minute. Come back. Wait a minute. Please! Come back!"

"Let's just get out of here, Brian," Melody told him while staring out the front side window. "We gotta get out of here. Now!"

"Okay! Okay!" Brian yelled. "I hear you, damn it. Just gotta make one more check, Melody."

"Check!" Melody screamed. "Check on what?"

"Fuck me before we leave, Brian," Lori yelled from her heavy intoxication, they shouted. "Fuck me! Now!"

"Shut up, bitch!" Melody screamed again, desperate to leave the campground. "You're really getting on my last freakin' nerve!"

"Brian, please fuck me," Lori said again, this time in a much calmer tone. "Brian, please."

"What the fuck!" Brian said after noticing Lori lying on the floor of the Winnebago and having taken her pants off, wearing only her panties. "Lori, it's time to go home."

"Tramp!" Melody whispered. "Bitch ain't shit!"

"Okay, look, Melody," Brian said, standing directly in front of her. "I just wanna make sure the tires and everything else is all right before we move this thing. I'm gonna need your full cooperation for this to happen."

"What about my cooperation?" Lori said. "Aren't you gonna need it, too?"

"Yeah, and yours, too, Lori," Brian said, nodding his head. "I'm going to need everybody's cooperation so we can get out of here."

"Where we going, Brian?" Lori asked him. "You still haven't told us. Oh, I know. You wanna fuck me. Well, so do I, wanna fuck me."

"Melody, you can't keep letting her get under your skin," Brian said, hoping Melody would help him get them on their way home. "You know she's had a little too much to drink. And really, it's not all her fault. It's ours too."

"What do you want me to do?" Melody asked Brian.

"Well, I'm sure you already know how to use that rifle," Brian said. "I want you to just pick it up and, you know, use it if you have to while I check everything underneath this Winnebago. Think you can do that?"

"I can," Melody said, still expressing her anger concerning Lori and her rude comments toward her while intoxicated.

"Check this out, Melody," Brian said, trying to whisper while gently and very slowly pulling Melody toward him. "She'll be fast asleep within a few more minutes, so try not allowing her to bother you for right now. We gotta get the hell out of here before them things make it back. You feel me?"

"Yeah, if you say so," Melody said, looking down at Lori, who was still lying on the floor, partially naked, wearing only her panties. "And what about her? We can't just leave her lying there like that, without—"

"Without what?" Brian asked. "Without what?"

"You know, Brian," she hesitated. "We can both—"

"What?" Brian asked, curious as to what Melody had in mind.

"I mean, the engine is running and warming up," Melody said, with a slight smile on her face. "What? You don't know, Brian?"

"I'm beginning to wonder if that's what you're asking me," Brian said.

"We're lesbians, Brian," Melody said. "But, as you now know, our relationship does consist of getting fucked by a man once in a while. You feel me on that note? We can both fuck her together before we leave this place."

"But what about the engine? It's still running," Brian said, somewhat afraid to move in either direction to turn off the engine or check outside the Winnebago.

"Just let it run for now," Melody told him, sliding out of her tightly fitted jeans and shirt top, revealing the smoothness of her erect nipples as her breasts stood firm, as if seeking affection. "Go ahead and pull Lori's panties off, Brian. And don't forget to open her legs wide so we can taste her together. Me and you, Brian."

But Brian just stood there, in shock from the thought of what Melody had requested him to do to Lori. "I, I, I," he mumbled. "Never, in my life, done anything like this, Melody. You know, I mean, never."

"Well, Brian," she told him, rubbing her now naked body up against his. "There's always a first time for everything, and this, this just happens to be that first time for you, Brian."

*

Here we can again see Satan at work, using both Melody and Lori through his supernatural approach to prolong their intent to get away from the deadly campground. From the outset, the entire scenario is continually put into motion, diminishing patterns that exist through the predictability Satan ultimately urges his follow-ers to follow.

The hateful belligerence and animosity brought about by Lori is an unfortunate element of this deadly scenario that serves her desires, much as Eve once matched herself equally to God through Adam, being the first woman and wife of Adam. In this case, Lori is attempting to prove herself equally; in other words, her initial of-fer to Brian was without concealment, though equally to that of Melody, even during heavy intoxication. To stimulate this evil scenario with an even more exhilarating flow of obligations, let us focus on the fact that Brian is just as astounded as Melody in a particular fashion, giving reasons why this scenario should be carefully examined.

The outset of Margaret's attack by something unknown and in no way belonging to the human race was indeed a fair statement in many instances and in more ways than one. However unruly the attack, she would eventually find herself accepting this unwanted character into her young life, distinguishing its features with mental characteristics like those of something made up in a play or novel system, with high complexions. The monster Margaret at-tempted to describe was none other than Lucifer himself. Al-though the spirit of Satan, Lucifer's realm had long become the grounds on which the entire Stonyford region had been built. This particular part of the region was his kingdom, his domain.

Virtually everything is geared toward the inauguration of the coming of Satan's fallen angels, who are, in preparation, readying themselves to once again take their place among the living. The fulfillment will continually flow, undoubtedly resulting in deadly effects, giving the account at hand factual truth.

Suddenly, there was an awful scream that echoed loudly and repetitively throughout the region. As the roaring continued, long, loud, and deep in tone, even those attending the festivity began to scramble hastily and urgently, confused as to what was happening. But without realizing it, they were about to witness a part of history that would take everyone attending the festivity and all its many colorful displays onto an elaborate platform put in place for submission.

This cheerful attraction, having the attention of so many souls, is the beginning of Satan's deadly ritual. It is enacted by none other than the evil fallen angels who were sent forth so that Stonyford and the entire region would finally, and for once, see them in their fullness and in plain sight. This display will be that of the fallen angels, solidifying Satan's military force, which in part consists of the deadly spirits of the old snake hunter and his snake.

The entire event is going to be like a musical composition with explicit dancing, clearly expressed and defined. The beginning is at hand, with circumstances that will be spoken gently and candidly using supernatural understanding, though ultimately, the outset will be like the blink of an eye.

Swift, with great speed.

Quickly accomplishing Satan's mission without alternatives.

*

"Oh, fuck! What was that?" Melody whispered.

"That thing," Brian said, rushing to the driver's seat. "It sounds like it's coming back."

"Who's coming back, Brian?" Melody asked frantically. "Just who are you talking about?"

"That thing," he said again while reaching downward to put the motor home's automatic gear shifters in drive.

"What thing are you talking about, Brian?" she yelled at him. "If you're not going to tell me, I'm just gonna open this door and find out for myself."

"Well, you just do that, Melody," he yelled back. "But I'm going to get the fuck outta here right now. That thing is coming back, and I don't intend to wait around just so it can do me like it did the other guys."

"Is it that chimera-looking thing?" Melody asked, looking aimlessly out different windows. "That's what it is, isn't it, Brian? That chimera.'"

"I don't really know, Melody," he told her. "But this time, it sounds like more than just one."

"What are you guys talking about?" Lori said aloud. "Tell me, I wanna know what's happening. Did you fuck me yet, Brian? Did you?"

"This isn't the time, Lori," Melody told her. "We're about to leave this place, and right now isn't the time for you to be talking like this."

"You know, what I might need you to do is keep close watch out these windows."

"Well, that's what I'm doing, Brian."

"Yeah, but what about in the back?"

"In the back? Where?"

"The bathroom. There's a window back there that I think you should, you know, check or something."

"For what?"

"Melody, that thing out there."

"What? That Chimera creature?"

"Look, Melody. Once we start rolling, I need you to be able to use that rifle."

"But what about Lori? Isn't that what she's supposed to be doing?"

"Come on, Melody. You know she's in no condition to be do-ing anything."

"I hear you talking about me, saying she's in no condition to do them things."

"Well, you're not, Lori," Brian told her while pressing down on the gas pedal with his right foot, causing the Winnebago to start moving slowly forward.

"Where're we going, Brian?" Lori asked, attempting to get up from the floor. "And who took my clothes off? You do this, Brian? And it better not have been this cunt—bitch," they shouted.

"Need to put you outside where you belong," Melody told Lori.

"What? You wanna tie me up to the front of this thing so Brian can have his way with me?" Lori said in an indistinct voice.

"Melody, really. I'm gonna need you to keep watch out the back window. At least until we get close to town."

"Why don't we just do as she said, tie her up to the front of this thing and hope that monster bangs her ass."

"Okay, here we go, you guys," Brian said, turning onto the road that would eventually take them back to Stonyford.

"Aren't you gonna turn on the lights?" Melody asked.

"What? And let them things see where we are? That's why I really needed you to keep close watch from the back window, Melody," Brian said. "With that rifle, you'll be able to blast them things."

All of a sudden, Lori finally got up from the floor completely naked, unwilling to put her clothes back on. She immediately reached for one of the rifles, bending over and exposing her nakedness without any embarrassment, revealing her beauty in full detail from behind. Brian, upon noticing her well-delighted figure, slowed to a near stop. He stared at Melody and then, without paying any attention to his actions, began once again to press slowly on the gas pedal without watching his steering.

Suddenly, there was a loud crashing sound within feet of the Winnebago that caused a considerable amount of thick dust and debris to fill the air in front of them.

"Oh, shit, man," Brian yelled. "What the fuck is that?"

"Brian," Melody screamed, they shouted. "What did you do?"

"I didn't do anything," he said, quickly slamming on the

brakes. "That had nothing to do with me."

"Well, what was it, Brian?"

"Man, I don't know. Something just came, I guess, crashing down from somewhere, and it smashed onto the ground really hard."

"You think maybe it was a car or something? Like, maybe somebody lost control of their car and came down the hill."

"Man, fuck! I really don't know, Melody," Brian said, confused. "I'm just as confused as you are. I don't know what happened."

"Well, can't you just go around it?" Melody asked him.

"I don't know," he told her. "I can't see anything. All this dust —"

"I'll go out there and see what it is if you want me to," Lori said.

"Think maybe you should turn the lights on?" Melody asked. "Can't see if there's anything in front of us."

"That's where it landed, Melody," Brian told her. "Whatever it is, it landed right here in front of us."

"Well, I can't see anything in back of us," Melody said, looking in one of the rear-view mirrors. "But it looks like there is something flashing back there."

"Red?" Brian said in a hushed tone. "What? You mean, red?"

"I don't know, but it's something bright red back there."

"You want me to see what it is, Brian?" Lori asked again, still naked as if unwilling to dress herself.

"No, that's all right, Lori," he told her. "I'll go back there myself and see what it is."

"But why don't you want me to check?" Lori questioned. "Want me to go with you?"

"No, that's all right, I told you," Brian said again. "Plus, you don't have any clothes on."

"Oh, my clothes," Lori said as if she didn't know. "I forgot.

Who took them off me in the first place? Was it you, Brian?"

"Melody, keep watch," Brian said while taking the gear shifter out of drive and moving it to the park position, then pulling up on the handle to activate the emergency brakes. "I'm gonna let the motor run for now. This shouldn't take long."

"Okay, now," Lori said, standing up with just her panties on. "Is this good enough for you, Brian?"

"Oh, hey. Wait a minute," Melody said, peering intently through the mirror. "I think that red light just went away or something. I can't see it anymore. I think it's gone from back there."

"Uh, hold up for a minute," Brian said, looking aimlessly out the mirror on the driver's side of the Winnebago. "You know what I think?"

"What, Brian?" Melody answered, curious as to what he was thinking.

"I think that red flashing light you were seeing back there was me," he told her. "You see, every time I pushed on the brake pedal, it made the brake lights come on in the back. That's what you were seeing in red, Melody."

"So, what about whatever that is that crashed on the ground in front of us?" she questioned. "Did you do that too?"

"Had nothing to do with that," he said. "Though—"

"Now, can I go with you to check it out?" Lori asked again while trying to put her pants on. "Anybody seen my shoes?"

"Well, I'm still going to go back and see what I can see," Brian told Melody. "Just keep watch on everything up here."

"How're you gonna see anything?" Melody asked him.

"Easy," he told her. "From in the bathroom. There is a small window in there that I can look out of to see if I can see anything."

"Just hurry up, Brian," Melody told him. "I'm really afraid up here."

"Okay, just hold on for a minute," he told her. "Lori will be here with you."

"Lori," Melody exclaimed. "I thought she was going back there with you? I don't need anything like that to depend on when I'm afraid of being alone in the dark. I'd rather have the monster anytime than to have her."

"Yeah, like I wanna be with you," Lori said, snickering, still in search of her shoes. "Just where are my shoes? I know they have to be here."

"Maybe the dingo got your shoes," Melody said, referring to the wild dogs of Australia, which have been said to have a reputation for entering campsites or small villages where certain groups are dwelling and dragging small children away into the night.

"You know, Melody," Brian began. "That could be true. I mean, just give it a thought for a second or two. That just might be happening around here."

"Yeah, like, I saw that dog out there when you were looking in that rear-view mirror," Lori told Brian. "He was just standing there, staring at us."

"What dog are you talking about?" Brian asked her. "What dog?"

"Yeah, Lori," Melody asked. "What dog are you talking about?"

"Don't tell me you guys forgot," Lori said, finding one of her shoes. "I am talking about that dog, you know, the one who ran away from us when we got here. You remember? It was trapped underneath that trailer that exploded."

"Oh yeah, I remember," Brian said. "Once we got it loose, it ran up this hill right here."

"Yeah, that's right," Lori said, grinning. "Now if only I can find my—"

"Are you sure you saw it, Lori?" Brian asked her. "I mean, that dog?"

"Yep!" Lori said sternly. "It was him, again."

"So, just where did it go?" Melody asked, slowly moving away from one of the side windows. "Did you see which way it went, Lori?"

"Uh-huh," Lori said, now down on the floor, searching underneath the sofa for her other shoe.

"Which way did it go, Lori?" Melody asked, hoping she would tell her.

"Where did it go, Lori?" Brian also asked. "Didn't you see it?"

"Oh, here it is," Lori said, holding up her shoe after finding it under the couch. "Don't know how it got way under there. It's still out there, just watching us. I think it walked around on the side somewhere. Maybe it went in the back somewhere. It's out there, 'cause I saw it just standing there, and it was staring right at us. Maybe we need to let it inside the trailer so it can get warm."

"No, I don't think so," Brian said. "But what I am going to do is check to make sure these windows are locked. You guys just stay where you are."

"Don't you want me to help you, Brian?" Lori asked him.

"Just stay where you are for now," he told her. "But, Melody, I'm still gonna need somebody to keep watch out the back window in case—"

"Oh, I'll do it," said Lori. "Please let me do it."

"Okay, but you have to fire that rifle if you see something following us," Brian told her. "You think you can do that, Lori?"

"Yep! Sure can," Lori said, standing upright without wearing anything on the top portion of her body.

"Uh, Lori?" Brian said, wondering if she even knew that she was topless as she stood slightly at attention. "Are you going to put on anything else?"

"Forget that, Brian," Melody gushed before Lori could open her mouth. "If she's going to be like that, I might as well do the same."

"What?" Brian was about to question when he suddenly noticed Melody undressing. "What are you doing?"

"If it's war those things out there want, then I'm going to give it to them," Melody said, standing firm as if she were some type of female Ramboy hero action figure. "Move out of the way, I'll keep guard from the back window. Oh, better not forget to get this rifle. Might need it."

"What's gotten into her?" Lori uttered, staring at Brian.

"Don't know," Brian said. "But it's time we get out of here."

"Well, now what am I gonna do?" Lori asked Brian. "She's taken my part guarding the back window. Now what am I gonna do, Brian?"

"I know what, Lori," Brian said. "You can keep an eye on this door."

"The door?" Lori exclaimed. "I wanted to watch out the back window, to make sure that monster thing didn't get us. So I could kill it if it did."

"Well, it might still try coming through the door, Lori," Brian told her. "That's why it's so important you keep an eye out to make sure none of them things try opening it to get in, and, you know, try harming us."

"What?" Lori said, staring out the front window. "Like making sure that dog right there doesn't try coming in to get us?"

"What dog?" Brian asked. "Where is it?"

"Look, right here, Brian," Lori told him, pointing downward toward the front right side of the Winnebago. "You see it? Hey, where did it go?"

"Melody, you see anything back there?" Brian asked in a low voice.

"I can't see anything," Melody said. "But maybe if I just pop this window open a little bit. But first I gotta get this screen off this thing."

"No, wait a minute, Melody, before you do that," Brian said, trying to stop her from removing the bathroom window screen.

"That dog just might be standing there, you know, waiting to try coming through that way."

"No, he isn't," Lori said. "He's right here. I can see him. He's right here, looking at me and wagging his tail. I think he wants to come in, Brian."

"Melody, don't remove that screen," Brian told her, heading back to the front of the trailer. "Whatever you do, don't remove that screen."

"But I need to be able to see if there's anything that's trying to, you know, climb up here to get in the window," she told him. "How am I going to see anything?"

"We're getting out of here right now," Brian said, sitting down in the driver's seat and repositioning the auto-shifter to drive. "Everybody hold on, we're getting outta here."

"Look, Brian," Lori suddenly yelled. "What's that right there in front of us?"

"Don't know, and really don't freakin' care," Brian said. "We gotta get the fuck outta here, Lori."

"Whatever it is," Lori said, "it's burning up really bad. And now that you know, all that foggy smoke is finally clearing up, you can see what that thing burning is, Brian."

"Like I said, Lori," Brian told her again. "Don't know what it is, and really don't care."

"It looks like one of the Jeeps we came up here in," Lori said, looking out the front window at the burning debris shaped like a square block of burning wood with tires on it. "It's all smashed up, Brian."

"Looks like something coming," Melody yelled to Brian.

"What is it?" he asked. "Are you sure?"

"Just thought I saw something flying in the air," Melody said.

"Flying in the air?" Brian asked. "What? A bird or something?"

"Maybe it's that Chimera thing," Lori said, looking back at Melody.

"Yeah, well, just come on, you motherfucker," Melody yelled, they shouted. "Come on and get your dinner, you son of a bitch."

"Just hold on, Melody," Brian yelled back at her. "Once I get this thing around this stuff out there burning, we'll be on our way."

Suddenly, there was another huge ball of fire and debris that came smashing loudly to the ground in front of them, causing another round of dark black dust and debris to scatter in every direction.

"Oh, fuck!" Brian yelled, they shouted. "What was that?"

"Lori!" Lori screamed, they shouted.

"What's happening?" Melody also yelled, coming out from the back of the Winnebago. "What's happening, Brian?"

"Don't know, you guys," Brian exclaimed. "Goddamn freakin' shit just came crashing onto the ground from out of nowhere. It almost landed right on top of us. Freakin' shit! Could've killed us all."

"Well, what is it, Brian?" Melody shouted.

They shouted. "What is it? Can you tell?"

"It's another of them burning things with wheels on it," Lori said. "I think it's another Jeep."

"Jeep?" Melody questioned. "Move out of the way, let me see."

"See, what did I tell you?" Lori said.

"But how did it come out of the air?" Melody asked Brian. "How did that happen?"

"Melody," Brian said, as though pleading with her, "I need you to keep watch in the back. You said you saw something that looked like it was flying over us or something. Well, please, Melody. Go back there, and just do what you gotta do. Start shooting at them motherfuckers. Kill all of 'em for us, Melody. Kill 'em all. Blow them bastards away."

"Well, I know we're not just gonna sit here, are we?" Melody asked.

"Hell no," Brian said, pressing slowly on the gas pedal. "We're out of here, you guys. Anything else come falling down out of the sky, it'll just have to fall, 'cause I don't give a fuck!"

"Well, let's do this, Brian and Lori," Melody shouted.

They shouted, with confidence.

"Anything come my way, it's going down!" Melody shouted.

They shouted.

"Do it, Melody," Lori shouted.

They shouted. "That's my—"

"Hang on, you guys," Brian said, pressing harder on the gas pedal while trying to see through all the fire and burning debris scattered in front of them. "Ain't no stopping us now!"

Suddenly, there was another loud sound of something crashing hard onto the ground. Huge balls of fire and debris slammed forcefully onto the ground within a short distance behind them as Melody could be heard shouting and cursing out loud, firing off the rifle at anything she felt was a threat.

As the Winnebago sped around curve after curve, without even any guardrails for protection in case of an emergency. Loud noises like deadly, thunderous discharges from clouds began to flash huge, dangerous vortexes of lightning and whirling pools of dangerous blowing wind throughout the region.

*

The lengthy inauguration is now at hand.

Satan is in the beginning development phase of the cyclic form of his appearance, in which the entire region will carry out his plan systematically in phases to introduce and eliminate those who refuse to follow him in many different stages.

The spiritual function is that of a physical depth inhabited by Satan's deadly army of fallen angels presently in attendance to wage their final war upon God and all mankind, like that of a dramatic production enterprise. The true manipulators are about to take revenge and inflict severe pain and punishment on a multi-tude of people throughout the region.

*

Steering in an effort not to lose control, Brian refused to ease up on his speed as the Winnebago continued at a high rate. It abruptly swerved from side to side around each winding curve and narrow path through the heavily rough terrain of the Stonyford mountains.

"Everybody hang on tight," Brian shouted.

They shouted, as the Winnebago did a quick fishtail around a curve just within feet from sliding off one of the many steep em-bankments.

"Hang on, you guys," he continued to shout. "We're almost there, just hang on."

It was at this point that another large chunk of debris struck the back section of the Winnebago, crushing its top and most likely killing Melody instantly. The huge impact nearly flattened the back of the Winnebago but did not prevent the back wheels from turning. The impact was like that of an explosion, as did those in the campground when the trailer exploded, killing Terry.

"Oh gosh," Lori cried.

They shouted.

"Brian, we're on fire. Everything is on fire back there, and Melody is back there on fire. You gotta stop this thing and help her. She's back there, on fire and burning up, Brian. You gotta stop so we can help her."

"I'm trying, but I can't," Brian yelled.

They shouted.

"The brakes are out, and they aren't working anymore. The fire burned them out, Lori. I can't stop this thing. We're going too fast."

"It's coming up here now, Brian," Lori screamed.

They shouted.

"It's coming up here, and it's going to burn us up."

"We're almost there, Lori," Brian yelled at her.

They shouted.

"Just hang on, Lori, we are almost there."

"Oh, no, Brian," Lori cried.

They shouted.

"My clothes are on fire. My hair! It's burning. We're gonna burn up in here. We gotta get out. Why don't you stop so we can get out?"

"Keep on over here by me, Lori," Brian told her, pulling her toward him. "The brakes are burned out, I can't stop this thing. It's going too fast for us to jump out. But we'll make it, Lori, just keep close to me. We'll make it."

"What's all that popping noise?" Lori asked Brian. "Is that the tires on this thing blowing out?"

"Not sounding like that. But what I think it is, it just might be those bullets from the rifle that Melody was using, exploding back there from all the heat."

"You gotta hurry up, Brian. My legs are starting to get really hot. It's beginning to feel like they're on fire or something."

"We're almost there, Lori," Brian told her, trying to reinforce her confidence and self-assurance. "Just hang in there."

"You think Melody could still be alive back there, Brian? She might be trapped."

"Don't know, Lori. This thing is really burning. I'm thinking maybe she could have possibly jumped out back there somewhere."

"But what if she couldn't? She might still be back there, Brian."

"Just keep close to me, Lori. We're almost there."

"What about the horn, Brian? Why don't you try seeing if it'll work?"

"Ah, man, Lori. Now why didn't I think of that?" Brian said, pressing down on the round-shaped device on the steering wheel, activating the horn on the Winnebago. "Man, I know somebody down there gotta hear that and see us coming down this hill. I know they gotta hear it, Lori."

"And what about the lights on this thing? Are they on? Maybe you should make them blink like an emergency. You know, like how they make them really light and really bright when they're blinking."

"I don't know. With all the fire burning on this thing, they're probably burned out by now," Brian said, flipping the light switch on and off, hoping to get someone's attention as the Winnebago sped faster and faster down one of the few hills and winding roads leading directly into the heart of town. "All this wind blowing past us is what's keeping the fire from coming up here. But the only thing I am really worried about is the gas tank going up. And damn, I forgot about the propane tank, wherever that thing is."

"Yeah, I forgot about that too, Brian," Lori said, occasionally looking back at the fire as each popping sound of bullets going off caused her to jump nervously. "When are those things gonna stop popping like that?"

"I really don't know," Brian said, slightly struggling strenuously with the steering wheel in his effort to keep control of the Winnebago. "I really don't know just how much ammunition was back there. But from the way it sounds from up here, there must have been quite a bit."

CHAPTER TEN

"What the?" Sheriff Blake Jr. found himself mumbling, they whispered, from the sight of the Winnebago coming down one of the winding roads heading for Stonyford fully engulfed in fire. "For Pete's sake, can somebody, anybody, tell me just what in the hell part of this goddamn celebration that thing is supposed to be in? Hell, if I'm not mistaken, the goddamn thing is really putting on one hell of a firing display. The kind of display we really don't need right now."

"Looks like it's on fire, Sheriff," one of his flunkies said. "That thing is really burning."

"Goddamn it, Jerome," Blake said, nodding his head in disbelief. "Now don't you think I can see that? That's quite obvious. I mean—"

"Hey, Sheriff," somebody yelled out. "Now that is pretty good. Tell me just how the heck did you come up with that idea?"

"What? Oh, that thing there?" Blake said as if taking credit for the firing display. "Oh, that's just something, you know, the guys and a few of us came up with at the last minute."

"Man, that thing is really lighting things up," somebody said out loud in the distance. "Just look at it, it's even pretending to be catching some of those bushes on fire up there. What an exciting display, you guys," they shouted.

"Just who the hell was that, Jerome?" Blake asked. "You know, somebody's gonna have to end up going up there and put out those goddamn fires."

"Isn't that really a part of the display, Sheriff?" Jerome asked while looking around aimlessly, wondering about the fire seemingly burning out of control. "I really don't quite know how they're driving that thing with it burning like that."

"Sounds like they're blowing the horn," a voice said. "Guess they just wanna make sure everybody's watching that thing burn."

"Hey, somebody better call the fire department or something," another voice yelled. "I don't think that's part of any display—burning like that thing is burning. And if it is, it's the best I ever seen," they shouted.

Suddenly, loud cheers could be heard from a crowd of spectators who were gathering in large groups in front of the Stonyford Supermarket, amazed at what they were seeing, as the flames from the Winnebago could be seen from miles away as it sped down the huge winding hill in their direction.

"I wonder just what the hell is all that popping sound, Sheriff," one of his friends asked curiously.

"Wondering the same myself," Blake said. "Maybe they got a bunch of those goddamn fireworks up there as part of their display."

"Yeah, but the only thing is, they ain't letting off any colored lights for real entertainment," his friend said, scratching his head.

"Sounds to me like they're shooting a gun or something to be making that kind of sound," Jerome said. "Just listen to it now: that ain't nothing like any firecracker I ever heard exploding."

"You know something, Jerome? I think you're probably right about that," Blake said, eyes fixated on the firing sight of the Winnebago, now practically engulfed entirely in flames. "I think one of y'all needs to get ready to go up there and put a stop to those sons of bitches before they end up really losing control of their display. Hell, if that happens, we'll really have a mess on our hands."

"Hey, Sheriff. I think you better get a fire pumper up there as quick as you can. If you know what I mean," a voice suggested. "Just look at that thing—it's catching everything on fire. If you don't do something, next it'll be rolling down here, and there's no telling what it'll have caught on fire by then."

Suddenly, there was a very loud, violent explosion. People screamed and yelled, shouting that one of the carnival rides had tipped over and people were trapped, needing help.

There was also mention of a second ride, and possibly a third, that had mysteriously gone completely haywire and wasn't functioning properly.

Suddenly, yet another explosion caused the ground to shake and tremble violently. "What in Christ's name was that?" Blake yelled as people ran in all directions in a panic. "Just where in the hell did that come from, Jerome?"

"Something blew up," Jerome said, as people cried and screamed about rides tipping over and trapping individuals in cages. Others shouted about thousands of extremely venomous snakes and other reptiles entering certain areas and attacking people spontaneously. "We got some serious problems, Sheriff."

"Sheriff Blake," somebody cried out, "you gotta do something. That one ride with all those people on it went up, but it never came down. We don't know what happened. And those people? They're gone. All of 'em."

"Jerome, go check and see what the heck he's talking about, will you?" Blake told him. "And somebody try to stop that goddamn motor home. All we need right now is for that thing to come flying down here and catch everything on fire."

*

Little did he know, Stonyford—the town he'd so loved and desperately served and protected—was about to be brutally destroyed under Lucifer's deadly concealment. The town's failure to comply spiritually was going to prove fatal despite the considerable number of people who didn't resist his calling.

As predicted by Margaret, Stonyford was indeed the only calculated area of misbehavior in the region, although nearby communities were not exempt from the initiated obligations, which were the result of Satan's beginning development stage of this sequence. The auction and sale of the deadly venomous Cobra by the auctioneer—who was about to destroy the snake only to shear its skin for amenity purposes—also played a role in the unfolding events.

The manifestation of these events would bring about the final alignment, at which time Stonyford would stand in opposition to God's heaven and Lucifer's Hell, created by an extremely violent collision between the two. This event would bring about the New Testament and a new doctrine for the entire universe and all existing space and matter that would be regarded as Lucifer's domain.

The new planet Earth is where God will undoubtedly be cast out of His once heaven, and Satan will reign with his regime forever, like under a new system and management, like a powerful military regiment or battalion, to bring about a new systematic order imposing strict uniformity and discipline upon the opposition.

And yes, the parade continued against Stonyford's odds, refusing to notice the catastrophic disaster about to take place throughout the region. As predicted, it was a very calculated plan designed to claim many casualties, render submission artistically, and create children of Satan's family.

*

"I think it's just a little too late for that, Blake," another voice said, sounding deeply saddened. "That thing is almost on the main part of the road, and the only way you can probably stop it is to crash something into it. But that's assuming they're really out of control."

"For Christ's sake, people," someone cried out. "Just look at that. It's out of control. That's why they're blowing that horn, trying to warn us about the problem they're having."

"Don't take a rocket scientist to see that," another voice said.

"Hell, I agree with you, buddy," another voice added.

"And here they come, you guys," someone shouted. "Everybody get out of the way of that thing because it ain't slowing down."

"It's really burning, Sheriff," another voice yelled. "Better get a fire pumper ready, 'cause that thing is really burning up."

"What about the people inside?" someone asked. "What about them?"

"We got a couple ambulances already here waiting," Blake said. "They are fully equipped to deal with this type of situation."

"Ooh, my. This is so awful," a woman could be heard crying. "Just think of those poor people inside that camper. They are probably burning alive."

Suddenly, there was another powerful explosion. People could once again be heard screaming loudly, yelling about the huge Mega Water Slide, slicing children as they raced down its multiple water lanes, through every winding turn, and ending at the Stonyford lake, where they were met by lifeguards and expert swimmers.

"Hey, uh, Sheriff Blake," someone said, rushing up to him. "It's at the water slide. Looks like somebody planted something all up and down that thing, and it's really cutting and slicing everybody, even some of the kids. Whatever it is, it sliced their little hands and some of their fingers right off. It's terrible, Sheriff. Really terrible."

"What in heaven's name are you talking about?" Blake asked. "Just how in the hell could that be happening?"

"Sheriff, we got a serious problem over there at the water slide," one of his deputies said. "I don't know what it is, but people are running around all over the place, screaming and crying, and saying crazy things, like kids are being cut and sliced in half by the water slide."

"Hey, I need a few good volunteers," Blake said out loud. "Are any of y'all interested? If you are, just step right over here and let me deputize you. And before I forget, if any of y'all have any outstanding warrants, your service to the community will automatically squash that problem. You'll have a pretty clean record once we get everything back to normal. But wait a minute—if you've been living like a goddamn criminal, out doing bad deeds like forcibly breaking the law or killing people, I'm just gonna have to lock your ass up. So, do I still have any volunteers?"

"Sheriff, thank God. I finally found you," a woman said, short of breath. "I am a nurse, and my girlfriends and I would gladly extend our services to this community. We'll help however we can."

"Well, that'll be mighty kind of you and your friends," Blake said.

"Y'all can just step right over here and let me deputize you for your services."

"No, we don't want to be deputies," the nurse said. "We just wanna help however we can as nurses. That's our job and profession."

"And might I ask where this profession is located?" Blake said. "You know, like, where are y'all from?"

"Oh, we're down here from—"

"Garberville," one of the other nurses quickly answered. "Just came down to enjoy ourselves, see the parade, and everything else."

"Well, um, hope y'all like what you've seen so far," Blake shrugged. "I guess I can say that all the way up until now."

"Sheriff, that thing on fire is about to come this way," one of his deputies said. "Think we better get everybody out of the way."

"Well, what about that water slide?" Blake asked. "Y'all got that taken care of yet?"

"Sheriff, we got problems," the deputy said, looking around. "That one ride, the 'Rip Cord,' went up but never came back down."

"Look, what the hell are you talking about?" Blake asked firmly. "Ain't never heard such a thing. What the hell are you guys out here talking about? This must be the second time I've heard something like that. Goddamn thing going up and never coming down. Bullshit."

"Think he's right, Sheriff," one of the nurses said. "The same thing happened with the 'Timber Wolf' ride. It's all over the place —scattered about five miles down the road—and people are lying everywhere needing help. It's really bad, Sheriff."

"Here it come," somebody yelled. "Everybody get out of the way."

Suddenly, the firing Winnebago came coasting past them in a straight line, burning intensely, with a huge chunk of debris dragging behind it, scraping the ground and scattering in countless fragments, sparkling and emitting thousands of tiny, gleaming particles on the dark road.

"Hurry up, it's slowing down," somebody yelled. "I think it's going to stop."

"Okay, nurses," Blake said. "Let's see what you can do. Got people in that thing burning alive. Gotta save them."

"Oh, God," somebody cried out loud. "We gotta save them. They're burning—I can see them from here. Help them. Oh, help them. They're burning up in there."

"It's stopping," another voice cried. "It's stopping. It's stopping down there by the ranger station. It's stopping."

"Did you see anybody jump out?" someone asked. "Did you see anybody jump out?"

Suddenly, the gas tank on the Winnebago violently erupted, as did the propane tank, sending huge amounts of flaming debris into the air from the natural gas and petroleum fuel. Another explosion followed. And then another. And another.

*

These explosions were coming from different areas of the festivity, illuminating the dark sky like blinding, fluorescent lights.

This was the beginning of Satan's return from the bottomless pit with all his fallen angels. It was also the start of Stonyford's horrible misfortune and the tragic ruin that would shatter every corner of the region.

Surrounding explosions and flaming debris could be seen in nearly every part of the town as fire moved swiftly and uncontrollably through Stonyford.

This was Satan's retribution for the community's outright refusal to obey and submit to his authority. With his degrading principles, he now sought to neutralize the town that had defied him. Such unrelenting vengeance, of violent intensity, was about to be unleashed under circumstances unlike anything ever recorded—or imagined—by the most distinguished mystery writers.

*

"Hurry up," a voice cried out in despair. "They're dying."

"Oh, my God. No," somebody whispered as they finally

reached the stopped Winnebago. "We're too late. They've burned up in there."

"Oh, heaven no," another voice cried. "No, no, it can't be. Look at them—they're still sitting there, burning in those seats."

"I can't look. I can't look," screamed another voice. "Oh, no, I can't. Those poor people... they've burned alive in there."

"Uh, hey, you guys, look," someone shouted, trying to get everyone's attention. "A car is coming down the road."

"Doesn't look like it's on fire or anything," another voice said.

"Not moving very fast either," someone else added.

"Don't nobody touch that motor home!" Sheriff Blake yelled to the crowd gathering around. "We got nurses here, and they'll keep watch until the local coroner and his team get here to see exactly what happened."

"Does anybody recognize that thing?" one of the deputized men asked.

"Is there really anyone still inside it?" a voice questioned.

"Can't you see, young man?" a woman answered. "Just come over here and you'll see the charred remains of at least two people. I can't tell if they're male or female."

"Uh, somebody get a canvas or something," Blake requested. "Don't need these bodies on display like this."

"Hey, look!" another voice yelled. "Looks like another car's coming, not far behind the first one."

"Yeah, and it's pulling a trailer," someone else added.

"They're all coming down out of the mountains," a woman said. "Just look—here comes another one, right behind them."

"What's going on around here, Sheriff?" a passenger in the first vehicle asked. "Did someone have a serious accident? We're seeing debris scattered all over the place up there."

"And somebody up there kept setting off loud explosions and rocking us just about all the way into the streams," the driver said, laughing. "Hell, I plumb forget about fishing anymore, Sheriff.

They just kept setting all those things off."

"To be truthful, Sheriff," the passenger said, "I think some-body up there must've gotten mighty pissed off at the fish and just outright decided to blow them all to kingdom come with a stick of highly explosive dynamite or something, 'cause I tell you, that campground was a-shakin', and I tell you, it just wouldn't stop."

"What y'all up here talking about?" a woman from the second car came walking up, saying, "Now, I hope you letting the sheriff know about that fool up there scaring away all the fish, ain't-cha?"

"That's exactly what we are doing, Elli Mae," the passenger said. "Crazy nut up there needs to be arrested and put in jail to pay for his actions, you ask me."

"What's that thing up there in the road doing, Sheriff?" the driver of the first car asked. "Is it part of the parade?"

"Look, I don't wanna be, uh, you know, scaring y'all any more than I'm sure you already are, but—"

CHAPTER ELEVEN

"HOLD UP! YOU GUYS LISTENING TO THAT?" I asked them. "Man, somebody was just saying something over the transmitters about some weird shit going on up in Stonyford right now, as I speak."

"What did you hear?" Tony asked.

"Man, look," I said, somewhat confused. "All I can say is that I just heard somebody saying that everything up there in Stonyford is going haywire, and that people are being found dead or something."

"Man, Murdock," Pee-Wee asked, "are you sure that's what you just heard?"

"Yeah, he's right," the medical examiner said. "That's why I'm going to release you people so you can get on about your business and go up there to see what's happening."

"Damn!" I said out loud. "Everybody back onboard your craft. Gotta move as fast as we can."

"You mean to tell me, after all this time on the ground, now we got a serious emergency jumping off up there in Stonyford?" the Cat questioned. "I mean, in the dead of the night?"

The Cat was right, I thought to myself. Here we were—we had landed out here on this highway early this morning, and now, late at night, this was happening. I couldn't believe it either, but I guess that's just another part of this strange life we live. Stonyford was supposed to be busy with their festivity celebration, enjoying all the supposedly joyous happenings. From my understanding, the town's rebound was going to be like the summers down in New Orleans when Mardi Gras is at its best. There were supposed to be carnivals, parade processions, and ceremonial marches of troops of people all dressed in bright, colorful costumes.

There was also supposed to be a bright, joyous display of elegant fashion for everyone to enjoy, an opportunity for people to place themselves on exhibit so the world could see their beauty displayed so lavishly. Even the elderly—and the not-so-elderly— were expected to leisurely walk and strut down the well-lit streets in their affectedly self-important gait and manner, just for such an occasion.

"All right, Mr. Murdock," Karen suddenly asked me, surprisingly. "Just what is it that you're thinking about? I know you have a lot on your mind, am I right?"

Little did she know, she weighed the most on my mind. I guess it was a serious challenge trying to balance my deep feelings and emotions for her. Truthfully, I really wanted to make love to Karen. I wanted to be inside her like never before, feeling her every move in response to my rhythmical movements—a rhythm without worry or stress, though lasting for a quiet duration. Making love to Karen would be like a smooth, recurrent pattern, formed by many soft, gentle notes of speech from our voices, and from the true sincerity of our hearts. To taste her would be like combining the depth of a jazz note with a strong backbeat from some downhome blues.

"Well," she said softly, "aren't you going to invite me into whatever it is that's captivated you so we can experience it together?"

"Didn't see you standing there, Karen," I said, wondering if maybe what I was telling her was a lie. "I was just thinking about this trip back up to Stonyford. Do you remember coming this way with me years ago?"

"Know, I can't say I do," she said. "Are you sure it was me?"

"Redding's just up the road from here," I told her. "Now do you remember?"

"No, Mr. Murdock," she said again, smiling. "I think you've got me mixed up with someone else."

"Remember these train tracks?" I asked, looking toward the state of Oregon.

"And why are you doing this to me?" she asked, forming a mental image of what she knew I was referring to.

"And what about that scar on your forehead?" I asked her. "How did that happen? How did you end up getting it?"

Silence.

"I don't remember," she said. "Why don't you remind me?"

I thought about the fact that if it weren't for Tony, I'd embrace Karen with all my might. This was something I yearned to do. I'm not ashamed to admit I cried many tears for this lady, but I am also fully aware that she too cried many tears because of the hurt I brought into her life after our marriage. A week or two into what was supposed to be the marriage of a lifetime—a fairy-tale wedding come true for both of us—and what did I do? I blew it within two weeks after we said our "I do's." I ruined the best wedding one could ever imagine. And yes, Karen was dressed like a real fairy-tale bride. The moment was perfect, with some of the best people in the world attending.

Being so near her was something I had yearned for most of my life. And here we stood, so close to each other. But now she belonged to Tony. Years had gone by, from then to now, and all I could do was nothing—absolutely nothing—to turn back the hand of time. And Lord knows, if I could, I wouldn't waste a second returning to that particular day, to stand firm with her beside me, and go home as I should have, hand in hand.

But I have to face the fact that I fucked up. I blew the best thing that could have ever happened in my life.

Am I suffering for it?

You goddamn right.

"That scar on your forehead will forever be my signature," I told her, doing everything I could to restrain myself from kissing those sweet, soft lips. "And although I didn't put the scar there, I'm still taking full responsibility for it being there."

The scar was considered unique and distinctive. It was like a token, a symbol—like a musical staff indicating the true essence and mark of the most important elements in a relationship. It represented the nature of her beautiful texture, containing an essential trait, a characteristic inherited from the best.

"You didn't put it there," she said.

"No. But I'm taking full responsibility," I told her regardless.

"Uh, what about this food?" an officer asked suddenly. "There's quite a bit."

"What food?" I inquired, wondering what he was talking about. "What is it that you're talking about? Food? What food?"

"These people are saying that somebody placed an order for this food," the officer said. "And it seems to me it's arriving just on time."

"Hold up, man," somebody said. "Uh, yeah. That's what I ordered."

"About time," a voice said. "I'm hungry as hell out here."

"Hey, Knucklehead," I called out. "Uh, you wanna check and see if June would like to, you know, be in charge of this?"

"That's a pretty good idea," Knucklehead said. "She's the lady for the job."

"And a damn good job," someone added.

"I'll check if you want me to," a female crew member said. "I'm really infatuated with the way she arranges everything."

"All right with me, if that's what you wanna do," Knuckle-head told her. "Nothing like having people like family assisting you, and that's just what she's got out here—family."

"Hey, can I help?" another female voice asked. "I'm riding with the Lodi crew."

"Sure you can," Knucklehead told her. "Just follow this young lady here and she'll lead the way."

"Now wait a minute with all that young lady stuff," a female voice said. "I know you're not talking about me being young, are you? But, on the other hand, I really wanna thank you kindly for the compliment, young man."

Everybody laughed.

"And speaking of the Chef," one of the female voices said, re-ferring to June, who was moving about. "Here comes our head chef now."

"Okay, you guys," June said, smiling. "Just what are you up to?"

"Uh, yeah. Well, uh, we really haven't met yet, but my name is Julia, and this here is, I think, Stacey," Julia said, introducing both Stacey and herself to June. "And we were just wondering—"

"They are wondering if you wouldn't mind taking charge of the evening meal," Knucklehead jumped in. "Cause they want to assist you, provided you accept the offer."

"Sure," June said without hesitation. "I'll be glad to. And I wouldn't have any problem with the two of you helping me."

"With all the food, you'll probably have a few more join you," I told her.

"Well, how would you want me to do this?" June asked me. "You know, I understand we'll be headed out pretty soon."

"That's right," I responded, realizing our mission to be air-borne in a matter of minutes. "Yeah, we gotta hurry up and get to Stonyford. Guess you guys can just pass this stuff out."

"Well, with enough help," June said, "we can just wrap everybody up a paper plate full of everything."

"Can you do that?" I asked her.

"Where're the paper plates?" June asked.

"We have plenty," one of the caterers said, pointing to a large box containing the plates. "As many as you need, plus doggy bags. All free of charge."

"Uh, you wouldn't happen to be part of that media crew headed up to Stonyford, would you?" one of the caterers asked Cat.

"Well, that all depends on what you've been hearing," Cat said, grinning.

"Man," the caterer said, smiling. "We've been hearing everything about you guys on the news. They were even talking about these helicopters and how dangerous they are to fly."

"I told you it was them," one of the caterers said to the other, excited at the thought of being in our presence. "I knew it, dude. I knew it was them we were bringing all this food to."

"Did you guys have any problem getting here?" the Cat asked.

"Well, that's how I knew it had to be for you guys," one of the caterers said, looking around. "At first, those police officers acted like they weren't going to let us bring this to you, but then all of a sudden, they said, 'Hurry up on up there.'"

"But remember what that one officer said?" one of the caterers asked the other, trying to jog his memory about what the officer told them as soon as they were allowed to deliver the food.

"No," he said. "What'd he say? I can't remember."

"Remember, he said that if we saw anything out of the ordinary happening, we were to turn around immediately and hurry back as fast as we possibly could," the other reminded him.

"You don't know what he was referring to?" I asked.

"All I know is that whatever it was," one of the caterers said, "it had me really afraid to even come this way. I mean, it had me paranoid as hell."

"Yeah, well," I muttered. "Let's just get this food onboard so we can be on our way."

"Wish I could go with you," one of the caterers said seriously.

"Me too," the other added. "We could help serve the food."

"Thanks for offering," Pee-Wee told them, "but this is a job I really don't think you're ready for."

"But we were thinking about driving on up there anyway," one of the caterers said. "That's where we're headed. I know the way; one of my friends lives not far from there."

"That's good," Pee-Wee said. "Then maybe you guys can help us out when it comes time to eat."

"I don't know about that," the caterer said. "With all the celebration and festivity they're doing up there, they already have more food than any of us could eat in a lifetime. Everybody's up in Stonyford partying tonight and getting drunk big time. Everything is happening up there. That's where all these people were headed on this highway before they started crashing into each other."

"What all do you guys have for us?" June asked the caterers.

"Let's see here," one of the caterers said, unfolding a list. "We've got all kinds of fresh, delicious fruit—mainly strawberries and blackberries. Cases of various sodas and Sunny D, yogurt, toaster strudels, chips, and Kroger Deluxe Ice Cream, both hot and fresh. Also fresh apples, grapefruits, bananas, tomatoes, and some California clementines—plus fresh oranges and peeled carrots."

"What about something with meat?" Tony asked. "You know, like pork loin chops or something."

"Was just getting to that part of the list," the caterer said. "Uh, yeah, here we go. Pork chops, boneless; fresh chicken breasts; boneless chuck arm roast; Honeysuckle ground turkey—"

"Yeah, and what about some seafood?" I had to interrupt.

"Uh, I was just about to get to that too," the caterer said, scanning his list. "Sockeye salmon fillets, Kroger jumbo shrimp poppers, deli boneless wings—we've got pounds of those. Pinto beans, kidney beans, Hormel chili with beans, catfish fillets. And for anyone who wants a special breakfast selection, regardless of the time—morning, noon, or night—the delicious hashbrown meal is perfect."

"What comes with it?" a voice asked.

"Well, let me see," the caterer said. "Ever how many hash-browns you want, with as many eggs as you want, all sunny-side up, with your choice of bacon, sausage, or both. Oh, and before I forget, we've got fresh frosted sugar cookies, Dutch country pumpkin rolls, Hostess Twinkies and brownies, several varieties of Sara Lee bread, and plenty of other things—you'll just have to check them out yourselves."

"Hey, Murdock," Knucklehead called, curious about something.

"Yeah, what's that?" I asked.

"I bet you anything that fella is gay," he whispered.

"Oh, yeah? Is that right?" I responded. "Well, I bet I can catch him and take him out on a date."

My statement surprised Knucklehead, but I was only trying to teach him a thing or two about judging people. I don't think that was his intention, but I wanted him to learn something about himself. One thing's for sure—after that, he never asked me anything like that again.

It had to be either Karen or possibly June who fixed me this nice bowl of some damn good chili beans, with crackers and a sprinkle of onions on top. I say Karen because she knew this was my favorite chili. For dessert, there was carrot cake and pecan pie —another couple of my favorites.

Just about everything a person could imagine when it came to food was there, and these ladies made sure we had it all.

And now it was time again for the trip to Stonyford. "Hey, guys," I said to the caterers. "Thanks for everything. You've been paid in full, and I'm sure you got a little extra for your services. Wish you could ride up to Stonyford with us, but laws restrict that privilege on our helicopters. I'm sure you understand. Just know we're looking forward to seeing you there, celebrating like never before."

Once again, the engines on our helicopters roared in deep, thunderous tones, every inboard and outboard light fully functional, cutting through the darkness to clarify our identification.

"Tony, Pee-Wee, Knucklehead, Cat, and MacDonald," I yelled over the transmitter. "It's time. Let's head for Stonyford, guys."

Within seconds, we were once again airborne, jamming to The Rolling Stones' *I Can't Get No Satisfaction* and AC/DC's *Highway to Hell.*

I found myself manipulating the throttle in the MH-53, peering to my left to see Pee-Wee doing the same, as did The Cat. With all the seemingly evil forces pushing hard against our crafts, it felt as if I were drilling my way through the devil's own body of thick wind, the powerful pressure pressing against me from every direction.

"Ain't no stopping me now, you fuckin' motherfucker," I cursed, directing my anger at the only one I felt responsible for everything unfolding and fighting against us.

My previous visit to this region had been when I had first started this story about Margaret. From the beginning, I knew Satan was responsible—and I also knew it was the mission of my team of news reporters and experienced journalists to bring to the world's attention what was happening throughout the Stonyford region.

Flying and navigating our crafts high above the huge mountains through the pitch-black night felt somewhat like a ship sailing the open sea, making its way to a particular destination. The feel of the wind pressing against my craft was truly awesome, especially when relying on my instrument panel as each of our helicopters penetrated the black sky.

"Hey, Tony," I said to break the monotony onboard my helicopter. "Whatever happened to that crazy dog you used to have? You know, the one who always used to growl at me?"

"What dog was that?" Karen interrupted, grinning. "What dog was that?"

"Mmm," Tony mumbled. "That used to growl at you? You mean bark at you?"

"No, I'm talking about that little brown dog you guys used to have that always stared at me but didn't want me staring at it. You know, the one who stared at me, but whenever I called myself staring back, the damn thing—for some weird reason—would always start growling at me for no reason."

"Man, when was this?" Tony asked, confused. "I mean, how long ago was this?"

"Well, I guess you can say it's been years ago, Tony," I said. "Far too many to think about."

"And how many is that?" Karen just had to ask.

"Okay, Karen," I told her. "Let's not go there."

"Mmm," she mumbled. "Must be something you don't want to remember?"

"Now there you go again, Karen," Tony said. "If he didn't want to remember anything, he wouldn't have asked me about some dog that I'm having a hard time trying to remember myself."

"That's all right," I said, taking a spoonful of chili into my mouth.

"Want me to feed you while you fly this thing?" Karen asked me in front of Tony, causing me to choke and cut off what little air I had left in my windpipe.

"No, thank you!" I quickly said in a grungy voice, gasping for air. "I got it. It's not the first time I've flown this thing while eating. Plus, at this altitude, you know, high up in the sky, if anything goes wrong, there'll be enough time for me to jump out."

At first there was complete silence, and then, "whatT?" both Tony and Karen shouted. "Jump out?" Tony exclaimed.

"Hey, you guys," I quickly said, laughing. "Man, I'm just playing."

CLICK! CLICK! CLICK!

CLICK! CLICK! CLICK!

"Scare Crow, you copy??" Sacro called.

"Copy," I answered. "Whassup, Sacro?"

"You picking up anything buzzing us?"

"Now, who the fuck is that?" I said, checking out my radar device. "Man, Tony, why didn't you tell me we had company on our tail following us?"

"Ah, man," Tony said, looking out the windows. "How can you tell when something like that's happening?"

"Man, check the radar," I told him. "See that little dot right there?"

"Yeah, I see it," Karen said, pointing. "It's right there, moving."

"Oh, yeah. I see it," Tony said. "What is it?"

"Somebody following us," I told him.

"Can you tell who it is?" Tony asked.

"Yep," I answered. "That's exactly what I'm doing right now."

"Who is it?" Karen asked.

"Well, from the looks of things," I said, "the object is an aircraft. I think it's something like the one we saw land on that highway. You remember? The Cat mentioned seeing them over in Nevada at the air show."

"Oh, yeah. Now I remember," Tony said, moving closer to the radar. "The Cat did mention seeing them at the air show."

"And, Karen, of all people?" I said, nodding my head. "I just knew you'd remember."

"But how can you tell who it is?" Tony asked.

"Well, pilots recognize certain types of objects," I explained. "It's part of our job—notice things, especially when we're flying."

"Okay," Tony said, curious. "What is it?"

"See the shape of that thing?"

"Yeah."

"Once you recognize shapes and objects, you can distinguish them for what they really are," I told him. "And clearly!"

"Okay," Tony said again. "Then what is it?"

"It's one of those new UH-72A Lakotas—a Light Utility Helicopter designed for law enforcement missions."

"So, who do you think is following us in that one?" Karen asked.

"Do you remember one of the pilots flying the Lakota asking, 'Who the hell are we?'"

"I think I remember something like that," Tony said.

"Well, when he asked, he looked at us really hard and then said something like, 'Never mind, don't tell me. You guys are that crazy group of reporters we've been getting all kinds of weird calls about—flying erratically all over those goddamn hills.' That was when Cat started grinning, because the pilot immediately recognized him."

"So, who's the pilot?" Karen asked me.

"All we know him by is the Commander," I said, peering out my side window to see if I could spot the Lakota. "Before he got pissed about Cat making that statement about him taking on this responsibility, the Commander just knew we had something to do with whatever's going on around here."

"So, that's him following us?" Tony asked.

"That's him, all right," I answered. "He's piggybacking on our tail on this trip to Stonyford."

"Uh, hey, Scare Crow. You copy?" a voice said over the transmitter.

"Copy," I said. "Who's calling?"

"Uh, this is Lodi."

"Whassup, Lodi?" I asked.

"Just thought you should know, we got company tagging."

"Copy," I responded. "But are you guys out there checking the radar screen? If so, I do believe a few more just appeared."

"Copy that, Scare Crow. Lodi on the low low."

"Just who's out there?"

"Let me get this one, Murdock," Tony said. "Do it."

"Uh, who's out there? Wanna know?" Tony asked. "This ain't nothin' but the Knucklehead riding up high with Sacro. You copy?"

"Copy that, Knucklehead," Tony responded. "What's happening?"

"Just that I get nosey on ya," Knucklehead said, snickering. "Hope y'all don't mind me in the convo?"

"Not at all, Knucklehead," Tony told him. "But you know we got company, don't you?"

"That's a big copy, my friend," Knucklehead said. "Got an eye on 'em."

"All right everybody, listen up," I said over the transmitter. "This is the Scare Crow. Keep strict vigil and be thorough at all times. Don't limit yourselves—use your judgment fully. Move deliberately and decisively to counter whatever is prowling in our region, stalking and destroying without mercy."

If you look outside your crafts, you'll likely see others following us on this mission. People are curious and eager to understand what's happening—and most are as inquisitive as we are about the strange events unfolding throughout the region.

Am I scared? Afraid of myself dying on this flight into the unknown? You damn right I am. That's the honest answer.

But people are dying mysteriously, and, as hard as it is to believe, there's evidence of some kind of transformation taking place. Cemeteries, mortuaries, even morgues are empty. Word is that these bodies have been seen walking among the living.

Please, don't bombard me with questions. I know a million things are running through your minds, but there are reasons to worry—and reasons to wonder. This mission was assigned to me, and I invited all of you because I knew you could handle it.

We still have quite a distance ahead. If anyone wants to call it quits, speak up now—save us valuable time. Yes? No? Last chance. Just like a marriage: forever hold your peace.

CLICK! CLICK! CLICK!

CLICK! CLICK! CLICK!

"Let's do this!" a voice said over the transmitter.

"Yeah, let's do this, Scare Crow!" another voice replied.

"I thought you knew? I'm already waiting on you guys," added another.

"Ain't never been there," someone said sharply. "But all of y'all better get me there—and quick!"

"I'm with you, buddy," someone said, sounding like a wild cowboy yelling. "Yee-haw, Yee-haw!" "People," I said out loud over the transmitter. "Welcome aboard."

By this time, everyone had begun to position themselves for the long flight to Stonyford. Settling in with a bodily posture as if with a very sharp attitude of tranquility, it was time once again to try stabilizing our thoughts through a mutual accord.

The dark evening sky felt calm and undisturbed as each heli-copter sailed smoothly and effortlessly, like sailing vessels moving between the huge mountains, steep slopes, and rugged terrain—with respect for the wildlife living in their natural environment.

Suddenly: Click! Click! Click!

Click! Click! Click!

"Uh, Scarecrow," a voice said, sounding curious. "You copy?"

"Copy," Tony answered.

"Man, uh," the voice began. "Uh, I just wanted to know, could you help me out with something?"

"Sure. What's that?" Tony asked.

"Well, I was just thinking," the voice said. "And, you know, um, I was just thinking about something you said a bit earlier, about these bodies having been seen walking amongst the living."

"And?" Tony said, trying to urge whoever it was to say what was apparently bothering them.

"Well, I was just wondering," the voice continued hesitantly. "Like, you know? Are you saying that this mission is really something like that movie *The Walking Dead*?"

"Not at all," I quickly interrupted. "No, that's not what I'm saying."

"Uh, excuse me, you guys," a female voice said. "But, that's the same question I wanted to ask you."

"No, this isn't about that movie," I told not only the people who were curious, but the entire team. "Whatever it is that we're up against on this mission, please keep in mind the facts that there is enough proof and data to substantiate the claim about some form of a serious metamorphosis that's taking place up there. There is a transformation going on, and from what has been related to everyone, the cemeteries, mortuaries, and morgues are all empty of their bodies. People are saying in just about every area of the region that some of these bodies have been seen, and that they have been seen walking amongst the living."

"Some creepy bullshit," Tony said, staring at Sandra and Regina. "What do you think, Regina? You guys haven't said a word."

"Just busy checking out everything on this laptop," Regina told him.

"Oh, yeah," Tony said. "Maybe that's what you need to be doing, Karen. It'll help you keep your mind occupied."

"Sounds like he's saying you're repugnant, Karen," I added.

"Not hardly," Karen said. "Though, it is somewhat annoying being, you know, couped up too long in such closed quarters with this man. But that's only if you really wanna know the truth about it. You feel me?"

"You're the one causing everything to be congested up in here," Tony said, smirking. "That's why I'm cracking this window to get some fresh air. I need some ventilation."

"Yeah," said Karen informally. "Talk about repugnance. I honestly do at times wish I'd never come on this trip. You're so full of fear, it's like embarrassing to think about."

"Is that right?" Tony exclaimed, staring out one of the side windows.

"You're so pathetic, Tony," Karen said angrily. "And the thing about your patheticness is that you know it's the truth."

"Yeah, well—"

"Mmmm," I quickly mumbled, interrupting their conversation. "Uh, before you get too carried away with your conversation, keep in mind the fact about this mission being serious. You feel me? We really haven't the time for all the bickering."

"Yeah," Karen said, smiling slightly. "Oh, I apologize. It's just that at times—"

"Yeah, I apologize too, Murdock," Tony said. "I'll leave it at that."

"Well, to be truthful," I began. "I'm really happy about the fact that both of you, including Regina and Sandra, could come on this trip with me because your presence is important to me and I want you to know it. I really do appreciate us being together again. Hey, being that it's been years since we've last had such an opportunity."

"I hear you on that one," Tony said, nodding his head. "Man, it's been years."

"And just think about all the people who didn't make it this far," I said, thinking about friends and family members who passed. "And, Karen, man, you just don't know how much I'm missing your people. I mean, I really wish they were here to see us now. I'd really like to talk to them and apologize for my behavior. I'm serious, Karen. I have always thought about them. I mean—they really put our wedding together. All the presents and everything. They just knew our marriage was going to last forever. But little did anybody see what was coming when I fucked it up."

"Hey, hey, hey now, Murdock," Karen said, interrupting. "Just like you put a stop to what me and Tony were doing, I'm going to stop you before your emotions start spilling over and you won't be able to fly this thing."

"Yeah, you're right," I told her. "It's emotional, and I could go on forever feeling sorry about what I did. You just don't know how awful I feel, Karen. I married you because I love you, just like I do today. It's like—"

"Oh no," Tony said. "Don't tell me we're going to have to find a violin to play?"

Laughing.

"You might," I told him seriously. "I'm crazy about this lady. But I also have to at all times respect the fact that the two of you are a couple."

"Not for long if he don't quit acting stupid," Karen said.

"Stupid?" Tony said, turning slowly around from looking out the window. "Just who are you calling stupid?"

"Y'all just don't know when to quit," Regina suddenly said. "What you guys need to be doing is getting some serious marriage counseling, 'cause it's like, ever since we been on this trip, all of y'all been on something. And that's including you too, Murdock. You guys need some serious help."

Click! Click! Click!

Click! Click! Click!

"Scarecrow, you copy? This is that there, uh, Knucklehead."

"Copy, Knucklehead," I responded. "Whassup?"

"Uh, I just wanted to know if any of y'all was listening to that? You know, something being said on the news station."

"Like what?" I asked him.

"Just something 'bout the situation we're heading into down there," he said. "Something 'bout a serial killer at large."

"Uh, excuse me for interrupting, but my wife was just asking me if I heard it," a crew member from one of the helicopters said. "But what she was saying was that the celebration going on there in Stonyford, well, it's in serious trouble. Or supposed to be in some sort of serious trouble."

"What channel are you guys listening to?" I asked, curious as to what I was hearing.

"Don't know for sure," the voice said. "She just happened to be trying to find her favorite music station when she came across it."

"Think it was coming from somewhere up there in Humboldt County, like in or around Eureka," another voice added. "But they're up there saying one of their residents had been possibly mauled by something they called a Bigfoot-looking thing."

"Are you guys really serious?" a voice sounding like Pee-Wee asked.

"Somebody's been drinking just a little too much," another voice said.

"Just what in seems name are you talking about?" a woman's voice asked the person who made the statement about drinking. "Ain't nobody on this trip and mission supposed to be doing any drinking. That's a no-no! So get your information right, buster."

Everybody laughed over the transmitter.

"Hey, I think what y'all been listening to is that crazy stuff about them people up there in the north seeing all them goddamn 'Sasquatches' all over the place running around," someone said. "It's the whole goddamn family of them Bigfoot creatures running amuck up there seemingly in a frenzy, you know, killing people."

"Like hell," a voice shouted. "Them things ain't no Bigfoot! It's a for-real serial killer out there in front of us terrorizing and intimidating that entire region."

"Okay, hold up, you guys," Karen quickly yelled over the transmitter. "Now check this out. Just hold up for a minute; they are about to say something about what's happening. Here it is:

'We're unsure how many killers are out there, but we do know a serial killer is likely responsible for the bodies we are finding throughout the Stonyford region. There had been speculation that a group could be responsible, but the theory now is that one person might be the lone culprit. Nearby communities are also worried because there is speculation that "zombies" have been spotted mingling among the living, and in this case, word is you can't tell the difference. The entire Northern California region is said to be experiencing such events. We'll keep you up to date should we hear anything.'"

"Now don't start jumping to conclusions, guys," Karen said. "That's not the thing to be doing at the moment. And don't forget our mission and the job we're supposed to be doing."

"Damn, Tony," I said, staring at Karen. "Just who is that lady sounding authoritative up in here?"

"Man, Murdock. Your guess is as good as mine," said Tony.

"Don't believe it," Regina said. "Sounds like somebody is taking power of command."

"I think you influenced her to do that, Murdock," Sandra said, grinning at Karen. "Now, you big woman in power in here."

Karen blushed broadly.

"Just look at her," I said, smiling. "Now the juice is on you, Karen."

Click! Click! Click!

Click! Click! Click!

"We copy, whoever you are," Tony said over the transmitter.

"Uh, just thought I'd tag along with you guys. But that's only if you don't mind the extra company?"

"Can't say I do," Tony answered. "Can't say I do. But who are you?"

"It's that goddamn Commander," a voice sounding like the Cat rang out. "I knew it, I tell you. I knew it!"

"Yeah, well. Welcome aboard, Commander," I told him. "Uh,

I do believe a member of this crew was already anticipating your arrival to join us."

"Is that right?" the Commander said somewhat arrogantly. "I was on your butts all the time, trailing you without you ever knowing it, young man. Could've shot you down if I'd wanted to, and mainly that stinking Cat! But my kindness decided to let you prevail so that you could do your good deed."

"Yeah, is that right?" I said.

"Goddamn skippy, youngster," the Commander said, snickering. "I'm the one ruling this shit up here during the night."

"Might be so," I told him. "But I just bet you didn't know the facts that you and your flunkies were being observed the moment you started, you know, trailing us."

"Like hell we were," the Commander said, surprisingly. "You ain't got that kind of power."

"No?" I said in an attempt to catch him off guard. "Just look around you and you'll notice what's been awaiting your arrival."

"Just what the hell they call you, youngster?" the Commander asked.

"Scarecrow!" somebody yelled out over the transmitter. "You don't want to fuck with the Scarecrow, Commander."

"Yeah, uh," another voice interrupted. "Uh, I hope I'm not being rude or anything by jumping into the conversation without being invited. But I just had to try and seize this opportunity as selfish and eagerly verbal attack it might seem from me. But I just happen to be out here on the sideline observing you too, Commander. Though—"

"And just who the hell are you?" the Commander asked as if he were screaming into his mic.

"Yeah, well," the voice began to introduce himself. "I'm Head Flight Commander, Robert Verge, and Commander of a Special Force Division in a particular branch of activities."

"Yeah, yeah, yeah," the Commander said. "I'm already fully

aware of who you are, now that you've mentioned it. Ain't got no kind of dispute with you there, Flight Commander."

"But, I think I just might have a question or two for you, Head Flight Commander, Robert Verge," I quickly said, jumping into the conversation. "I recall hearing you say something about 'Special Force.' Is that right?"

"Special Force," Flight Commander Robert Verge answered. "That's just what you heard."

"Cool, got no problem," I told him. "Only thing is, on this mission we have only one force: us! Do you copy?"

"As the Commander said, and without any doubts whatsoever," Commander Robert Verge said. "But one thing."

"And that is?" I asked.

"Just who are you?"

"I'm Murdock," I told him. "Navigator of the Scare Crow. This is my team. And you, Commander Robert Verge, just where are you from?"

"The Midwest," he said. "Missouri, Kansas, and whatever. I'm there."

"Man, Murdock," a voice yelled out. "Just call em KC, and be done."

"Just how the hell you know if or not he wanna be called that?" the voice of a woman said. "I think y'all should call him Midwest!"

"I'd second that motion," another voice said.

"Third it," another voice said in agreement.

"Damn, too many KCs out there as it is," someone else said. "Midwest will do just fine if you ask me."

"Well, what do you think, Flight Commander Robert Verge?" I asked.

"I copy that motion," he said.

"Cool," I told him. "Welcome aboard."

"Copy," he responded.

"Hey, Midwest," somebody called out. "Man, what's the name of the helicopters you guys are flying? Are they Lakotas?"

"Uh, no. That's a negative, buddy," Midwest said. "We're flying these badass AAS-72X+s up here. High on performance that I'm sure no other class can touch or even match."

"Ah, shit!" someone said. "Here we go again."

"Nah, you guys," Midwest again said, attempting to explain himself.

"Eventually, on this mission, you have a chance to prove yourself," I told him. "Plenty of time to swallow your pride. Or, choke! One or the other on this mission."

"Hey there, Scare Crow," Midwest called out.

"What's that?" I answered.

"We in the Midwest have been told that there's a lot of exorcism taking place there in Stonyford. Is that true?" Midwest asked.

"To be truthful, guys," I said to everyone involved, "it's a lot of everything going on up there. From copycat killers to serial murderers, from my understanding. Some of the people are really serious about believing that Lucifer's dragons are about to be unleashed from the bottomless pit. And those things the people up there in Humboldt County are calling 'Big Foot' or 'Sasquatches,' what is that? Those are Satan's fallen angels. Huge giants from heaven accused of trying to overthrow God's kingdom. They have been described as huge giant monsters.

"Unfortunately, the entire region is in serious trouble. Many of the people in the region, considering themselves Christians, are believing that it is God who is going to save them from the harsh, brutal intimidation that's been violently bestowed on the entire region."

"So, you've been there before?" a voice sounding like Midwest asked.

"On numerous occasions," I answered. "In fact, Stonyford has a few very memorable moments for me that from time to time I find myself looking back on. Though not my favorable."

"So, you know all about that place?" the voice suggested.

"Is this Midwest I'm talking to?" I asked.

"Copy!" he answered.

"Check this out, Midwest," I said, curious. "You know, like, under the circumstances and having such an opportunity. Tell me something. Just what is your mission on this journey? I mean—"

"Excuse me?" Midwest interrupted.

"No! What I mean is, what is your purpose for, you know, really wanting to be a part of this mission?" I asked him. "Like, are you even at all in any way familiar with—"

I was trying my best not to sound too personal by being, I guess you can say, too inquisitive or even furtively prying into his personal life. But there was just something about this guy that I had to find out. And from the sound of his voice, it was like the tone when I'd asked him the question—the sound of his voice was somewhat miffed when I began questioning him.

"Scare Crow, right?" Midwest asked. "That's what they call you?"

"That's right," I answered again, curious.

"Years ago, a group of people went up there to, I guess, investigate the situation of a reported call for help," Midwest began saying over the transmitter. "All that I can say is that they were from the Sacramento Division. A guy they called Sheriff Johnny Blake Sr. was leading the team. He was the Stonyford top sheriff on duty at the time. The group of people from the Sacramento, California division were supposed to be investigating the death of a little girl there in Stonyford named Wanda Johnson. This girl had been very savagely brutalized in a horrible, horrible manner with such an extreme taste to where, for some strange reason, the entire town just began placing the blame on her other sister, named Margaret.

"It was like this entire region, for some unknown reason, had an itch to blame Margaret. From just reading the report, I too was shocked and dismayed. I couldn't believe what I was reading. It was a feeling of pure horror, like what you'd read in a mystery book or even see at the movies.

"That's when I heard about you, Murdock. The firm that I worked for out of Missouri began mentioning your name daily, about how you had come to the state of Kansas, there in Wichita, and had done an interview with Margaret. It was something to hear about. And I guess you can say that my wife became as fascinated and as attracted to the story as I did, like when becoming a true fanatic for something with an irrational attachment to it. We couldn't stop reading about the situation there in Stonyford.

"I mean, sure, you hear about stories like the Amityville killings, which were committed by their son, Ronald 'Butch' DeFeo Jr., back in 1978 at that human-like face-looking house on Ocean Avenue. And you also read about the Lutz family, who purchased the classic Dutch Colonial waterfront estate for a discount price.

"And then, you read again about how within four weeks after purchasing the house, the Lutz family was gone, claiming to be driven from their home by bleeding walls and disembodied voices. This prompted a best-selling book by Jay Anson, *The Amityville Horror: A True Story*, followed along with a parade of movies.

"Throughout the Midwest, the situation there in Stonyford has been dubbed 'Stonyford Submission.' That's because it has been said that all of the people throughout this particular region submitted themselves to Satan. And the old Johnson estate—everybody knows it's haunted. That's an apparition from visits during certain times from that of Satan and the time of the ghost of Wanda to appear. Quite frequently, we hear and read in our reports about how different spirits have been seen, lingering throughout Stonyford.

"But, supernatural beings (ghosts) are something quite frightening, and especially to those of you who fear the unknown."

"And just how does this connect to you, Midwest?" I asked. "I mean, I understand you a little better now that you described your past, but—"

"It's like I was saying, my wife was just as curious, and I, I would guess you'd say we became fascinated. She was called to Sacramento due to her specialized qualification and having met the requirements for such a task, holding her specific position."

"So, just what are you saying," Karen just had to ask. "Like what, I mean, is she still working on this?"

"Yeah, that's what I was wondering," Tony said, peering out one of the side windows, trying to see what helicopter Midwest was flying.

"Remember, we're talking about years past," Midwest said in a rather doubtful tone, as if uncertain about the outcome of the mission. "And all I can say is that she's still up there. Somewhere. And I gotta find her."

"Jesus Christ, man," someone could be heard saying loudly over the transmitter, obviously disturbed by the thought of what Midwest had said.

"Look, I understand where you're going," Midwest said. "But no, she was born quite a few years later. She isn't elderly. She grew up, went to school, and later graduated from law school. She joined the military, receiving her degree, and worked at GE Aviation on extremely critical missions. She's a highly skilled aviation machinist, skilled with both Harrier jets and helicopter engines. In fact, she's also one hell of a pilot. She's flown in combat for our troops, and God knows she served this country well from an expeditionary unit. Hell, you think you can fly that MH-53, Scare Crow? She's a master at her game—MH-53Es, MH-60s, MV-22s, and the CH-53s, and also the UH-1N Hueys, to name a few."

"Hey, damn," someone said. "Got no problem with me."

"Me neither," someone else said.

"I'm here for you, Midwest," another voice said.

"Got room for me?" someone else added.

"We're all here for you, Midwest," I told him. "You can believe that I can feel your pain. Just ask my co-pilot's wife."

"What's her name?" someone asked Midwest. "I'm talking about your wife, man?"

"Goldsby," Midwest said out to everyone over the transmitter. "It's Goldsby. She's still up there, and I intend to find her."

"Uh, God bless you, Midwest," someone said. "But I'm sure you know it is going to be like a freakin' needle in a haystack up there. From listening to what FEMA is saying, the Coast Guard sent teams up there to try helping out on a search-and-rescue mission. They got C-178s and C-5s from all over the place. They're coming from everywhere, you guys."

CHAPTER TWELVE

"And here we go again," is what I said to myself after noticing such a large number of helicopters following in formation behind us. Except this time, there were groups of people joining this mission from different states and counties on what they knew could potentially end up being a lengthy journey.

I couldn't help continuing to think about the massive size of the MH-53 J-Pave Low. I can also honestly admit with excitement that this particular type of aircraft had become my pride and joy. Better yet, it's like a crown jewel—always ready to prove just how valuable it has become to me.

Every so often, I have to restrain myself from wanting to just burst out loudly in laughter. Such thinking comes from the realization of who is responsible for flying this big bird. The MH-53 is enormously huge and outrageously beautiful. It's in a class of its own with first-rate qualities, and the deadly dingy-looking gray and black blades are themselves extremely massive, rotating rapidly in horizontal forceful support of the craft while visibly keeping this very threatening, impressive-looking giant piece of machinery airborne.

Looking around aimlessly, I found myself staring intensively out a few of the half-size gazebo-shaped windows. I then thought to myself that whoever placed such emphasis on the design of the MH-53 really deserved applauding. This particular craft is just about everything needed, especially when it comes to fast geographical acceleration during moments requiring quick, urgent movement through the northern California mountainous region. Such craftsmanship enabled me to maneuver the MH-53 with accuracy while maintaining the proper altitude needed during flight.

The touch, feel, and grip of something so powerful humming in my hands is unlike anything I had ever felt before as this baby shook vibrantly, seemingly itself dancing to an accompaniment of old-school musical classics such as *Does Anybody Really Know What Time It Is?* By Chicago, *You Made Me So Very Happy* by Blood, Sweat & Tears, and *You're Still a Young Man* by Tower of Power.

Another steep, smooth, 60° bank to my right got my Airspeed Indicator, Artificial Horizon, Altimeter, Magnetic Compass, VOR Indicators, and all the RPM gauges suddenly jamming like crazy to every musical instrumentation pounding loudly in conjunction with what was being heard in each of the helicopters flying in formation alongside the MH-53. This very powerful piece of machinery forcefully banked to the left and then into another steep, smooth, downward descent, subjected to heavy wind turbulence. Such agitation was brought about by strong streams of violent unrest within the wind's current that tried to reduce my speed to no avail.

"It's my guess that you don't believe in warning anybody ahead of time to put on their seatbelts," Karen suddenly said while gripping a few of the adjustable leather hand straps inside the helicopter. These straps were used to hold and secure objects during flight. "You must still be in your own little world as usual, Mr. Murdock."

"I don't think he heard you, Karen," Tony said, grinning at her statement. "Better say it again, so he can hear you."

"What's that?" I asked, pretending I wasn't aware of anything.

"I said, you must've forgot to let us know about the seatbelts in here."

"Hold up, wait a minute," I said, pretending to be monitoring the instrument panel and acting like I didn't know what she was talking about, which, in some aspects, was the truth. "OK, now. What's that, Karen?"

"I was talking about what you did," she said, referring to the 60° bank I had made that I was more than sure caused her to feel somewhat drowsy and lightheaded from such a thrusting, heart-gripping rapid descent to a much lower altitude.

"What was that?" I asked again, all the while knowing what she meant. But I guess I just wanted to hear her say it again. It was like I was somehow enjoying hearing Karen repeat herself. Something men have a habit of doing when it comes to a lady we're pretending not to be interested in. We can't seem to help it. It's habitual. Something men find ingrained in their brain. "What is it you're talking about, Karen?"

"Never mind, Mr. Murdock," she said, as though wondering if it was even worth asking or if I was just being silly. "That is quite all right, Mr. Murdock. I know you know what I'm talking about."

"What?" I said again, knowing I was annoying her. "What's that?"

"I said, that's all right," she repeated, staring directly at me with piercing eyes. It was as though she were visualizing herself outright socking me with one of her tightly clenched fists. "Keep it up, Bennie. Just keep it up. You're going to make me put these hands on you."

"Oh, yeah. That reminds me, you guys. Make sure you put on your seatbelts right about now. Things can get a bit rough in here, turbulent-wise. You know what I mean? There isn't anything gen-

tle in this neck of the woods when it comes to airplanes and helicopters," I said, just trying to aggravate Karen by getting under her
skin.

"Yeah! Fine time to let us know," she said harshly. "And I do
believe you know it."

"Just what is it that she's talking about, Tony?" I asked him,
trying my best not to laugh. "All that mumbling and grumbling
she's doing."

"Man, I already told you, Doc. She just don't have it all," Tony
said.

By the end of the conversation, I was back once again in my
own little world just as Karen had said. "Look out everybody down
below, these freakin' helicopters ain't taking no bullshit off nobody," I intended to say to myself, but apparently, I had spoken it
aloud into my microphone-headset, not realizing the entire crew
could hear me over the transmitter. "We coming at you with
deadly force!" Most of the crew found themselves agreeing with
much of what they were hearing from a revolutionary point of
view, feeling it was radical and an abrupt attempt to overthrow the
governmental power of whatever we were about to encounter in
Stonyford.

But as it was well known, it was also time for me to get a much
better grip on things. Realizing that we were now thousands of feet
in the air, in pitch darkness, with our crafts seemingly dancing and
steadily rocking back and forth to the song "Rock Steady" by
Aretha Franklin, while climbing to a very unpredictable altitude
and elevated velocity for helicopters, I knew it was time to start
maneuvering this baby into another uncomfortable steep downward descent while still holding steady altitude.

The MH-53 J-Pave Low, AKA Scare Crow, being the largest in
its class, responded as I made a sharp 45° bank to my right, followed by another quick 65° bank to my left. Coming out of the
climb with a descent at 400 feet per minute, I had far more power

than expected, with everyone following behind, caravanning on this wild venture like a pack of vicious wolves on the hunt.

The instrument gauges in the Scare Crow seemed hyped and hypnotized by the music blasting through the interior communication system. Each instrument was jumping, rocking, and jamming to the heavy rhythm section of "Chase Me" by Con Funk Shun, in time with every maneuver, while the engine hummed along to the beat of "Rumours" by Timex Social Club.

I would guess this entire trip to Stonyford could be summed up in very few words: this group of professional journalists and media personnel were at the moment flying their crafts as if enjoying themselves on a vacation. I was also hoping that, while embarking on this venture, we hadn't, by any intentional means, accidentally harmed any wildlife during the flight in darkness.

But, unfortunately, as is often the case with misfortune and mischievous mishaps, there is sometimes, on most occasions, always a sad event—what you could also call a very unhappy ending —when dealing with the massive rotating blades of such powerful helicopters in motion.

Still, I could only imagine the amount of wildlife we had most likely disturbed or destroyed while sailing smoothly with extreme acceleration through their natural environment throughout the night.

There were many deep, dark valleys, and what could only be described as numerous steep, inclining slopes. There also seemed to be a large number of very dangerous obstacles, all slanting in different directions. Detected on the radar were some of the most astonishing huge mountains and hills, appearing to point upward like thousands of deadly projectiles.

From what could be read on the instrument panel, the vast majority of the obstacles below us appeared to be surrounded, each with a covering that seemed to conceal them. This form of concealment was carefully noted on all the helicopters' radar screens. The description of these obstacles was of a notably thick, rough body surface, like brush encircling them, and they were within a particular proximity of each other.

As I continued to adjust the radar screen in the MH-53 J-Pave Low for a clearer view of the area below us, I could see that the mass of thick brush resembled very sharp, piercing bristles, covering the entire surface like a large furry blanket.

Countless oddly shaped branches protruded outward from the brush, resembling long woolly arms—arms extended or extruded outward in an embracing manner—which was indeed fascinating to observe.

This was the view detected below us on all the screens in each of the helicopters as we continued over the Northern California mountainous region. It was the moment when most of the crew realized not only what we were up against, but that we were venturing profoundly deep into the most extreme parts of the region's terrain.

At times, violent undercurrents could be felt, resembling either rushing water or air flowing heavily against the underbelly of my craft. The swift-moving currents caused the entire crew to experience rough, violent turbulence and a powerful uproaring commotion.

"All right, you guys. Listen up. This is the Scare Crow," I began, addressing the crew. "I'm more than sure we have all by now come into contact with very large flocks of some of the most notorious nocturnal birds, known for flying at night. You can sometimes see these strange nocturnal birds alongside other species like bats and various wildlife, all trying their best to stay clear of the powerful suction and deadly stronghold created by engagement with these helicopters."

"But, sadly, for any group of species or organism, living or dead, when it comes to the power and strength of the birds that each of us have found ourselves in complete control of, the massive blades are something I am more than sure each of you is fully aware would be a horrible experience for anyone to contend with."

A smooth 30° bank to my left, and then another 45° bank to my right, all while at the same time losing more and more altitude. My instrument panel is finally beginning to mellow out.

By now, it had become quite obvious. The town of Stonyford was still within miles ahead of us. This is also when I decided to bring an end to our seemingly joyful, monotonous, unvarying tone and uttered pitch sound that was being made with our voices. This was something done in the first place to try and refrain from re-curring thoughts and ideas. But I'm also sure the crew had sensed the activity as something that was only momentary.

There were thousands of many different colorful lights, much like both Bell-Howell Tac lights and the old customary flashlights, seemingly flashing upward in the distance ahead of us. This is when I began maneuvering the MH-53's throttle, which regulates vaporized fuel flow, while simultaneously checking all the instru-ment gauges and the carburetor heat lever. This important con-stituent element is what's used in aircraft as a very meaningful device during atmospheric flights. It's used particularly when weather conditions are at times unstable. I was checking and making sure there wasn't an excessive amount of ice built up on my craft after coming down from such an altitude as quickly as I did. But one thing for sure, there's no doubt about it after checking the instrument panel. The Directional Gyro, as well as the MH-53's Rudders, had all had one hell of a workout.

Still, we had miles to go ahead of us before we would be ar-riving near our intended destination.

While in deep thought with emotional feelings of empathy, my eyes swelled to a complex situation arising from the song "Dreaming of You" by another of my favorite artists, Selena. I found myself thinking about just how important this crew of some of the most tenderhearted people meant to me. They were ready to give their own lives for the sake of a community of people they really knew nothing about. The only thing on their minds was that the town of Stonyford, California, would be our final destination for this mission. Our intentions were to hopefully do everything we could to rescue and free, or to extricate from danger and confinement, a region of people residing in the most undesirable state.

*

Such an extrication of deliverance would be from the hands of Satan, who had personally sought after this region for himself. Our mission was to bring about an interruption, which included his inauguration, where he would then reinvent himself, making his creative innovation available for everyone to see.

The inauguration of Satan is said to have been described in incredible detail, as though it were being read from something like an ornamental design resembling a scroll. From many perspectives and current official investigations, materials found with the scroll were said to have highly constrained levels of something in the form of Covid-19 on its surface. It's said that such material has been kept confined within the scroll throughout many centuries, and that upon the ceremonious inauguration of Satan, and the release of his multitude of angels, bound together in great chains from the bottomless pit of the Abyss, the highly toxic material would itself be released from the scroll.

A strong wind shall scatter the material amongst many nations. Everyone will bear witness and render as a testimony the birth and death of a loved one during their deep sadness caused by the material's bereavement.

Many nations will undoubtedly categorize the material as an established chemical compound from a foreign country. But however catastrophic the blame is placed, the disaster will be widespread and prevalent, an affliction much like a deadly plague with an impact on everyone regardless of their nationality, traditions, or the constitution of their faith.

*

I'm more than sure the residents of nearby communities that we most likely flew over very swiftly during what we thought was late night or early morning found themselves surprisingly startled and terribly frightened from the sound of all the helicopters. It's also my guess that the people who could hear us, and were able to get a vague description, found themselves experiencing what's known as a sudden emotional shock while observing our crafts flying at such a low shallow altitude over them, and within feet of their homes.

I'm also sure the people observing us thought perhaps a few of the helicopters were going to end up crashing into one of the farmhouses. Inasmuch as what was expected, there were groups of people anticipating seeing one or more of the helicopters crash and burst into flames from flying at such a low altitude in pitch darkness.

But I was, without them knowing it, very much aware of the area and intended location we were headed, being that I was once one of the young kids who resided at the boys' ranch at the lower basin of Snow Mountain.

I was fully aware of any possible danger lurking and concealed in the wee hours of the night sky, like that of utility poles, or very powerful high-hanging electrical wires, and far too many connections and structural support systems. I was also fully aware of systems with wires that were all bundled and twisted tightly together to form heavy-duty cables that carried high-voltage power lines and electrical current throughout the region.

There could again be seen quite a large number of various bright lights in a short distance ahead of us. Some of the lights seemed to be pointing in an upward position, as though directly at each of the helicopters. From our point of view, the lights could only be described as something in the form of highly powerful searchlights. These lights were once used with a strong beam to illuminate enemy aircraft attempting to violate territorial space. But in preparation for this mission, everyone was fully aware of the fact that Satan and his fallen angels were still miles ahead of us. The searchlights caused no real alarm for any of the crew members to act out aggressively or in any type of hostile manner in relation to an enemy down below becoming the target of one of our sharpshooters.

"I bet you that someone down below most likely became so frightened by the roaring, thunderous sound of these helicopters that they immediately went and notified local authorities, reporting unknown UFOs flying around at a low altitude," I said to Tony.

"Yeah, and that they were all flying as if out of control, and about to crash into something," he said with a chuckle, staring directly at Karen.

"People be doing and saying some of the most out-of-the-ordinary things at times," I uttered in a low voice. "Just look at that. Can you imagine what must be going through these people's minds right about now? People can at times end up being a for-real pain in the butt. You feel me?"

"Uh, roger that, Scare Crow," a voice suddenly said, sounding as though with a lot of static.

"Damn! Who the heck was that?" Tony questioned. "He plunged headfirst into the conversation—didn't he?"

"Never mind," I said with a quiet laugh under my breath. "I'm not even going to ask who that was. But I do know one thing I gotta do—it's now time for me to once again take these helicopters higher up in altitude, and on over to the other side of the ridge within a mile or two in front of us. What I need to do is slow these crafts down before we end up staring at Stonyford in our rearview mirror. Those people are expecting us to arrive on time. Therefore, if some weird freak did indeed end up reporting us, there is no way they will be expecting these helicopters to be coming from the southwest. But instead, they will most likely be expecting us to come from the southeast of Stonyford."

"So, what you're saying is that, if in fact someone really did call the local authorities to report the sighting of numerous unidentified aircraft," says Tony, "then the route we've taken will only cause those making the UFO claim to look really stupid—am I right?"

"Exactly, Tony," I said, agreeing. "I knew there was something mentally sharp about the way you think—regardless of what Karen's been saying."

"I knew that," Tony said, smiling.

"Excuse me. What was that?" Karen asked.

"Okay, you guys. Check this out," I then said on the transmitter. "What we are about to do is make a 45° turn to the north. This will have us flying over some very dangerous mountains and hills that should take us on up to the northern tip of the Stonyford region, and out over the boys ranch. This is an area and location where you will then be able to see the lower basin of Snow Mountain."

"Excuse me for interrupting," the voice of a lady suddenly said. "But I was just wondering what it is that's so important about this particular area?"

"That voice sounds just like one of the sweet ladies from Montana," Tony said with an expression of remembrance on his face.

"All depend on what it is you're referring to," I responded.

"I guess you can say, I'm referring to Snow Mountain," the lady said. "I was just wondering what's so important about it, and why it's called by that name in the first place?"

"Good question," I then said, agreeing. "But before I get into what's so important about Snow Mountain and its legacy that was passed down by families of numerous generations, let me remind you people listening about the fact that the old snake hunter and his snake ended up becoming Stonyford's discourteous nightmare on every street. And what has made this area of the region important is that Satan officially declared this section of the Northern California region a place of pleasure to fulfill and to satisfy the selfish appetites of his followers. This is the place and location of his inauguration. There will be cowardly murderers of children, the vile, and those who practice magic, as well as the idolaters and the liars. They will all be attending the festivity. Stonyford is at present without any form of correctness, for Satan has taken complete possession, confining its residents within something much like an enclosure after the capture of an animal and placing it into a corral. The entire region is about to undergo a transformation so deadly and unstable that such a metamorphosis and its alteration will be like an experiment, and the interpretation is going to be overwhelming."

"Is that it?" the lady asked. "Can you describe in greater length details about this region that were told to you by Margaret?"

"No doubt. Believe it or not, and from my personal understanding," is how I began to attempt explaining the fictitious fairytale story to the group about the mysteriousness of Snow Mountain. "You see, from what I was told by very reliable sources, there was once, from my understanding, an ugly-looking tiny imaginary creature. I'm told he was in the exact likeness of human beings and that he could on most occasions be seen roaming around aimlessly as though lost in the area where we are presently headed.

"But check this out. It wasn't until a few hikers, who, while exploring the creature's inhabitant, just happened to be scaling a particular section of the mountain, when they unknowingly ventured into his space in an effort just so that they could see the tiny creature for themselves.

"This is when the tiny being up there in those mountains just happened to be out roaming around in search for something we haven't any knowledge of. Well, it just so happened that, while the hikers were in the midst, you know, making one of their most daring upward scaling attempts on a particular section of this mountain, and from my understanding, took a lot of balancing and courage, and also bravery and strength, the story is that they ended up, you know, meeting face to face with the tiny being, startling them in an amazing way to see for themselves that the so-called tiny creature they'd heard many tales about ended up not being so tiny after all."

"What's that?" someone asked curiously.

"Yeah, I was wondering the same thing," another voice questioned.

"Hey, I was waiting for you to say something about the tiny being ended up, like, you know, being Peter Pan, or somebody," the voice of another lady said with a chuckle over the transmitter.

"Oh, well," I then said. "Sorry to spoil the overindulgence of the fairy tale fantasy you've been living in. But from what I have been told about the supposedly tiny creature, it ended up being well over twenty feet tall, and supposedly spoke with a heavy, rough, and very sluggish, discontented, deep bass voice that sounded as though it were hoarse and very disagreeable to one's ears, being that it also sounded as though his way of talking made all of his words sound as if he were muttering and grumbling as that you'd hear from an old moody, grumpy person."

"Did they ever say anything about him being like a Big Foot creature or anything?" another voice asked over the transmitter.

"You guys gotta remember, this was supposed to have just been, you know, just another of those old-time fairy tales that the folks there in the town of Stonyford sat around talking about during those moments when they hadn't much else to talk about, except share stories about everything they knew that would be of interest to whomever it was that wanted to listen. They were always hanging out talking and sharing conversations about any and everything that came to mind."

"Plus, the gathering at the Stonyford grocery store was always the best spot in town to get the best seat, where you could get away with telling your most favorite, fascinating tale of all times, as you'd do your very best to make an attempt to capture everyone's attention. But that was providing such a tale was really worth listening to in order to get the attention of those who were themselves willing to listen."

"Uh, Scare Crow," a voice suddenly said to get my attention.

"Yeah, what's that?" I responded.

"Uh, just how long did these people hang around the grocery store, you know, like, doing this stuff?" he asked me.

"Man, I tell you no lie. Them folks would be sitting around that grocery store there in Stonyford for hours and hours on end, without blinking an eye, listening to each other tell one fascinating story after another from far too many creative imaginations," I told 'em. "And yeah, I have to admit, that some of those old-time stubborn, pigheaded formers, who, you know, could always be seen gathered around standing next to some wooden square boxes with round openings like holes on the surface, playing a game they call 'Corn Hole' and tossing small-looking beanbags into the openings, they were all the same."

"That's all they be doing, other than telling stories?" someone else then asked me.

"Oh, hell no!" I exclaimed. "Quite a few of those people were, I'd guess it be all right to say, tending to indulge in some really highly imaginative shit like fanciful stuff, with all of their supernatural elements; and all of that witchcraft and magical power, and also some of that, you know, old-time VooDoo stuff that's marked by the belief of Sorcery and Primitive Deities and Fetishes and Spells and Curses that these people held, proving that they, uh, you know, really possess magic power.

You see, at the Stonyford grocery store, you could always, during most occasions, hear how voracious, or, on other occasions, hear how eager the tiny being was said to be during its attempt to consume very large amounts of food such as that which you'd see a predatory vulture doing, or a predacious greedy person.

You could always, on many occasions, hear the town's residents gossiping how hunters and hikers who ventured Snow Mountain complained about being stalked and attacked by something hard for them to describe. Word is that some of the venturers and those just out exploring the mountain never returned, leaving the speculation for curious minds to believe they had become themselves victims of various large carrion-eating birds that resided up high on that mountain."

"Carrion-eating birds?" someone asked me, curious about my statement. "I know you're not talking about the carrion bird that eats dead, rotting flesh like those nasty-ass opossums, are you?"

"Yep. That be exactly what I am referring to," I responded. "You see, it's from what I was told that you could always see these carrion birds seemingly floating and sailing through the air as though they were gliding smoothly with the hot summer breeze in search of food. They could be seen with their, uh, you know, dark plumage, naked head, and weird-looking neck.

Another part of the mystery about this story was that people were, you know, claiming to have seen a few of these carrion scavengers out openly in the midst of transforming themselves into the likeness of human beings. They were saying that this transformation seemed to be taking place while these, uh, you know, carrion birds were feeding on, or had just finished feeding on, dead decaying bodies that were, from what was being told, discarded outside of local nursing homes and hospital facilities."

"Man, are you really for real?" someone asked me.

"Now, remember, you guys, this story is still dealing with what most of the folks in this town thought was a tiny imaginary human being that, you know, somehow ended up becoming a twenty-foot giant.

But, check this out. Now this is when the story really gets weird. The individual who was telling the story had also mentioned the fact about this, uh, twenty-foot or so giant possibly being one of the fallen angels who was eventually cast out of heaven during Lucifer's unsuccessful attempted reign in which to exercise his sovereign power to try overthrowing, yes, the kingdom of heaven in order to bring about its destruction."

"No way," another voice said over the transmitter.

"Man, let him tell the story," another voice then suddenly said.

"Go ahead, Doc," somebody shouted.

"Well, if any of you have been reading your Bible, then you should know that this attempt by Lucifer was his biggest downfall, bringing an end to what has been said about him being the most attractive figure of God's creation. He was, by all means, perfect and indeed the most beautiful figure you ever wanted to meet, with widespread influence and dominant power throughout heaven."

"It was also said that Lucifer was a true musical compositionist, and that he was in charge of conducting large-scale arrangements of very deep-sounding unified artistic parts that were said to be composed of elements far beyond the scope of our human capacity to comprehend.

"Lucifer was said to be the beginning adjustment of every poem, created into memorable songs, produced into beautiful arrangements, with the most distinct components, that were said to have been deeply characterized like that of a sweet rose bush of flowers.

"Now, as each of you can use your imagination, I am without any doubt whatsoever that you, yourself, were all just then able to smell the roses. Uh, am I right?"

"Ah, man, Doc," a voice said on the transmitter. "How did you do that?"

"I know I smelt something," the voice of a lady said.

"Yeah, I think I smelt it, too," someone else said, laughing.

"Man, what'd you do, use hypnosis on us or something?" I was asked.

"Just remember, the influence of Lucifer is still very much alive, which you should by all means be aware of," I told 'em. "And please do remember: 'The natural man receiveth not the things of God; for they are foolishness unto him; neither can he know them, because they are spiritually discerned.' (I Corinthians 2:14)

"Although our Heavenly Father has given all of us something in the form of supernatural wisdom and understanding, and the knowledge to at least learn to leave well enough alone, it's really strange how our minds have seemed to have somehow turned all of us into mad scientists, philosophers, and some of the most en-thusiastic scholars, with an out-of-control and very unrelenting sweet tooth, just craving for something to devour ravenously.

"But the ultimate truth about the individual telling this story is that little did anyone know that upon Lucifer being cast out of heaven along with his multitude of fallen angels, their spirits were never cast into the bottomless pit. In fact, from what has been proven by modern scholars, these are the same spirits that reside amongst the living to this day, causing alarming havoc, wide-spread famine and confusion, and some of the most severe de-struction ever known to mankind throughout the universe, im-pacting species of every category."

"So, what you're saying is that we've all been, in one way or another, impacted by this act brought about by Satan, or Lucifer, or, though," a voice said on the transmitter.

"Precisely, and most certainly, I can say, definitely, that I am categorizing this very unique situation that has been proven to be effective and presently at hand. It is functioning, in particular at the present time, throughout the entire Stonyford region.

"The weapons onboard our crafts are what each of you will soon find yourselves having to use in your effort to strike at anything that is a threat, or that you feel is a threat, intending to inflict harm, or of any type of imminent danger. You must defend yourself."

"Hey, Scare Crow," a voice called out to me that sounded very familiar. "Uh, this is Rico, a member of the Commander. You copy?"

"Copy that, Rico," I responded. "Whassup?"

"Gettin' a bit, you know, tasty out here on the limb cultivating some of that sweetened beverage. You feel me?"

Indistinct chattering and chuckling came from crew members on the transmitter while listening to Rico.

"Uh, Rico," I said. "Whatever it is about the beverage, toss that overboard."

"Yeah, I second that motion," someone else said. "Shit ain't no good for you."

"Hey, Scare Crow. This is one of the ladies onboard a CH-47 Chinook from the highline of Montana. You copy?"

"Copy," I responded. "So nice to hear from someone coming from Montana. What part?"

"Sweetgrass," she said with a chuckle.

"Damn! I should've known. Thank you for joining us on this journey. And just how can I help you, Sweetgrass?"

"Yeah, and thank you, too," she said. "What's happening is that I was just sitting here in my co-pilot seat when the thought came to mind about Stonyford—the situation that took place there concerning Margaret Johnson."

"Sounds like you're somewhat familiar."

"Oh, that I am," she said again with a chuckle. "Very familiar."

"Okay, and just what is it that's on your mind?"

"Well, it's Margaret," she said, curious about something.

"And," I said in anticipation, "just what is it that's bothering you?"

"Well, from reading over the report, you seem to have had an opportunity to talk to Margaret. Is that right?"

"Uh, yeah. That is correct."

"A very lengthy conversation with her. Is that also correct?"

"Uh-huh."

"And, also from the report, the conversation with Margaret was said to have been quite exhausting, and at times somewhat confusing. Is that also correct?"

"Uh-huh," I said, a slight lump forming in my throat.

"Well, I was just wondering if it could be at all possible that you could, you know, just share a little something of that conversation with us?" she asked.

"No problem," I said. "Anything I can do to help you guys get a better description of what you're venturing into. Hey, the presentation is about to start.

"You see, as told to me by Margaret herself, I am now going to share with you. From what she told me, the belligerent scenario of Satan was indeed extremely brutal and violently intimidating under all the conditions and circumstances in Stonyford. It was far more powerful than any of us on this mission can even begin to imagine. I just pray that each of you, during this very lengthy battle, periodically take the time to at least remind yourself who you really are and your reason for volunteering for this mission.

"The information provided to me by Margaret is what I am trying to provide to each of you, to always keep in mind and to remember. I'm only trying to keep you focused. Your undivided attention should be without any foolishness during this mission. I want each of you to be fully equipped and completely ready to comprehend the depth of everything I am speaking to you.

"Remember, that so-called tiny figure ended up being quite a giant—a deadly giant, to be frank. However, those who ventured onto this mountain with all their investigation, exploration, and expedition in a very careless, systematic way never anticipated that the deadly giant would be in pursuit of them. We, too, will now venture into this same area, but our journey will undoubtedly be without those same deadly penalties."

"What's the story about the old snake hunter?" Nate Bell asked. "Can you shed any light on him and his supposedly evil snake? I heard they were up there somewhere, always attacking prospectors."

"Well, I see somebody's been paying attention to this legend," I said over the transmitter with a chuckle. "And so, this indeed brings to mind the story about the old snake hunter and his snake. To this day, some of the people residing in Stonyford still consider it Spiritual Truth. But when combined with all the other fairy tales, and even with deliberate deceptions meant to trick listeners, it's amazing how most people still find themselves believing the legend to be true.

"Just let me remind you that at some point, while so many people had made it their mission to gather in front of the Stonyford grocery store, they never really anticipated any of what is presently happening and taking place to actually come into existence. Each of these deadly, horrendous, and deeply dreadful occurrences just seems to continue, one after another. It's like it just wouldn't stop happening to these people."

"What was it that was happening?" someone asked over the transmitter. "What kind of occurrences are you talking about that were happening and wouldn't stop?"

"Well, for one thing," I said, wanting to make sure I was perfectly understood. "The occurrences in question are the terrible unexplained events, tragedies, and misfortunes brought about by the mysterious and unfathomable situation that Margaret herself experienced throughout the region."

"Tragedies?" another voice rang out, sounding emotionally upset and questioning what he'd heard me say.

"You heard me right," I quickly responded. "Tragedies, unpleasantly ugly in every aspect of the term for something being disliked. But this situation can best be described as something extremely shocking or dismaying, and everything else that can be added to an event so tragically horrible in nature. There was something or someone outright snuffing the life out of every living creature throughout this part of the Stonyford region. It was said that maybe it was someone pretending to be the devil, and that this individual was out for some type of revenge, inflicting serious injuries upon the people residing mainly close to the town of Stonyford, California.

"There were people claiming to have personally witnessed the brutal assaults and deadly attacks upon their friends and family members, who they said were being violently hit, badgered, tossed, and thrown about as they simply walked to and from different locations. Some were even claiming to have heard the sounds of someone screaming loudly, laughing, and crying late in the night, only to find no one to account for such frightening activities and distasteful events.

"For whatever reason, for the awful, unfair treatment bestowed upon the vast majority of communities throughout this part of the region, there seemed to be an unwanted dreadful obligation that residents feared had been established and put in place by the devil himself, implying the inauguration time in Stonyford, for which there will be the gearing up in preparation for the rebirth of Lucifer's fallen angels, who, according to the Spiritual Matrix, are in developed progressions, waiting to emerge from the bottomless pit, at which time each will appear first, starting in the town of Stonyford, California."

"Seriously?" a voice suddenly said.

"Seriously," I responded. "You see, everything is in place and geared up in accordance with the confessions of a community of people who submitted their souls to Satan in order to try and obtain his form of justice without guilt. But, consequently, the sad results following such confessions are undoubtedly going to prove fatal to everyone involved.

"As you guys already know, this is a technique used by Satan time and time again throughout history. It's a scenario with a deep chronological record proving these terrible events, all caused by Satan, are indeed facts incriminating the entire Stonyford region."

"Ah, man, look at all of those flashing lights down below," someone said on the transmitter, referring to a cluster of lights gathered together.

"Damn! That looks like a bunch of emergency lights all gathered in one huge circle or something," another voice said, pointing out to everyone.

"Hey, Scare Crow," someone called out to me on the transmitter. "Aren't those people down there, like, doomed?"

"To be completely truthful," I said, while myself wondering about just what I was being asked. "Hey, it's like, you know, I guess it's all right for you to look at it that way. But that's only if you really understand the circumstance. I mean, it can really cause you, at a time like this, to wonder if possibly everything heard about these old story tellings could actually have some truth to them.

"But just think about it. It's really not at all difficult to form an opinion and understanding about the situation at hand, especially when we all damn well already know for ourselves that something about this picture just isn't right."

"Hey, you guys," someone yelled out on the transmitter in an effort to get our attention.

"Yeah, what's the problem, Potna?" a voice asked.

"Take a look at what's happening down below," the individual on the transmitter said with excitement in his voice. "Looks like a bunch of planes all lined up in something like a caravan, waiting their turn to take off from that rinky-dink-looking runway."

"Oh, yeah. I see what you mean," someone else said. "I know they're not finished celebrating already. Damn! We just now making it here to be a part of the freakin' festivity."

"Festivity?" a voice questioned. "What's that all about?"

"Hey, Scare Crow. You copy?"

"Copy," I quickly responded, already knowing what it was about. "Whassup?"

"Uh, yeah. This is Cat," he said, identifying himself. "Are we still on our original course?"

"Proceeding as planned," I told Cat. "Is there any reason why you have become somewhat apprehensive and worried about our course?"

"Naw, it's not that," Cat said, sounding a bit uneasy with anxiety in his voice. "I was just thinking about all the traffic down below us that would soon be airborne. And I was just wondering the reason for them to be lined up in a take-off position as though in formation."

"Do look rather strange," said Tony, staring down at the sight below.

"Yeah, well. I was just thinking it was possibly, you know, one of those night flight air shows done under darkness or something going on down there," I said, keeping my personal opinion to myself. I could've allowed my imagination to run wild, especially after all the weird stories already floating around about the town of Stonyford. I then said, "Whatever the case, they're wasting very little time getting off the ground. So, uh, check this out, you guys. Let's all turn our frequencies to whatever channel they are on and find out what's happening."

"Uh, already there, and been there, Scare Crow," another familiar voice came over the transmitter, saying, "Sacro is always on time, and be listening, big time, to all the latest sensational gossip."

"Yeah, well. Why don't you share with us what you've been hearing, Sacro," I had to ask. "Should've been there myself way long before now, but as it is well known, other distractions had the Scare Crow's attention."

"A million and one conflicting stories," Sacro said, his emotions seemingly flaring up and intensifying at times. "I'm just trying my very best to stay focused and keep my full attention in place right about now. But I just want you guys to know that what Sacro is hearing is really some weird, for real, bullshit going on all over this freakin' place. Conflicting bullshit coming from everywhere! One minute you hear someone screaming for help, and then the next minute all that we can hear is some crazy stuff like laughing or something. Man, it's really crazy, Scare Crow. It's all kinds of weird stuff going on down there."

But we proceeded as planned and were on schedule to arrive in Stonyford on time, all the while realizing that something wasn't quite right about the situation there. I knew I had to get these helicopters clear of whatever was presently happening.

"Uh, everybody listen up," I said over the transmitter. "We're almost there. Try not to crowd each other too closely, but stay together as if in formation. Keep in mind that we are about to cross over the area where young boys are sometimes sent after being involved in, I believe, mischievous behavior—some form of unlawful misconduct or, at times, an altercation with law enforcement.

In other words, this is where these youngsters are sent after getting into trouble. Rather than having the courts send these kids to a place such as the California Youth Authority, the courts are giving them a chance to get themselves together. These are judges influenced by members of the community who, on most occasions, find it feasible and appropriate to send them to a place like the boys' ranch instead of prison, where they'll be housed with men."

"And what's the age of these kids?" someone asked me.

"Uh, preferably, no older than seventeen," I answered.

"And what type of crime are they sent there for—in specific?" another voice over the transmitter asked, coming from one of the AAS-72X military helicopters, which I immediately recognized by the sound of its high-performance engine.

"It's for kids who have somehow been involved in, I would say, some minor delinquent acts and are desperately in need of a stable, home-like environment for developmental purposes."

"So what you're saying is the courts chose to send them to this particular boys' ranch instead of prison, where their little badasses belong?" a lady asked, sounding concerned. "I mean, why here instead of jail or a penitentiary, where I believe they should be if they broke the law?"

"For Christ's sake, lady," someone exclaimed in disbelief. "We're talking about little kids here, not a gang of out-of-control thugs, ravaging murderers, or insane maniacs joyously stalking and killing innocent people."

"Well, I don't know," she said, sounding somewhat confused. "After reading and hearing about what happened to that poor little girl, it left an unpleasant feeling in the pit of my stomach. It was so horrible."

"I know one thing for sure," a voice came over the transmitter. "I'd really hate having someone like you as a judge, or even a juror, if I was on trial. I know for a fact that you probably wouldn't even look at the evidence. I'd be convicted because of your emotions."

Indistinct chattering followed on the transmitter.

"Well, anyway," I said, trying to break the strange monotony. "Just keep in mind that these are just kids in that place—maybe yours, maybe mine. Some, due to severe problems during growth, are still a few steps away from functioning as mature individuals. But that's the truth of it.

"These kids have all, at one time or another, been severely—and I mean severely—beaten and whipped for no reason other than being on the receiving end of some sick abuser's rod. Suffering unknown punishment, just because they were born into the arms of abusive parents who either didn't want anything to do with having children, or, perhaps worse, got some sick thrill from outright abusing and mistreating helpless kids in the most inhumane way.

"Whatever the case, these kids have experienced troubling trauma—beaten, bruised, severely injured, repeatedly raped by family members, and many even left for dead by the very parents whose job was supposed to be protecting them from monsters. And the monsters they feared under the bed? Only this time, the monsters were the ones they looked up to for shelter.

"My personal opinion? I honestly believe the boys ranch here at the lower basin of Snow Mountain is the ideal place for these troubled kids. It's the appropriate setting for the treatment they need, considering what they've endured before arriving here."

"And you were once yourself at the boys ranch?" I was asked.

"Yes, I was," I answered. "Not just once—I ended up there twice."

"For being abused?" another voice asked.

"No way, my friend. I was just out doing mischievous things. And, as you now know, I got caught," I said with a slight grunting chuckle.

"So you were there twice, you say?" someone asked on the transmitter.

"Uh-huh," I responded.

"Do you think it did you any good?" the person asked.

"Well, just let me put it this way," I started. "Fate ended up having an altogether different plan for me throughout my life. I really did end up at the boys ranch twice—and without any regret whatsoever. I did a damn good job there, yes, without any real problems. Well, I did get into a little trouble once or twice for having fun throwing rocks when I should have been working.

But check this out—my success speaks for itself and tells you a thing or two about me and who I've become today."

"Uh, hey, you guys," a voice suddenly interrupted over the transmitter.

"Whassup, man?" I asked. "What's happening?"

"Is anybody listening to what was just being said on the transmitters?" the voice asked.

"What'd you hear?" someone else called back.

"Man, there's really something weird going on down below. Sounds serious, if you ask me."

"Hey," another voice jumped in, "I think I heard it too. Whatever it is, it sounds like Stonyford might be having some serious problems."

"Uh, Scare Crow. You copy?" someone called urgently.

"Copy," I responded. "Whassup?"

"Uh, yeah. This is Midwest," he said, identifying himself. "One of my crew members was just browsing through a few channels, and—Damn! Man, you won't believe it—but all of a sudden we could hear loud yelling and screaming for help. It sounded like something was really screwed up. People were screaming, crying, calling out for help."

"Hey, Scare Crow. This is Knucklehead, on that there Sacro, man," Knucklehead said, breathing slightly hard. "Yeah, uh, we heard it too."

"Uh, yeah, Scare Crow. This ain't no joking around or playing games. The Lodi ain't shittin' you, man," another voice added.

"Identify yourself," I immediately said.

"Oh, yeah. This is McDonald, and that crazy-ass Cat," he replied, making sure we knew exactly who he was. "We just happened to be browsing around too when—well, I guess it would be safe to say—we also heard what sounded like somebody scream-ing and yelling and crying out loud for help. It sounded like a bunch of little kids' voices in the background, screaming and crying."

As I listened to the crew describe the situation coming from Stonyford, I realized I was already tuned in to the same frequency.

I immediately began manipulating the throttle on the MH-53 with careful dexterity, keeping a sharp eye on the instrument panel, which by this time was brightly illuminating in thousands of colors as I maneuvered the craft shrewdly, often deviously.

I could feel moisture building on the helicopter from the heavy humidity in the damp atmosphere, carried by the silky wind currents sweeping through the valleys of this region.

This is where the boys ranch was located, at the lower basin of Snow Mountain. Here, the strong wind currents pressed hard against the massive blades of the MH-53 as the helicopter sliced and chopped through the heavy, swirling air, which seemed to reach out and wrap around each craft.

The downstream of blasting air felt as though it were re-minding us who truly controlled the region.

I could only describe this powerful manifestation as a signal to the entire crew: no matter how large or powerful our bird, we had to prove the strength of our craft before being allowed to pro-ceed to our destination.

With all these opposing forces at work, the crew began to feel a sense of stagnation. It was as if each helicopter were suspended in midair, caught in suspense, while apprehension grew from the uncertainty pressing down on us.

It wasn't hard to spot the boys ranch within a very short dis-tance ahead of us. Beyond it, the huge mountain in the background created a picture-perfect portrait, almost like a philosophical icon captured in a photograph.

Naturally, the mountain resembled, in many ways, the Himalayas' highest peak, Mt. Everest. Snow Mountain, however, is one of America's largest mountains, and here we were, staring at it in Northern California. Its highest peak reminded me of Japan's Mt. Fuji, in central Honshu, with a similar majestic presence.

I could finally make out the runway that pilots from various states and county agencies used to land when transporting kids to and from the boys ranch—particularly when driving by car was too far a distance.

As I continued manipulating the throttle while guiding the MH-53 closer to the runway, I suddenly noticed something unusual. A thick, grayish cloud—or perhaps a low, dense fog—was forming across the surface, spreading over the Stonyford region in the still-darkness of the night.

Click! Click! Click!

Click! Click! Click!

"Scare Crow, you copy?" a voice called out.

"Copy," I responded. "Tell me about it."

"Did you hear that weird clicking noise just now?"

"That you, Pee-Wee?" I asked.

"Uh-huh. Roger that," said Pee-Wee. "Man, something isn't right."

"Hey, I would agree," someone else said about whatever was happening around us.

"Who is that?" I quickly asked. "Identify yourself."

"Midwest, Doc," the person said. "I think I'm having some problems with my instruments. This has never happened before."

"Me, too," someone else suddenly spoke up.

"Yeah, me, too," another voice added. "Shit all over the place."

Indistinct chattering, clicking, and short rattling continued over the transmitter.

"Everybody just try and be cool," I told them. "Stay calm. We'll be touching down in a few minutes. Keep vigil."

There was no question about it—something wasn't right. I

could feel the engine vibrating and humming loudly as I pushed the throttle to full.

I could just imagine how everyone else must be feeling, having to do the same thing. But we had to reach the runway at all costs. It was only a very short distance in front of us.

For reasons unbeknownst to the crew, something strange was beginning to happen, making everything feel like a challenge. It was as though our crafts were in a serious battle with a forceful entity trying to prevent us from proceeding, bringing to mind the possibility of an emergency landing.

It was then that I realized I could barely see the runway ahead as I continued maneuvering the MH-53 in and out of a slightly steep descent, while simultaneously coming out of a very sharp 45° bank to the right, holding a certain amount of altitude and adding extra pressure on my tail.

I am more than sure that each of the navigators found themselves having to apply more throttle than normal in an effort to prevent too much drag and to avoid coming into contact with the many bushes, trees, and wild overgrowth of shrubbery. Sharp, pointed rocks seemed to protrude upward and outward from the hills surrounding the boys ranch on just about every side.

These hills were covered by the region's rough terrain, as though buried under heavily wooded branches that were like a thick overgrowth, woven almost like silkworm threads, practically covering every area of open land.

With our navigation lights brightly illuminating the entire area and reflecting a somewhat shiny, glossy perception emitted by the surrounding hazy, foggy atmosphere enclosed by the dark sky, I could visibly see the many rough trees and very thick, pointed branches from all the wild vegetation. They were now plainly visible, as though spread violently outward and connected, like a million people reaching toward each other, embracing tightly together.

From our vantage point and the position of our crafts, it looked as though the mass of land before us was like a huge shaggy mass of hair that, in my opinion, had become entangled as if dreadlocked. This is a hairstyle created by twisting and braiding hair into numerous thin locks.

The shiny gray foggy haze had started to thicken. I then noticed that I could barely see anything in front of me as Tony and the rest of my crew began to readjust themselves, preparing for the inevitable.

It was at this point that I began to sense my crew's slight feelings of apprehension and paranoia trying to take control of them. I thought to myself that being in such a vicarious situation is much like being in a state of intense delusion. Such an experience was the last thing we needed—especially while we were in flight, attempting to land with roughly three hundred feet of altitude remaining.

Well, that is what I was reading from my instrument gauges.

But, when really thinking about it, my instrument gauges hadn't been working properly ever since coming into this particular location of the region. In fact, my entire panel seemed to have, all of a sudden, decided to just outright malfunction without any warning. From what I do recall reading from the MH-53's suction gauge, and ever since feeling all the moisture and humidity in the air, the suction gauge was now indicating something about there not being much moisture in the air. And the humidity? Well, the gauge was now indicating that it was at times as though none existed, or that the humidity was extremely low.

What was really strange about the entire situation was that we just couldn't understand how all of the fog could have suddenly appeared out of practically nowhere in the dead of night, without any of us seeing or noticing it beforehand.

"Sacro, Lodi, Midwest, and Commander, and everyone else," I decided to call out over the transmitter. "You guys give the Scare

Crow a copy, please."

Click! Click! Click!

Click! Click! Click!

"Sacro, Copy!" he responded.

"Lodi, Copy!" he, too, responded.

"Midwest, Copy!" he also responded.

Indistinct blurring.

"Commander, you ass still with us?" a voice called out.

Silence.

Suddenly—"Commander, Copy!" he finally responded.

"We all out here, Scare Crow," the voice of a lady responded. "We copy."

"Anybody got a vigil on the Wolfman out there?" I asked.

"Wolfman?" Tony uttered. "Who the heck is that?"

"Uh, yeah. Last time I saw he and his team of rotten spoilers, they were flying them UH-72A Lakotas high in behind us in perfect formation," someone came on the transmitter.

"Any of you guys see where they went?" I asked.

"I sure don't see any sign of 'em anywhere to our right," a voice said.

"Well, they sure ain't out here on the left," another voice said.

"Not up here," someone else added.

"And they sure ain't nowhere down below us," another said of the Lakota crew.

"I think maybe the Dingos got 'em," a lady's voice said humorously.

"Yeah! Since when did we end up in Australia, fool?" someone said.

"Just hold your horses. I hear you talking," a voice that sounded like the Commander suddenly said on the transmitter. "Uh, yeah. I copy you, Scare Crow. All this cloudy shit out here that's happening kinda got me a bit, you know, disoriented. You feel me? It's like I've lost my sense of direction or something. I'm a bit confused as far as my direction and my location. My doggone instrument panel seems to be having some serious problems. Got all of us somewhat disorganized or something."

"Hey, you're not alone," one of the crew members said of the situation.

"Now, you see what I mean?" a voice sounding like Cat suddenly said on the transmitter. "Don't you guys remember me telling you that we, too, were experiencing some problems? I got McDonald checking everything out to see if he can find out what's happening."

"Yeah, Midwest and his crew are having the same problem," a voice came on the transmitter sounding like Midwest said. "We're just out here following in behind you guys, but this fog is really putting a damper on things."

"Any sightings on the Wolfman yet?" I again asked the crew.

"That's a negative," someone said.

"Well, everybody just keep together in formation," I then told 'em. "I can barely see the runway just ahead of us and the area and location where I am intending for us to land. So, I think it's time to start, you know, trying to descend downward a bit toward the runway. Keep a visual on each other."

Before we knew it, the thick, heavy fog-like substance and its material belongings had increased around us with a snowball effect. But just as the fog had seemingly built this huge swell of a wall around us, there was suddenly a slow, gradual dwindling of the fog-like cloud with a decreasing process, which in the most part had resulted in reducing the incoming rate of the fog and was now appearing as though something was allowing us to see our surroundings.

I have to admit that after everything we had priorly experienced all the way up to this point of our journey, whatever it was that we had now found ourselves going through, the mere thought of what was happening seemed to have taken the entire crew through one hell of a loop.

I mean, it was just like a few minutes ago we were all seemingly somewhat confused about our directions, but now, after all the maneuvering and all the desperate, extreme manipulation of our throttles, rudders, and instrument panel gauges, it was hard to believe what we were now seeing.

Peering over the instrument panel, I then looked at Tony. I then looked in the direction where Karen was seated. And then in the direction of Sandra and Regina, who were just as lost and looked as confused as I was after finally realizing what had happened, which began to reveal our plight.

I then immediately looked out my captain's window, and then the windows on both sides of my craft in search for a safe place for these helicopters to land. Everything around us began to become partially into full view.

And then, the thought of what I am more than sure everyone was seeing with their own eyes was enough to freak the fuck out of the entire crew.

Every last one of these goddamn helicopters had somehow, apparently and mysteriously indeed, landed by themselves and were now on the freakin' runway that I just knew was at least about a little under a half mile from the point that I had thought to be calculated with careful estimation.

It seemed as though everyone in these helicopters were just as curious about these strange phenomenal occurrences as my crew was. This is also when I suddenly noticed that I could see no movement while staring intently around me as well as on the outside of my craft's windows.

Observing that my crew had now become as if unable to move about the craft from the thought of whatever it was that we had just gone through, and while knowing that it was my job, duty, and responsibility to try figuring out just what it was that happened, I knew without any doubt whatsoever, I had to be completely honest about the situation.

But then, I thought about my honesty, and how none of the crew knew about the fact that I, with such leadership qualities, and could on the spur of the moment make very appropriate decisions, was scared as hell. Deep down inside the pit of my stomach I wanted to just outright scream out loud from fear and confusion.

But, I then thought to myself, saying, "No, not yet. No, no, no. Don't you dare. Not yet. Not ever!"

But that is what I kept telling myself. I had every right to express my fears. I'm only human. Anticipation was driving me something crazy. It really wasn't that hard to sense that something wasn't right. Something with morally bad intent and an obnoxious vile disgusting odor had apparently, and yes, very inconveniently, invaded and seemingly conquered the entire Stonyford region by means of encroachment in which to violate the livelihoods of its residents.

And again, and to be completely truthful about the situation, I have to honestly admit the fact that I did indeed think about just slapping, uh, you know, everything out of myself for thinking maybe this was just another one of those horrible dreams I've had throughout my life. But then, just the thought of such an attempt, I would guess, made me feel really stupid. I also think the feelings of being stupid were caused by me thinking about the reality of possibly being somehow asleep somewhere before taking this trip to this area of the region, and that now it had become somewhat impossible for me to wake up.

"Yes, that's right. I'm just having a very bad awful dream," is what I was telling myself. "Soon, I'll wake up and everything will be back to normal and I will be myself again. Ever what that mean."

In the process of unbuckling my seatbelt, it was then that I remembered motioning to Tony and asking him to help me turn everything off. But it was for reasons unknown that I started resetting the instrument gauges, while at the same time, listening to see if or not I could hear anything coming from the blades rotating.

I was also checking to see if or not they were even moving, being that everything had now seemingly come to a complete standstill.

After a minute or two of hesitation, I then noticed the massive blades on this MH-53 had indeed come to a complete halt, and in my estimation, there was a temporary suspension of movement that to me was in pure quietness.

It was a sudden quietness.

It was a quietness not brought about by any doing of mine or my crew.

Not a sound could be heard. Not from my craft, and not from any of the others.

Just a very still quietness.

Something in the exact likeness of a true sense of pure tranquillity.

But, then, I just had to break the silence by interrupting such tranquillity by asking, "Can anybody hear me?"

At first, there was a tremendous amount of something in the form of what I can only assume was electrical static. And then, clicking sounds like never before—repeatedly.

Click! Click! Click!

Click! Click! Click!

Click! Click! Click!

Click! Click! Click!

"Uh, yeah. Copy you," a voice suddenly said responding. "Sacro, copy."

"Lodi, copy."

"This is Midwest. I... I can't—"

"Midwest, you copy?" I again asked on the transmitter.

Indistinct high-frequency static filled the channel.

"Commander, copy," he then finally responded. "Can barely hear you guys, Scare Crow. I guess I'm having some slight difficulties. But nothing I can't seem to manage."

"We all copy you, Scare Crow," the voice of a lady again said with her usual chuckle. "Even that crazy ass, Wolfman, copy you this time."

"You damn skippy," a voice sounding like the Wolfman suddenly said with a huge chuckle. "We back, everybody."

"Midwest, copy," he then said again making sure he could be heard.

Suddenly, everyone seemed to be breaking up terribly. It sounded as though there was a large amount of continuous air or water flowing into each of the helicopters' correspondence systems. The breaking up was accompanied by static creating the effect of a serious malfunction somewhere inside the instrument panel. This malfunction had failed to function properly and was, for reasons unknown, emitting some of the most disturbing electrical charges with high-pitch random noises.

It sounded like an atmospheric disturbance somehow attempting to impede our progress. It was using our voices and had created a speech defect as a means of obstructing communication, preventing any direct instructions and operations on our radio receivers and transmitters.

The transmission equipment capable of being moved from the panel was immediately checked, fixed if needed, and mostly remained unchanged. The majority had been built directly into the instrument panel. But during our otherwise constant attempts to communicate, there continued to be a breaking up of our voices, as if a collapse had occurred in each of the craft's communication transponders.

Such a collapse had apparently, in one way or another, become weakened to the point of being rendered completely ineffective.

It was then that I immediately, though very slowly, rose upward from my captain's chair and began checking all the instrument gauges and stabilizers, still not quite understanding what had taken place.

But there wasn't any doubt whatsoever. I had to make it more than perfectly clear to myself that, in no way, were my crew or I responsible for landing the MH-53 J-Pave Low. Truthfully speaking, none of us was responsible for bringing any of these helicopters in for what could be considered a perfect landing. When really thinking about it, it seemed that everything was somehow predestined and unaltered, with each of our craft already set in perfect formation, arranged, and now facing in the intended direction for us to take off from the runway.

Strangely, nothing seemed to be in any way damaged other than the pride of each of the crew members. But other than that, I could see no signs of any structural damage nor any impairments to the interior or exterior surfaces. There was nothing to prevent us from taking off from this area in a hurry if needed under emergency circumstances.

The entire ordeal had begun to seem as though nothing had ever happened.

This is also when I suddenly thought to myself about the possibility that maybe, just maybe, this entire event we were presently experiencing was just a setup. That someone—like the Federal Government—was using us to accomplish an important undertaking operated by some of the most highly trained professionals, with numerous elaborate skills, most likely engaging in some form of highly classified intellectual process and operation which mandated my crew's uninformed knowledge and complete cooperation.

I thought maybe there were tracking devices constructed and attached to our crafts, mainly the MH-53. And assuming that I was indeed correct, I was willing to bet just about anything that the company's administration in Napa, California, had all this time been busy tracking the MH-53 and had now decided to somehow, in their power, with the usage of modern advancements in technology, flip a switch and land not only this huge particular aircraft but just about any of today's aircraft without ever needing the skills of a pilot in the cockpit. I just knew that whatever it was we were presently going through, Napa was somehow involved as the main corporate entity pulling the strings.

I also thought that maybe, and being that each of us were very highly skilled and among the most elite professionals, and were pilots licensed to operate just about any aircraft as legit helmsmen, we were probably, without knowing it, presently operating some type of new experimental craft without realizing that we'd indeed become the company's guinea pigs.

But then I thought, what if I am wrong?

But just how could this be happening?

And just why would any meaningful company in good standard just outright use people like us? We're all just a group of journalists for Christ's sake! And to use us for any type of selfish experiment would be completely ludicrous!

We're a bunch of adventurous journalists, not scientists.

However, after checking everything inside my craft, it was then time for my most daring challenge. It was time to check on the outside of my craft in the hope that maybe, after this experience, we could just consider this one of those weird and very strange phenomena that do sometimes tend to occur.

Take the Bermuda Triangle, for instance. Now, this weird phenomenon has for thousands of years captured the imagination and attention of people worldwide. The Bermuda Triangle is universal. But does that make it real? You can't answer such a question honestly or truthfully, can you? But I can tell you one thing for sure: it's fascinating to read about and to watch on PBS documentaries that's presented in factual but artistic form.

The only thing that could be heard on the transmitters was a bunch of loud random noises that sounded like very annoying high-pitch electrical charges and static, obstructing any form of communication on our radios.

The transmission equipment onboard our helicopters was built supposedly to withstand any type of severe weather condition or storm, or just that of any type of disagreeable atmospheric weather under such circumstances.

This equipment, mainly that onboard the MH-53, was supposed to have been built to withstand just about anything. But, to everyone's surprise, each of our crafts seemed to be experiencing the exact same thing. It was equipment failure under unusual circumstances.

Attempting to contact any of the crew members by radio was impossible. The only option was for me to open the door and face whatever consequence I was to deal with. But then, I thought to myself just how foolish it would be for me to step out into a mysterious situation where everything seemed to be operating in the supernatural.

"You know something?" Karen suddenly said, breaking the silence, as well as practically scaring the everything out of us.

"Damn, Karen!" Tony quickly shouted in a low whisper, while at the same time jerking himself forward as though being pulled or thrusted forcibly in a violent motion. "What's your problem doin' something like that?"

"Something like what?" she asked, curious as to what he was talking about.

"Scared the everything out of me," he told her, still whispering. "That's what I'm talkin' bout."

"And, just how'd I do that?" she asked.

"Yeah, well. Never mind if you really don't know."

"Know what?"

"Nothing. Just forget about it."

"I know what you mean, Tony," I just had to say with a chuckle. "I think she just caused us all to be a bit more jittery."

"And I know you ain't playin' into that, Ms. Regina," said Karen.

"Girl, you mean to tell me you really don't know what you did?" Regina asked while moving her head in a round circular motion.

"Well, if I did, there wouldn't be any need for me to be asking any of y'all what I did—would it?" asked Karen while moving her head in the exact same manner. "And what about you, Ms. Sandra, sitting over there all quiet and everything, like yo ass is all that. I just know you got something to say."

"You scare me, too," said Sandra, staring at Regina. "I thought it was scary monster talking. But it was you."

"Y'all asses done gone crazy up in here," said Karen while again moving her head in a circular motion and pointing an index finger at random. "I know one thing, whatever it is that's going on around here, it got all y'all up in here trippin' on some for real bullshit."

"Just what was it that you were about to say, Karen?" I asked her.

"Uh, I don't know. I can't remember," she said, smiling, "Y'all made me forget what it was. Though."

"No. Really. What was it, Karen?" I again asked.

"Never mind. That's all right," she said. "I forgot. Really. I forgot."

"Like hell you forgot, Karen," said Tony. "Since when did yo ass start forgetting anything? You don't forget nothing, no matter what it is. You never forget."

"Oh, well," said Regina, grinning while staring directly at Sandra.

"You know what I think?" said Sandra, whispering to Regina. "I think we never leave here alive. We die here."

AUTHOR'S STATEMENT

Wrongfully Convicted

To support Bennie Ray Murdock's defense fund, contributions can be sent to:

Bennie Ray Murdock
c/o Clarence Murdock 607050309
Bank of the West
3400 Lakeshore Avenue
Oakland CA 94610

www.ingramcontent.com/pod-product-compliance
Lightning Source LLC
Chambersburg PA
CBHW011431170626
46808CB00010B/3112